D0417233

The Winter Orphan

Cathy Sharp is happily married and lives with her husband in a small Cambridgeshire village. They like visiting Spain together and enjoy the benefits of sunshine and pleasant walks, while at home they love their garden and visiting the Norfolk seaside.

Cathy loves writing because it gives pleasure to others, she finds writing an extension of herself and it gives her great satisfaction. Cathy says, 'There is nothing like seeing your book in print, because so much loving care has been given to bringing that book into being.'

Also by Cathy Sharp

The Orphans of Halfpenny Street
The Little Runaways
Christmas for the Halfpenny Orphans
The Boy with the Latch Key
An Orphan's Courage
The Girl in the Ragged Shawl
The Barefoot Child

A Daughter's Sorrow
A Daughter's Courage
A Daughter's Choice

CATHY SHARP

The Winter Orphan

HarperCollins*Publishers*

This novel is entirely a work of fiction.
The names, characters and incidents portrayed in it are
the work of the author's imagination. Any resemblance to
actual persons, living or dead, events or localities is
entirely coincidental.

HarperCollins*Publishers*
The News Building,
1 London Bridge Street,
London SE1 9GF

A Paperback Original 2019
2

www.harpercollins.co.uk

Copyright © HarperCollins*Publishers* 2019

Cathy Sharp asserts the moral right to
be identified as the author of this work

A catalogue record for this book
is available from the British Library

ISBN: 978-0-00-8286712

Set in Sabon LT Std 11.5/14.5 pt by
Palimpsest Book Production Limited, Falkirk, Stirlingshire

Printed and bound in Great Britain by CPI Group (UK) Ltd,
Croydon CR0 4YY

All rights reserved. No part of this publication may be
reproduced, stored in a retrieval system, or transmitted,
in any form or by any means, electronic, mechanical,
photocopying, recording or otherwise, without the prior
permission of the publishers.

This book is sold subject to the condition that it shall not,
by way of trade or otherwise, be lent, re-sold, hired out or
otherwise circulated without the publisher's prior consent
in any form of binding or cover other than that in which it
is published and without a similar condition including this
condition being imposed on the subsequent purchaser.

MIX
Paper from
responsible sources
FSC™ C007454

This book is produced from independently certified FSC™ paper
to ensure responsible forest management.

For more information visit: www.harpercollins.co.uk/green

PROLOGUE

Snow was falling, coating trees, bushes and fields with a thick covering of soft, cold whiteness. From the landing window of what had once been an impressive family home and was now the local work-house, a young girl of perhaps eleven summers watched the heart-wrenching scene as the young mother begged for help in the drive below and tears stung the child's eyes. She had heard the story of how she herself was found on the steps of the rectory on such a night. Had her mother also begged for entry here and been turned away to die in the bitter cold?

'Give me back my child,' the young woman below wept as she was thrust out of the huge wrought-iron gates of the workhouse. 'I know my babe lived, for I heard her cries!'

'She died an instant after drawing breath,' was the reply from the hard-faced warden, who had ordered her ejected from the property. 'Your child died, Jane! Accept it as the will of God and be gone.

1

If you dare to come here again I shall have you whipped.' Dressed in black, her thin features showed no hint of sympathy or concern as she ordered the servants to shut and lock those formidable gates.

'You are a wicked, evil woman!' the wretched mother cried. 'I know not my name, but it was not Jane – and I swear that my child lives. I feel it in *here*.' She placed her hands to her left breast, tears running down her pale cheeks. It was but a few days since she'd given birth in great pain, her strength almost gone, but even so she knew she had heard a strong cry from a living child and the words of the midwife who had birthed the babe and from somewhere she'd summoned the will to live. 'I know my child did not die and I know she was healthy for I heard them say that she was beautiful!'

'The babe is dead to you,' the spiteful voice said. 'You are a whore and you do not deserve a child. If you ply your trade once more no doubt you will bear another . . .'

The gates shut with a clanging sound that was like a death knell to the unhappy woman who pressed herself against them, desperately looking at the grey walls and stout door. She'd struggled here in a raging storm to give birth in safety. Would to God that she had given birth under a hedgerow for her child might then be here in her arms!

It had begun to snow harder now and the wind was cold, biting through her ragged gown and thin shawl. Her feet were bare and felt frozen as she stubbornly stood staring at the door of the work-house, which remained firmly shut. They had stolen her babe! Jane might not know her true name, for when she'd arrived at the isolated workhouse – ill, close to starving and near to giving birth – all her memories had gone. She knew not where she had been, nor where she was trying to go. Her own name, as well as that of her child's father, had vanished from her mind with all the rest.

The women who cared for the sick in the work-house infirmary had named her Jane. She had heard them talking when they thought she was dying. For some reason they were triumphant that the babe was healthy and spoke of someone being pleased that she was such a beautiful girl – but Jane had not died and when she finally began to look about her and ask for her child, they told her the babe had been all but stillborn.

Jane knew it was a lie. She would never believe that her babe had died soon after it drew breath, but if she stood here from now to kingdom come she knew they would not tell her what had happened to her child. Tears ran silently down her cheeks as she turned away. Night was closing fast and the snow was beginning to lie thickly. She was a mile from the nearest village and she knew that even if she reached it no one would help her; they would merely send her here. She was a vagrant. Nothing. No one. If she died this night it mattered not, but if she lived she would return and somehow she would have justice for what had been done here.

As she lingered at the gates, a young girl came rushing from the rear of the house. Jane knew her, for this girl had helped her in the infirmary, had given her a cup of milk and a piece of bread when she lay weeping after they'd told her that her babe was dead.

'Thank you, child,' Jane had whispered, because something in the girl's face had touched her heart – and there was such sadness in those big brown eyes.

'I am called Bella,' the girl had whispered to her then. 'They will beat me if they find me giving you sustenance, because you have angered the mistress . . .' She'd gone quickly, afraid of being caught and punished.

Bella was dressed now in just her nightgown and a shawl, shivering with cold.

'What are you doing here, child?' Jane said. 'You will catch your death on this terrible night.'

'I had to tell you,' Bella gasped. 'I saw you from the window and I got out the back way! Don't believe them when they say your babe died. She lived for I saw them take her out to the gates some two days later and give her to someone in a carriage. You were still ill and would not have heard her even if she cried, but I did.'

'You saw it? You saw them give my child to someone?' Jane clutched at the child's arm, hope soaring. 'Did you see her, Bella? Do you know if she lived?'

'She did not die as they told you. Your babe was

4

crying as they carried her away. I heard her and I saw them give her to someone in a carriage – but I am sorry, I do not know who it was.'

'Thank you!' Jane reached through the bars of the locked gate to catch Bella's hands. 'Go quickly before they discover you or you will be punished.'

The child had been going to say more but she nodded and, giving a little sob of fear, Bella fled the way she had come. Jane's eyes filled with tears but her heart grew stronger. She had *not* imagined those cries. Her daughter lived somewhere and one day she would find her and take her back . . .

Raising her hand, Jane waved to Bella as she paused at the corner of the house, before disappearing round the corner. If she found her child perhaps she might come back and take Bella away from this terrible place . . . but for the moment it would take all her strength just to survive.

Once inside the scullery, Bella paused, listening for sounds, but the other inmates were in their beds and she knew she must hurry – if the mistress discovered her here at this hour she would be accused of stealing food from the kitchen and beaten. Her eyes stung with tears for she could not forget the look of despair in Jane's eyes. There was nowhere the young woman would find proper shelter on such a night, for even the church was locked during the hours of darkness to deter those who would steal from God and the poor. It was likely that Jane would die unless she found a barn or a haystack to crawl inside. Bella shivered, feeling chilled, for there was little hope that Jane would recover her babe even if she survived the night.

'God grant you peace,' she prayed, knowing that Jane's chances of survival were as small as Bella's of finding happiness in this life. 'If there is a God I think you need him this night . . .'

CHAPTER 1

On the lonely road, a carriage bowled smartly through the gathering gloom of a bitter night, both coachman and horses eager to find an inn, stables and warmth. Inside, the man, his eyes closed as he endured the jolting of his well-sprung vehicle, let out a cry of pain, but it was not for physical discomfort. In his mind, he had seen again the dying agony of the woman he loved, cradled in his arms but beyond his help.

'Katharine . . .' he murmured, tears on his cheeks. 'Katharine, why did you leave me?'

Yet it was not her fault that she now lay in the icy ground. The brute who had killed her was punished but that did not ease Arthur Stoneham's grief. It was for her memory that he was set upon this road this dread night, because she would not let him rest and he knew he would carry this agony until he had fulfilled his promise to her – a promise to find the sister she had loved.

After weeks of following clues that led nowhere,

Arthur was no closer to discovering what had happened to Marianne Ross more than twelve years earlier than he had been when he left London. He had visited the man Katharine Ross had spoken of in her dying fever. Squire Thomas Redfern had seemed a pompous young man to Arthur and uninterested in Katharine or her sister and so he had simply told him of Katharine's death and her wish that Arthur would look for her sister.

'It is my intention to do all I can to find Marianne,' Arthur told the squire, looking for some flicker of feeling but there was none.

'I do not believe you will find any trace of that unfortunate young woman,' Thomas said in a voice devoid of emotion. Married, with two young sons, he had clearly ceased to mourn her long ago. 'A search was made at the time. Marianne unwisely walked home through the woods, though she had been warned gypsies were camping there. My father and hers made searches but no word of her was ever heard. I think she was murdered and her body concealed . . .'

For a moment there was a flicker of something but then it was gone. If this man had ever loved Katharine or her sister, he had only a fleeting interest now. Arthur decided that he must have mistaken Katharine's last words; she could not have loved someone as unfeeling as this man! He would not give him another thought, nor, if Marianne were found, would he pass on news of her to such an unfeeling oaf.

The resolution helped to soothe his wounded heart

a little, for he could not be jealous of such a man. Katharine must have been trying to say something other than the words that had burned into Arthur's soul: 'Tell Tom I loved him . . .'

He would not think of this man as a rival for Katharine's love again. Perhaps she had meant to say, 'Tell Arthur I loved him,' and the words had come out wrong.

The squire had no clues to help Arthur find Marianne Ross, nor did any others he questioned in the household. It was no different in the village. No one remembered much of the old tragedy. Marianne had simply disappeared that night and never been heard of since. Most who remembered the old story believed her dead. Arthur himself thought it was the most likely explanation, but he would do his best to exhaust any leads that might help him to discover the truth, though they were few indeed. Gypsies had been in the woods and one of Marianne's shoes had been found so it seemed to him that there were two possible explanations: either Marianne had been attacked and killed or she'd been abducted by the gypsies. He was unlikely to find her whatever the case, but he must exhaust all possibilities before admitting failure for his own peace of mind.

Arthur lounged back against the comfortable squabs in his carriage, closing his eyes as his coachman drove through the icy night. Although his journey had been fruitless, he was still in Hampshire and not ready to return to London and give up the search for Katharine's lost sister. As Hetty, his true friend and colleague, had told him, he owed it to the memory of the woman he'd loved. Hetty ran Arthur's refuges for women and children in London and had been Katharine's friend, nursing her when she lay dying.

Katharine's tragic death was still like a stone in Arthur's breast and he could not face the anxious looks and concern of his friends, especially those who had also loved her. The man who had caused her death was locked away in a cold cell from which he would emerge only to meet death at the end of the hangman's rope. The rogue's fate was assured, but that did not ease Arthur's state of mind. His grief was too bitter, too personal, to be shared – nor did he wish for sympathy, and together with the grief came the doubts and the guilt.

Was it Arthur's fault that Sir Roger Beamish had seized the chance to send his beautiful Katharine to her death in front of that brewer's waggon? Sir Roger's insane jealousy was certainly one cause for the spiteful act, but Arthur now knew that the man had been ruined, his fortune lost, and that in his twisted mind he'd blamed Arthur, who'd caught him cheating and accused him publicly of it, for his downfall. Or was it because Katharine had refused him and accepted Arthur's proposal that he'd given her the vicious push that ended her life beneath the flailing hooves of the heavy horses? Arthur knew he would never discover the answers to his questions and it haunted him.

He groaned and pushed his tortured thoughts to a distant corner of his mind. Katharine was lost to him and nothing would bring her back. His only hope of finding peace was to unravel the mystery of her sister's disappearance. Perhaps then he might be able to sleep at night.

Suddenly, he heard a shout and his carriage was brought to a screeching halt as the coachman reined in his horses abruptly and Arthur was flung from one side of the carriage to the other. By some miracle, his man managed to hold the plunging, screaming horses and the coach did not overturn. Recovering swiftly, Arthur wrenched open the door and jumped out into the road.

'What happened?' he demanded of his driver, but even as he asked, Arthur saw what looked like a huddle of rags lying a few feet in front of his carriage. The horses were still snorting and stamping their feet, disturbed by being so misused, their breath white on the frosty air, and Arthur went to their heads to quieten them, whispering against their faces so that they calmed and responded to his voice before he walked on to investigate the bundle.

Arthur looked to either side of the road suspiciously for it might be a trick to take them unawares. Some thirty-odd years earlier, highwaymen had been the plague of these roads, but none had been seen since the last known gang was caught many years before. It was now 1883 and Arthur did not fear them but there were still rogues and thieves aplenty who might offer violence on a dark lonely road such as this, so

11

it was best to be careful. Indeed, it was only the previous year that Her Majesty Queen Victoria had been shot at, so Arthur went prepared wherever he travelled. He patted the pistol in his greatcoat pocket, ready for the worst if this was a trick.

'Be careful, sir,' his groom warned. 'It may be the work of rogues . . .'

Arthur had reached the huddle of rags and saw at once that it was a young woman lying there. Her face was pale and for a moment he thought her dead. Kneeling on the frozen surface of the road, Arthur felt for a pulse. It was faint but it was there. He swept her up in his arms as his groom came to join him.

'What is it, sir?'

'A young woman – and she's barely alive, Kent. Had we not chanced on her she might have died this night. We need to get to the nearest inn.'

'There's a small one about a mile ahead. Let me help you, sir.'

'Open the door of the carriage,' Arthur said. 'I have some brandy in my bag and I'll see if I can get her to swallow a little. As soon as we reach the inn, I want you to discover the nearest doctor and bring him to us.'

Kent nodded, glancing at the woman as Arthur lifted her gently on to the seats and sat next to her, holding her against him. Another servant might have observed that she was a vagrant and warned his master, but all Arthur's people knew that such a remark would earn them a severe glance. Arthur

Stoneham would never leave a woman to die on the side of the road, even if, as it looked, she was a beggar.

'Yes, sir,' he said. 'I'll tell the coachman to get on now.'

He shut the door carefully and left Arthur to settle the unfortunate woman. Arthur took a small silver flask from his pocket and opened the stopper, then gently lifted the woman in his arms so that she was propped up against his shoulder as he put the flask to her lips.

'Try to swallow a little please,' he said gently. 'It will warm you . . .'

Whether she heard or not, Arthur could not know, but she moaned slightly and, as her mouth opened, he poured a tiny drop on to her tongue. Her throat swallowed and he poured a few drops more. He thought she sighed and her body seemed to sag against him. He sat with his arms about her, holding his greatcoat around her frail body, instilling his warmth and vitality into her, willing her to live.

'Be brave, lady,' he murmured. 'I have you and you are safe now.'

As the coach slowed to a halt and his groom opened the door and helped him ease the woman out, he saw a small inn with a lantern above its door and welcoming lights from a parlour window.

'Run and secure rooms for us, Kent – and then fetch that doctor!'

'Yes, sir.'

Kent ran ahead while Arthur gave instructions to

his coachman about stabling the horses then assisted the shivering woman to walk. By the time he reached the lights and warmth of the inn hallway, Kent had secured a room for him and accommodation for himself and the coachman.

'There is but the one room in the house but I thought it would do as you will want to watch over the young lady, sir – and me and Barrett are over the stables and the landlord has given me the doctor's direction,' Kent told him.

Arthur nodded to the landlord. 'I shall require a fire lighting and food for us all. My companion is not well, so some warm milk, perhaps, if the doctor thinks it advisable.'

'Yes, Mr Stoneham.' The landlord bowed respectfully. Kent had made sure to speak of his master's consequence, no doubt, for the landlord took a brass oil lamp and lit their way up to a large chamber at the rear of the house. 'I fear there is but the one bed, sir.'

'She is ill and must have it,' Arthur said. 'I shall take the chair and be comfortable enough; besides, she will need watching. I do not know what has befallen this poor girl, but I shall not let her die if I may prevent it.'

'Your man said you were a philanthropist of the highest order, sir. My wife would take in all the waifs and strays if she could . . .' He tutted as he saw the condition of the young woman. 'She cannot be past twenty, sir. It is sad to see one so fair brought to this.'

'Yes, you are right,' Arthur agreed. 'I fear it happens all too often but, with God's aid, we help those we can.' The landlord nodded and looked pious.

'Amen to that, sir,' he said. 'I'll send the chamber-maid up to light the fire straight away.' He paused, then, 'Will you dine here or in the parlour?'

'I'll dine after the physician has been and we hear what he has to say.'

The host nodded and left Arthur to place the girl between the clean sheets and cover her. Despite her wretched clothes, he thought she had washed recently and her skin had a pleasant perfume of its own. She was pretty, he decided, as he pushed the long fair hair back from her cheek. If she lived, he would be interested to hear her story and would help her if she was willing to be helped. He could take her to Hetty, who would find her a bed at the refuge and perhaps a place to work, he thought as he turned away to take off his coat.

'My baby! Give me back my baby!'

The cry from the young woman's lips was so desperate that Arthur turned sharply and saw that she was sitting up in bed staring about her wildly.

'Where is she? What have you done with her?'

'I saw no baby . . .' Arthur felt a stab of doubt. Had he missed the child? He had seen nothing of it when they rescued the woman. No, there had been no child nearby that he'd been aware of – but had it been lying hidden by the side of the road? 'Forgive me, where was your child, madam?'

15

'They took her. They said she was stillborn but I heard her cries,' the woman said clearly, in the voice of one gently reared, and then fell back against the pillows, her eyes closing.

Arthur bent over her, fearing for a moment that a relapse had taken her life, but she was sleeping now and her breathing seemed a little easier. He was relieved, but the poor girl was feverish. He decided that he would not go and look for the missing babe for she seemed confused. Perhaps she had recently given birth to a child that had died, which might explain her distress, but why had she been lying in the middle of the road?

It was more than half an hour before Kent returned with the doctor. By that time the maid had a good fire burning and the room was pleasantly warm. The doctor examined his patient and confirmed Arthur's belief that she had recently given birth.

'She still has her milk,' he told Arthur, 'though I would say it was some days since the birth – perhaps more than a week.'

'She was asking for the child and seemed confused. Do you think she has been attacked?'

'I see little wrong with her,' the doctor told Arthur. 'I imagine she may not have eaten for some hours and she was probably on the verge of dying of the cold. It is a bitter night, Mr Stoneham – too cold for any of us to be out.'

He seemed a little annoyed that he had been brought from his warm house to tend a woman he did not

16

consider sick, for bearing a child was the law of nature. Arthur kept his counsel, paid him generously and thanked him for his advice – which was that she should have rest, good food and be kept warm.

'She is young and with some food inside her will soon recover her strength, sir. I think these young women are often back in the fields within days of giving birth.'

'You think her a country woman?'

'She is dressed like one of the travelling folk,' the doctor said disparagingly. 'Be careful, Mr Stoneham – these people can take advantage if you let them.'

Arthur nodded, giving no answer except to thank him for his time once more. He was angry, for he had seen nothing in the young woman's features to suggest she was Romany and would not have cared if she was, but he would have thought by her speech that she was more likely to be of good family, although he supposed the clothes she wore might have belonged to the kind of woman the doctor had mentioned.

A knock at the door made Arthur turn to greet the plump woman who had arrived with a hot toddy and a glass of warmed milk.

'I'm Sally, the landlord's wife, and I thought you could do with something to warm you, sir,' she said. 'I brought the milk in case the young lady was feeling able to drink it.'

'At the moment she sleeps,' Arthur said. 'I wonder if you could bring me up a cold supper – I do not feel able to leave her just yet.'

'How would it be if I sat with her for a while, sir? You go down and my husband will bring you soup, bread and then cold meat and pickles – if that will suit?'

'It sounds like a feast,' Arthur said and smiled, for Sally had a kind face. 'She woke once and I think she has recently lost a child.'

'The poor girl,' Sally said. 'I know how that feels, for I lost one of my own – though I now have two strapping sons.'

'I am glad to hear of your present happiness,' Arthur said and drank some of his hot toddy. 'I shall take this with me, Sally. Please watch this lady while I avail myself of your husband's hospitality.'

It was an hour and a half before Arthur returned to the bedchamber. The landlord's wife was bathing the young woman's forehead and smiling as she tended her. Clearly, she had taken to her patient and was caring for her as she would one of her own.

'Thank you for your kindness, Sally.'

'It was a girl I lost, sir. She would have been just a little younger than this young lady if I am not mistaken, for she can be little more than eighteen.'

'You think her gently born?'

'Oh yes, sir. Her hands have known work but only in the past few months – and her skin is soft and white, her features gentle. I believe her to have been ill-treated, Mr Stoneham – there are marks of a beating on her back no more than a few months old.'

Arthur's eyes narrowed in question. 'You bathed her to ease her fever and discovered scars?'

'Aye, sir, I did. Who would beat a young woman who was bearing a child? I do not understand such cruelty, for my John is a good man. What kind of a man could do such a thing?'

'I fear there are many such,' Arthur told her, frowning. 'I daresay there is a sorry tale behind her appearance but she is not alone in her suffering; there are many more . . .'

Sally nodded but made no further comment. She took her tray and left the room, saying she would return later but he must ring for her if he needed her help. Arthur thanked her and sat in the armchair by the fire, stretching out his long legs and leaning his head against the winged back. He felt warm and he had dined well. The young woman seemed to be resting and he might as well sleep if he could; time enough when she woke to discover the mystery that had brought her to a lonely road for him to find on such a night. It could not be mere coincidence. This was meant to be and Arthur sensed that he was meant to find her.

CHAPTER 2

'I had thought Mr Stoneham would have returned by now,' Ruth Jones said when Hetty visited the kitchen at the refuge in the East End of London for fallen women where the pair both worked and lived. 'You don't think he would . . . you know, in his grief for the poor lady?' Her distress showed in her eyes at the thought and Hetty was quick to reassure her.

Made warden of this spacious and comfortable home for unfortunate women, by a man she both admired and cared for, Hetty smiled. It had, she thought, once been the house of a wealthy merchant and had several good bedrooms, which enabled them to take in more women needing a place to call home.

'No, Ruth, I do not think that Arthur Stoneham would take his own life, no matter how much he loved Katharine. He knows that too many people rely on him – besides, it is the coward's way, and Arthur is no coward. You must not think such things.

21

I daresay he has been delayed for some good reason and will return when he is ready.'

Ruth nodded and looked more cheerful. 'Bless you, Miss Hetty, thank you for puttin' my mind at ease. The master had seemed restless for a while and then, when Miss Ross agreed to wed him – well, I'd never seen him as happy. It was such a tragedy.'

'Yes, it was,' Hetty agreed, though privately she had her doubts that Arthur would have found lasting happiness with Katharine Ross. No doubt Katharine had felt some tenderness towards Arthur, perhaps loved him in her gentle way – but not with the wholehearted passion he deserved. But perhaps Hetty was biased, because she loved him herself, loved him with a passion she knew matched his own capability for love, though she would never have stood in his way. She cared only that he found peace and happiness for he had surely suffered enough remorse for any man.

At that moment a knock came at the door and Ruth went to answer it. Hetty looked for her to return, hopeful of some news concerning Arthur. Instead she was followed by a young girl Hetty had come to know well in recent weeks; she had, no doubt, brought medicine for one of their ladies.

'Here's Eliza come with herbs for our Sarah's cough . . .' Ruth announced. 'I asked her to step in and take a glass of milk and a biscuit.'

Hetty nodded her approval. Eliza worked and cared for the apothecary, taking her cures to those in need and sometimes visited them at Hetty's behest, for her ladies had often suffered and needed medicines to help them overcome their ills. A young, pretty girl, Eliza had both compassion and courage, for she had survived the cruellest upbringing in the workhouse.

Hetty knew that Arthur believed Eliza was his child, born of a young country gentlewoman, long dead now, and through misfortune given to a workhouse where she had suffered terribly before being rescued.

'I am happy to see you, Eliza dear. Come, sit with us and tell us how you are – and Miss Edith, too.'

Eliza smiled. 'I am well, ma'am, though I fear Miss Edith is not as strong as she might be.'

'I am sorry for that,' Hetty said looking at her with sympathy. 'You know you may come to us if you are worried or distressed and we shall do our best to help you. My door is always open to you, Eliza.'

Eliza smiled at her sweetly and in that smile, Hetty saw something of the man she admired, and in her heart had always loved. Arthur only needed to see that smile to know for sure that she was his daughter, but Hetty knew that for the moment his grief had made him blind to anything but his memories of Katharine and her loss. He worried what to do for Eliza for the best, because she loved Miss Edith and to take her from the woman who had given her a home might distress her, and yet he wanted her to have the life she deserved. Once he'd managed to set his grief aside, he would undoubtedly put his mind to ensuring Eliza's future happiness.

'Miss Edith told me to make sure that Sarah knows the dose is once every six hours, Miss Hetty,' Eliza said. 'She should not take more.'

'We'll look after her, don't you worry . . .' Ruth said and smiled at her. In the workhouse she had looked after Eliza as if she were her own child for she had none to love and truly cared for the girl.

Hetty knew it was on Ruth's mind that she needed to tell Eliza the secret she'd kept all these years, to give her the diamond trinket she'd discovered pinned inside her shawl – placed there, Ruth had no doubt, by the mother who had been forced to give her up. However, she agreed with Hetty that she needed to ask Arthur Stoneham's permission before she did so and in all the distress of the past weeks she had not dared to ask.

'Has Mr Stoneham returned from the country?' Eliza asked suddenly.

'Not yet – did you wish to speak to him?'

Eliza hesitated and then nodded. 'Yes, ma'am but it is not important. I know Mr Stoneham is a busy man. I only wished to ask if he had found any record of who brought me to the workhouse. He did say he would help me if I asked . . .'

'Arthur will return soon I am sure and you may ask him then. He has spent the weeks since Katharine's death, at Christmas, searching for her

24

sister, but I fear too many years have passed for him to succeed. Only a little miracle would bring that to pass.'

'Her death was very sad, ma'am. We were sorry to hear of it . . .'

Hetty sighed. It would take a miracle and a persistence few could muster to find someone who had disappeared all those years ago. No one but Arthur Stoneham would have attempted it. She had calmed Ruth's fears, but she too wondered where Arthur was, for she had expected his return before this. His cousin, Matthew Soames, who was also his secretary, was taking care of business in Arthur's absence, but Hetty felt it keenly. Arthur Stoneham was never far from her thoughts or her prayers these days. Yet she believed that if he had not returned from his search there must be a good reason for his tardiness.

Bella sat on the stairs, hugging her thin arms about her body as the tears trickled down her cheeks. She hated this place – and most of all she hated Mistress Brent. Mistress Brent was the warden in charge of the female section of the workhouse but her husband was the master. He ruled the house with a rod of iron and even his wife had been seen with black eyes after he'd beaten her. It was after he'd taken his wrath out on Mistress Brent that she vented her spite on the women and girls in her charge – but most of all on Bella.

Bella had no idea why the mistress despised her and ill-used her so much more than the other children. A harsh, thin-faced woman, tall and skinny but very strong, when Mistress Brent gripped Bella's arms, her fingers dug in so hard they bruised her and she had black and mauve marks all over them. The mistress had a long thin cane, which she used whenever she felt inclined, striking out at anyone she thought was being disobedient or impertinent. She made the children line up for everything – food, visits to church or the schoolroom, which was a privilege reserved only for those the mistress favoured, despite the law that said children must be educated between the ages of five to ten years. Bella had learned to write her name, but she could not read more than a few letters nor could she reckon numbers, even though some of the women inmates said that it was a disgrace she had been denied this right.

'It's the law that all the children should be taught their letters, numbers and to read, as well as sewing and other things and the child's ripe to learn,' they'd said amongst themselves, but no one dared to say it to the mistress's face. All the women and girls obeyed their mistress almost by instinct, their spirits long subdued, and it was Bella alone who refused to march in time to her tune. She ran when she should walk and talked when she was ordered to be silent and took her punishment without tears. Something told Bella that, whatever she did, she would be beaten and ill-used and a fierce pride inside would not let her lie down and let the mistress wipe her feet on her.

Bella was good with a needle. Her eyes were sharp

and her stitches were neat, and because of that she was given most of the mending to do. She was allowed to sit in the special room reserved for the seamstresses and help them in the afternoons, but in the mornings she was set tasks like scrubbing the floors or washing dishes. Yet she suspected that if her needlework had not been so neat, her life might have been harder. There were far worse jobs in the workhouse – the laundry, which was hot and damp and smelly; picking oakum, which made hands bleed, and slopping out the latrines. They stank, especially in summer, and they were cleared manually by the men, but children had to wash them down after the men had taken the stinking effluent away. Bella had been given that job once but since then she'd been fortunate enough to be sent to the sewing room.

Bella had learned about the woman who had given birth to a healthy child but was told it was dead while she sat quietly mending. The other women had gossiped about the young woman who had arrived earlier that bitter afternoon on the point of giving birth.

'She does not know her own name nor whence she came,' Florrie said as she cut the delicate pattern out of expensive silk. Florrie was the head seamstress and her work was so fine that word had spread to Lady Rowntree, whose family had founded the workhouse. Lady Rowntree had started by asking for some alterations and repairs, but then she had asked if Florrie could make some fine underwear for her daughter, Rosalie, who was soon to be wed.

'I think a man betrayed poor Jane – for so the mistress said she should be called – and beat her and she lost her mind, poor wench.'

'She would be better off if the babe dies at birth for she cannot care for it,' Marta said as she paused in her own sewing. 'In any case, I know the mistress and master sell the healthy ones – it has always been so, except in her case . . .' The woman nodded her head at Bella. 'Why do you think she kept her?'

'Hush, Marta.' Florrie shot a warning look at her friend. 'If someone tells her what you say, they'll shut you in the cellar and starve you.'

'They can't let me die,' Marta said in a belligerent tone. 'It's not lawful – and Lady Rowntree would close this place down if she knew some of the things they do. It was she and her husband who endowed this place and they are still the guardians of it.'

'I think he is too ill to care what happens here,' Florrie said, shaking her head. 'Her ladyship might – and Miss Rosalie would be shocked. She's a lovely young lady, she is – and so grateful for our work. She told me that she has not seen better embroidery than ours, Marta.'

The chatter had turned to other things then, but Bella did not forget the woman who had lost her mind. When the poor lost woman had given birth, Bella had been sent to the sickroom with cloths and saw a healthy child born – but later she heard that Jane had been told it was dead and, in pity, stole a cup of milk and some soft bread from the kitchen and took it to her. The woman had looked so sad and ill and Bella had felt drawn to her. Poor Jane had wept and thanked her and her tears had remained in Bella's memory.

Bella saw everything that went on in the workhouse. She was small and slight and no one took much notice of her – unless the mistress chanced to look her way when she felt inclined to punish someone. Bella had seen Jane's babe carried from the workhouse one evening, two days after the birth, wrapped in a thick blanket. It could only have been Jane's babe, for there were no others in the house, and she knew that the babes of young unmarried mothers were routinely sold to people willing to pay for them; fine ladies who longed for a child and could not bear them would pay well for a healthy babe, particularly a boy. If a family entered the workhouse and a woman gave birth, she would be allowed to keep her babe until the father took them out in the spring to find work. Only if the woman was alone and had no one to help her was the babe stolen from her.

Bella had felt so sorry for the woman they had named Jane. It was the reason she'd gone down to the yard the previous night and told Jane that her child lived and what she'd seen. She had tried to help her, but she'd been caught when she was returning to the dormitory and that was why she was sitting on the stairs now, awaiting the mistress's summons. She knew she would be beaten and it would hurt, but she would try not to cry. Mistress

Brent liked to see her cry and would just beat her all the harder.

'Bella, come here!' She rose and walked up the last few stairs to the woman waiting for her and her heart raced wildly. Mistress Brent was smiling and that meant trouble. She was looking forward to inflicting punishment. Bella was sure it made her happy to see others in pain and distress. 'Come in, girl.'

Bella went into the dark room that the mistress called her office. There was a desk and a chair and a mahogany tallboy, in which she kept her cane, her papers and other things, but no pictures or ornaments or anything personal.

'You stole from the kitchens last night. No, do not try to lie to me. It is the only reason you would be coming from the kitchens late at night – and, I'll swear, it is not the first time,' Mistress Brent said and glared at her. 'You will be beaten and then you will go without supper. I despise thieves – and I have decided that I shall not keep you here. The gypsy threatened that I should be cursed if I sold you and swore she would come back for you – but she lied. I no longer believe in her or her curse.'

'What gypsy?' Bella looked at her fearfully, for it was the first she had heard of this curse. 'I do not understand you.'

'No, nor shall you – but know that you are scum, the child of a whore, and deserve all that you get. Your mother deserted you, left you to die in the snow on the church steps and then gave up her worthless life. You are cursed and I should have sold you years ago but I thought – well, now it is time.' She shook her head as if shaking off something that haunted her, a flicker of something like fear in her eyes. 'Yes, I shall keep you no more, for you have proved that you are a thankless wretch.'

Bella shivered, the terror mounting inside her. She had been beaten before and half-starved – but from the look in the mistress's eyes there was worse in store for her.

Raising her head, she looked into the cold eyes that raked over her. 'I do not care if you sell me – anywhere would be better than here!'

'You think so, do you?' Fire flashed in the mistress's eyes. She was angry and Bella was suddenly frightened. She had spoken out of turn and defiance was always met with more punishment. 'You may think you are ill-treated here, girl, but there are other places much worse and you will soon discover that you had a life of ease here within these walls.'

Bella kept her head high, but inside she was frozen with terror. What did the mistress intend to do with her?

'It is time you knew the truth of who and what you are! Your mother was an impertinent bitch too,' Mistress Brent said harshly. 'She came here weeks before you were born but she was too proud to accept her lot and she defied me.' A cruel smile touched her mouth. 'She begged me to send you to her sister if she died but I refused and so she ran away. I know not how she lived, but she came back here, begging to be let in hours before she gave birth to you. I turned her away and she crawled off to die in the fields where she belonged. However, the vicar found you at his door and brought you to me, demanding that I take you in. She had wrapped you in her own wool shawl – far too good for one of her kind! – and so I knew you for her brat. I kept you here to let you learn humiliation, but it seems you are as defiant as the bitch that spawned you. So now you will learn to regret you defied me . . .'

Thin spittle had come from the mistress's mouth as she ranted, trickling down her chin. Her eyes flashed with temper and her arm jerked back and forth as she lashed Bella's back and shoulders.

'The gypsy came one night. She threatened me with terrible things if I did not keep you and care for you, but she never came back.' Mistress Brent's arm arced once more, bringing down the cane across Bella's shoulders. 'She dared to threaten me – but I'll not harbour a gypsy brat a moment longer!'

Bella set her teeth, refusing to cry out as the thin stick bit into the flesh on her legs and back. The tears would come later as she lay in her bed being tended by some of the women, but no – it seemed that this time she would not be given even that courtesy. She was to be sold to a new master.

'Defy me to the end, would you? Well, you leave tonight. You will feel the pain as your wounds fester and the maggots eat your flesh, and then see if you do not feel like crawling back to beg my pardon,' she said and laughed. 'But do not bother, for I shall not admit you.'

Bella raised her head and looked at her. 'You are a wicked evil woman. You lie and you steal people's babies – and I hope you rot in Hell!'

Mistress Brent lashed out, striking her across the face twice. 'Get downstairs! Someone will come for you soon.' She thrust Bella from her room and pushed her so that she stumbled on the stairs outside, but managed to save herself from falling.

Bella's face and legs stung and her back felt sore and tender as she walked slowly to the bottom of the stairs and made her way towards the hall. Florrie was waiting there and she looked at her with pity in her eyes.

'Why did you do it, Bella? If you were hungry I would have given you some of my food.'

'I took some food to Jane whose child they stole,' Bella said as the tears coursed down her cheeks. 'They lied to her and I told her the truth – the babe lives.'

'Oh, Bella, no wonder the mistress picks on you,' Florrie said sighing. 'Let me bathe your legs and back.'

'Mistress said I was to wait here until someone came.'

'Well, they can ask for you. I'll not let you go before I tend your hurts, child.'

'I don't want you to be in trouble . . .'

'Oh, she dare not punish me for Lady Rowntree

33

favours me and I could ask for a position in her house. I stayed here because of you, Bella, and my friends – but if she raised her hand to me I would leave.'

Bella let Florrie lead her to the kitchen where her hurts were tended and she was given a cup of milk and a piece of bread to eat. She had ceased crying when another woman came looking for her.

'He's come for the girl,' she said. 'You'd best hurry, Bella, or goodness knows what she'll do – I think the devil has got into her today.'

Even the women chosen to help the mistress disliked her. Bella felt fear ripple through her, because she knew that wherever she was being sent must be much worse than this house. The trustee took hold of her arm, holding it firmly.

'You have to go, Bella. She's made up her mind to it and there's no help for you here.'

'Please, I don't want to leave you . . .'

Bella looked back at Florrie imploringly but the woman gave a little shake of her head. 'I've done all I can for you, child – may God be with you . . .'

Bella shook her head. Sometimes, she did not believe in God. How could there be a God when he let people like Mistress Brent rule their lives? People said they were lucky to live in the work-house, because otherwise they might starve – but folk who said that knew nothing of the hardship and cruelty behind those impressive wrought-iron gates.

As she was taken into the hall, she saw a large

man standing there, waiting. He had big arms and shoulders and untidy lank hair that hung about his shirt collar. His ruddy face was unshaven and there were black marks all over his skin. She could smell a sharp, metallic odour that seemed to emanate from him.

'So this is the brat,' he bellowed in a voice calculated to put fear into the stoutest of hearts. 'She'll not last five minutes – but I've been paid to take her so come on, brat. I've got no time to waste.'

Bella was given a little push towards him. Now the stink of him was much stronger and her stomach rebelled. The food she'd been given in the kitchen rose up her throat and splashed out of her mouth on to the floor, some of it landing on his boots.

'Little pig!' the man yelled and gave her a smack on the side of the head. 'You'll learn not to waste your food – and never to spill it on Karl Breck. I'm your master now, brat, and you'll clean these boots as soon as we get back to the works.'

Bella found her arm taken in a grip of steel and she was propelled out of the house. A weary-looking horse and a wagon stood outside and Bella was unceremoniously tossed up into it, landing on a pile of old sacks. She felt the pain of her back and legs where she'd been beaten, but the tears that spilled now were because she feared for the future, not for what she had suffered at the mistress's hands.

Where was she going and what would happen to her now? Bella had no true friends, though Florrie had been patient with her, teaching her how to refine her skills as a seamstress, so she would not break her heart over those she left behind, but she was terrified of this man who said he was her master and she lay shivering as the dusk gathered around them and they were driven away from all she had known.

CHAPTER 3

Florrie's anger had begun to smoulder after the brute she knew to be a chain-maker in the village of Fornham, which was some four miles or so from the Sculfield workhouse, took Bella away. She liked the young girl who had refused to be cowed by the harsh regime at the workhouse, enjoying the time they spent together in the sewing room and teaching her to improve her skills. Now the talent Bella had shown in her needlework would be wasted. She would be put to the drudgery of chain-making, which was hard enough for strong men but a destroyer of women and innocent children. The young ones often lasted only a few months, for the work was both tiring and dangerous – the heat of the furnaces was intense and it burned the unwary, scarring arms, legs and searing faces. Bella's delicate complexion would be lost if she toiled over those wicked fires.

Women and children earned only a few pennies a day, because the work was paid for by weight.

Men made the thick chains used by ships and heavy industry and were paid a fair price for their labour, but chain-making was known to be a bad trade for women and girls. The chains they made were smaller and lighter and yet they took many hours to fashion; it was a trade only the desperate would choose, when there was no other work to be had – and Bella had no choice. She'd been indentured to a master who would work her to death and that was what Mistress Brent hoped for. Florrie suspected it was unlawful for the Mistress to sell Bella the way she had, but Mistress Brent cared nothing for the law. The guardians of the workhouse trusted her and neglected to inspect or control her and she ruled much as she pleased with none to gainsay her. Bella had dared to defy her – as had Bella's mother – and this was her revenge, Florrie knew.

Florrie recalled the delicate young woman who had spent some three weeks in the workhouse before running away from its strict regime. Later, Florrie had heard that Bella's mother had given birth one cold winter's night and died in the fields. She had told the warden that her name was Marie but Florrie thought it was not truly her name. She herself had only recently come to the workhouse at that time and had formed a friendship with Bella's mother who'd told Florrie a part of her story.

'I was attacked,' Marie had confided as they sat together over their sewing, her eyes dark-shadowed as she remembered. 'I was alone in the woods and

– and I was attacked and – and violated. I never saw his face, for he was masked with a thick scarf . . .'

'Oh, you poor girl,' Florrie said.

Marie smothered a sob. 'I was unconscious when Jez found me, Florrie. He and his sister Bathsheba are gypsies. They took me in and cared for me, and I was ill for a long time.'

'How awful for you!' Florrie could hardly envisage such a terrible fate. 'Why did they not take you to your home?'

'I did not remember my name or where I lived, then – and besides, Jez was afraid he would be blamed for what had happened to me. He was not supposed to be in those woods.'

'But you remember your past now?'

'Some things,' Marie said. 'I remember that I had a sister named Kathy and Papa was a parson but I do not remember where we lived or anything more of my life and I do not know why I was in the woods that night, though I think I may have quarrelled with someone, but I cannot remember him.'

'I am so sorry,' Florrie had told her, holding Marie's hand as she saw her tremble. 'Could the gypsies not help you find your home?'

'Bathsheba wanted to take me back to where Jez had found me when I was recovered from my fever. She thought then I might remember more and she could help me find my family.'

'But then you discovered you were with child?' Florrie guessed and the young woman nodded. Marie was of a good family, a parson's daughter, she thought, and would have been too ashamed to return to her home once she knew of her condition, even if she could.

Marie's face clouded. 'Yes . . . I could not go home to shame my family. Kathy would never have found a husband and Papa could never hold up his head again. Jez told me I should stay with them.'

'Then why are you here?'

Marie shook her head. She could not be persuaded to finish her story and a few days later she had run away from the workhouse. Florrie had been distressed, especially when she learned that the girl had died in the fields. But why had she run from the gypsies who had befriended her? It was a mystery and had haunted Florrie all these years. During that time Florrie had found work outside the workhouse, but it never lasted for more than a few months and so she had returned to seek shelter – and something else drew her back time and again.

When Marie's baby was brought to the work-house, Florrie had asked to be allowed to care for her. Florrie had never had the chance to marry and have a child of her own and she'd been glad to do what she could for the motherless babe. She cared for the babe as if Bella were her own and, even when she left the workhouse for a short time, her thoughts were with the child she cared for, though she did not dare to show it for fear of reprisals from the unkind mistress.

For the first few years of Bella's life she was left to the care of anyone who took pity on her. Mostly, that was Florrie and a young woman, Maggie, who had taken her to her own breast. Maggie had given birth to a stillborn child in the workhouse and so was able to suckle Bella. She'd been kind enough in her way, but she ran away when Bella was weaned. She'd told Florrie what she intended and asked her to care for the child.

'I would take her with me, but I must find work as a housemaid and with a babe I would have no chance. Still, she is like my own and I pray you care for her.'

Florrie had promised. She would have cared for Bella in any case, because she too loved the child and she'd shielded her as much as she could from the mistress's spite, but it was impossible to prevent Mistress Brent venting her temper on the girl as she grew older, for the more she resembled her mother, the more the mistress hated her. Had Florrie been able to find permanent work she might have taken the child with her, but that had never been her fortune – especially after she had been accused of theft, and though it was a lie, most employers believed it and dismissed her once they learned of it. So, in the end, Florrie had given up all hope of a life outside the workhouse and took what comfort she could from her work and the child.

Florrie had never understood why the mistress hated little Bella so much. How would the child fare at the chain-maker's forge? Florrie could not think that she would survive the terrible conditions for long – but what could she do to help the young girl she loved? She had only a few shillings and she feared she would starve if she left this place, as so many did when they could not earn their keep.

The only person who might help her was Lady Rowntree. Florrie only ever visited her grand home when she was summoned. The work was more usually sent in and the mistress received payment but Florrie was given a few shillings a week and excused rough work so that her hands were always soft. She had considered it a reasonable exchange for her labour, because outside the workhouse she would have to find her own board and lodgings and, even if Lady Rowntree had still given her work, she might struggle to pay for rent and food. Yet now she wondered if it might be possible to make a home for herself and Bella elsewhere. She made up her mind to speak to Lady Rowntree when they next met – but what of Bella in the meantime?

Florrie's eyes stung with tears. She knew that a change in her circumstances might come too late for Bella. Even if she could find regular work and a place to live, she would still have to save the money to buy Bella's bond, and by then the girl might have fallen ill and died . . .

'Mistress Brent asked me to put her to chain-making,' Karl said to the woman who looked at him wearily when he brought Bella to the cottage that first evening. It was situated outside the village, backed by open fields and a wood. 'She must want the brat dead, because she'd not last five minutes in the furnace room. I'll give her to you, Annie. You're near yer time and exhausted, and I'd not see yer die before my son draws breath.'

Annie nodded, putting a hand to her back. She ached so much that all she wanted was to lie down and sleep forever. Her life was almost as hard as the wretches that worked for her husband in his forge; he worked them hard and showed no compassion. It surprised her that he had given this girl to her to ease her burden – she knew that he cared little for her – but of course, she thought, he wanted a son! Their first two children had been girls – and both had died in their cots within days of being born. If Annie had been rebellious enough to have such thoughts she might have wondered if her husband had smothered her daughters; he had not wanted them, scowling savagely at her each time he discovered that she'd given him a daughter. However, she was a docile girl and accepted that she must obey her husband in all things. Her father had beaten her when she was at home and Karl had not yet raised his hand to her, even though he never praised her for keeping a good table and a clean kitchen. Yet she had fallen for three children in less than three years and knew that she pleased him in this. If she gave him a healthy son he might be kinder to her.

Annie breathed easier as her husband went back to his forge. He never liked to be away too long for he believed the men and women who worked for him would cheat him if they could – though as they were paid for the work they did by weight it was not possible.

'Well, girl, what is yer name?' Annie asked irritably. She felt tired, dirty and huge and she wanted to be rid of the burden inside her womb but knew that only if she gave birth to a living boy might her husband let her rest for a while. If she lost this child, or bore a daughter, he would make certain her belly was full again before she'd had time to heal.

'Bella,' the girl said in a whisper. 'What can I do for you, mistress?'

Annie sighed with relief. She'd feared the girl would be sullen and a trouble, for why else would Mistress Brent wish her dead? Now she saw that Bella was lovely, her sweet gentle face looking anxious but not cowed. She smiled, because it seemed Karl had given her a more precious gift than he'd realised.

'My name is Annie but yer had best call me mistress or Karl will have the hide off yer back. He's a harsh man, though he's never beaten me yet, but there are other ways to break a woman's spirit and at times I've been close. Yer lucky he brought yer to me, Bella, for yer would have died in the heat of the forge. I shall need yer to work hard, for I'm near worn out carrying his son – and I do not want to lose the babe.'

'I can scrub and clean, sew and write my name – but I do not know how to cook,' Bella said and looked anxious.

'Yer can peel spuds fer his dinner,' Annie said, 'and put the kettle on the hob, Bella. I need to sit down afore I fall down. I'll teach yer to cook – me ma taught me afore she died and there was not another cook better than Ma in the whole of England.'

'The food in the workhouse was terrible,' Bella said. 'We ate gruel and bread and a thin stew sometimes – on a Sunday.'

Annie nodded, for she knew the workhouse near Sculfield, which was less than five miles from her own village of Fornham, its reputation well known to locals as being an awful place where none in their right mind would go unless they were starving.

'You'll eat better than that here,' Annie said. She went to the table and cut a slice of fresh bread, spread it with butter and then a thick layer of strawberry preserve and handed it to Bella as she placed the kettle on the hob. 'Get that down yer, child. Yer will labour 'ard because there is much to do 'ere. Karl has two nephews who live with us; they work in the furnace room and oversee the others – and they're always 'ungry. I never seem to stop washing and cooking – and the mess they make!' She shook her head. 'Karl is jealous of his brother for having two sons. His first wife died 'aving a fourth child – and none of them lived beyond a few weeks. They were all girls. Karl wants sons to take over the chain works when he dies. It would grieve him to leave it to his brother's sons.'

Bella ate her bread and jam quickly, half fearing that the huge man would return and snatch it from her. She wiped her sticky fingers on the dark-blue apron she wore over her workhouse dress.

'Didn't they teach you to wash yer 'ands at that place?'

'We wasn't allowed to,' Bella said. 'Only in the mornings and at night.'

'Well, there's a sink over there – so go and wash them now,' Annie directed. 'You'll wear that thing you've got on for workin' and I'll get yer another for when I take yer to church.' She smiled and nodded. 'See that wicker basket over there?' Bella nodded. 'That's their shirts and breeches – and they all need ironing. You'll have to heat the flatiron on the range and yer need to press hard, but they're still damp so they should be easy ter smooth.'

Bella nodded. She fetched the basket to the table and Annie spread the ironing blanket, which was covered by a piece of old sheet. She nodded to the pile of washing.

'Get on with it then, girl. I could do with a rest – and if you want some supper, it had best be finished when I come back down.'

Annie left the girl to it. She was too tired to care what Bella did. If she ruined some shirts Karl and his nephews would be furious, but he'd brought the girl here so it was hardly her fault if Bella proved useless. He would probably thrash her and might take her back whence she came, but at this moment Annie didn't really care . . .

Bella hesitated for a moment before picking up the first iron that her new mistress had put to heat. She held it a little way from her face and felt the fierce heat, then tested it on the edge of a shirt, as Florrie had shown her when she worked in the sewing room at the workhouse. Because the linen was damp, it hissed and smoothed over the coarse material. Bella nodded and proceeded to iron the first of what looked like more than a dozen similar shirts. When the iron was no longer hot, she replaced it on the range and picked up the second before testing it at the edge of the shirt as before.

It was hard work, because she had to press heavily to achieve a smooth surface that she could hang over the back of a chair to air. Her back was already beginning to feel the strain but she knew that she was lucky. They had passed the forge on their way here and Bella had smelled the awful stink coming from it. It was the smell of heat, molten metal and sweat. Even outside the heat met them and she could not imagine what it must be like inside. She was fortunate that the chain-maker's wife was close to her time and she'd been given to her as her servant. Bella knew that it would have been much harder for her at the chain works.

She had been fortunate, despite her surly master, and she decided that she would help the mistress, who seemed more weary than unkind, as much as she could. Indeed, she was probably lucky, more fortunate than poor Jane who had been turned out from the shelter of the workhouse on a snowy night. Regardless of her own plight, Bella spared a thought for the woman she'd seen from the landing window.

'I don't know where you are, Jane, but I hope

you're warm and I pray that one day you will find your baby . . .'

Arthur's attention was caught by a slight noise. The young woman was stirring at last. She'd slept all night and most of the morning, swallowing a little brandy and water when coaxed to it, but falling back into her state of semi-unconsciousness almost at once. He stood looking down at her as she opened her eyes and stared at him, more in puzzlement than fear. Arthur thought her eyes were a lovely shade of azure fringed by golden lashes. With her hair washed and dressed in decent clothes she would be a beauty and he thought it was probably her looks that had brought her down: many men would desire a woman like this one.

'You are awake at last,' he said as he saw the first awareness and unease in those wonderful eyes. 'How do you feel? When we found you on the road I feared you might not last the night.'

She pushed herself up against the pillows, glancing down at the clean linen nightgown that was much too large for her. 'Who undressed me?'

'Sally – she is the landlord's wife and she made you comfortable. I understand what you were wearing fell to pieces and she burned it. We shall find something for you to wear, ma'am.'

'Why do you call me, ma'am? I – I am not wed.'

'You have borne a child and I thought perhaps . . .' She moved her head negatively, the hint of tears in her eyes. 'I do not recall much but they called me

48

a whore. They said I wore no wedding ring.' An anxious look came to her face. 'I cannot remember clearly . . . but I know I bore a child, a living child. They told me the child died immediately after she was born, but they lied; I heard her cry – and I heard them say she was healthy. Bella told me they gave the child to someone in a carriage.' She whimpered with distress. 'They stole my baby and threw me out. It was so cold and I did not know where to go . . . I wandered across the fields until I found the high road in the hope I might come to a place where I could find work. I saw a sign for Winchester, where I think I once stayed for a time though I do not recall anything of that city, but it was in any case many miles hence and I knew not where to go . . .'

Arthur shook his head for Winchester was a good day's journey by carriage pulled by fast horses and would take days or weeks to walk that far – and she was in no condition to go anywhere.

'Who are "they"?' Arthur asked gently, realising that a great wrong had been done her.

She took a deep shuddering breath, then began, 'Mistress Brent is the mistress of the workhouse near the village of Sculfield. I was close to my time and the villagers told me to go there, but I wish I had given birth in the fields for then I might still have my babe.'

'You are not Romany?'

'No, I am sure I am not,' she said. 'I was wearing clothes that might have belonged to a gypsy but I think they were given to me before – before I lost my memories . . .'

'Perhaps you travelled with the gypsies? Perhaps they attended a fair in Winchester and that is why the name attracted you . . .' Arthur suggested. 'No, do not struggle to remember. It does not matter for now. In time we must hope that your memories will return but for now, what shall we call you?'

'They called me Jane but it was not my name.' She gave a cry of despair. 'Please, do not call me by their name! I think . . . I believe the name Meg means something to me, though I know not why.' She nodded and looked at him in appeal. 'Please call me Meg – and your name, sir?'

'I am Arthur Stoneham – and you need have no fear of me. I shall help you if I can, Meg.'

'Yes, I have been aware of you,' she said and a smile lit her face for a brief moment. 'You gave me brandy when I could feel nothing but icy cold.'

'So you were aware of me.' Arthur nodded. 'I will make no promises, except that I can find you a home to stay in while your memory returns. As for your child, I shall see if Mistress Brent will yield the truth to me.'

'She will lie to you as she did to me.'

'Very likely, but there are other people who may not be as tight-lipped. Money will make some folk talk – and as it happens, I know one of the guardians of the Sculfield workhouse slightly. Now, you mentioned someone called Bella?'

'Bella is a child of perhaps eleven summers. She

brought me food and milk and, the night I was thrown out, told me she had seen my babe given away. But I do not think she knows more. The master of the workhouse is a man called Walter Brent and his wife is the mistress. He is a harsh man. I have seen him strike an elderly man down, and the boys go in terror of him. I think even his wife suffers at his hands, though she is spiteful and cruel. You should take care, sir, for they are evil people.'

'As I said, I promise nothing except that I shall try.' He smiled at her. 'I shall leave you and Sally will bring you clothes that belonged to one of her maids. Perhaps not what you would wish to wear, but better than the rags we found you in.'

'Thank you, you are very kind. The clothes will do very well.'

'I shall find better for you as soon as it may be arranged.'

'Why will you do so much for me? You know nothing of me.'

'I hate injustice,' Arthur said. 'I believe that Fate brought you to me last evening and who knows, She may yet be kinder still. I shall visit this work-house and discover what I can . . .'

CHAPTER 4

'You wished to see me, sir?' Mistress Brent looked at Arthur uneasily as he was shown into her sitting room. She offered her hand a little tentatively. 'I am Norma Brent.'

'Good day, madam. My name is Arthur Stoneham,' he said and he spoke evenly, giving no hint of his anger. 'I have come to make inquiries on behalf of my cousin by marriage – Mistress Meg Stoneham. She recently gave birth within these walls to a living child – a girl. Meg tells me that you took the babe from her and told her it had died.'

'That gypsy wretch your cousin?' Mistress Brent looked at him in disbelief. 'I do not believe it – how could that be?'

'She had an unfortunate accident upon the road and was set upon by some rogues. My cousin and I have been searching for his wife for some weeks and had almost given up until we were told of a young woman taken ill and brought here,' Arthur lied easily. He had decided that this woman would lie whatever he did and the only way was to scare her – or bribe her. 'We had offered a reward for her recovery because my cousin loves her and is anxious to hold his child . . .'

He could see her mind working as her eyes tried to avoid his. She was deciding whether it would be worth telling him the truth and risk being accused of stealing a child or easier to lie to him.

'Then I wish that I had better news for you, sir,' she said, making up her mind to stick to her story. 'We called the young woman Jane, for she could not recall her own name, and she wore no wedding ring . . .'

'We believe it was stolen from her along with her clothes, all of which were expensive,' Arthur said embroidering on his tale of misfortune. 'But you have news of the child, I hope?'

'I fear that the babe died almost immediately it was born.' Mistress Brent held fast to her story. Arthur was sure she lied. There was something in her eyes and a slight unease in her manner. He had not been sure of the truth until then, for Meg might have been mistaken. Though he believed her an honest woman, a woman in the aftermath of a hard labour could easily have misheard, believing she heard her child cry when there was no cry at all. 'We tried to tell her but she became abusive and we were forced to put her out.'

'Into the bitter chill of night? Had she not been found and cared for she might have died,' Arthur said sternly. 'I do not think that Sir Arnold and

Lady Rowntree would be pleased to hear of such heartless behaviour, madam. Nor do I believe that the babe died. There are witnesses who will testify otherwise.'

'Liars all!' Mistress Brent said furiously, her face red with temper now. 'Besides, none would dare to speak against me. And if you blacken my name you will be sorry. You can prove nothing!'

'You think not?' He smiled wryly. 'I have met bullies before, madam. I assure you that my word goes a long way in influential circles. As it happens, I know Lady Rowntree – we have served on a charity committee together in the past. She and her husband set this workhouse up to help the poor of this parish. I cannot think she knows what goes on here. Once I tell them of your cruelty – and explain that I think you sell the children and babies—'

'Lies! You can prove nothing.'

Arthur's eyebrows rose. 'I wonder how many more children you've sold, madam. How many years does your reign of tyranny stretch? How many lives have you ruined or blighted?' He was merely guessing, using Meg's rather vague memories of her time here and his own instinct, gained from years of experience, but the look in her eyes was enough to make him certain he knew, though he had no proof.

'My husband will thrash you for slighting our good name!' she blustered but Arthur had seen the fear and guilt in her eyes. It was as he'd thought, and his bold verbal attack on her had paid off. She must have many lives on her conscience.

'He is welcome to try, madam,' Arthur said. 'I shall be speaking to Lady Rowntree and I think you will both find yourselves dismissed before much longer. Indeed, that may not be the limit of your woes. I shall do my utmost to see you both behind prison bars!'

Arthur left her fuming. As he went down the stairs he saw a woman of perhaps forty years standing at the bottom, clearly waiting for him.

'I heard some of what you said to the mistress,' Florrie told him and clutched anxiously at his arm. 'I pray you will not believe her lies.'

'I do not,' Arthur said. 'Meg believes her child lives and someone told her that it was given away.'

'I know the child lived at birth,' Florrie said, 'and Bella saw the babe given to someone in a carriage but I did not – though I know it has happened in the past. And I know she sold Bella to a brute who will work her to death. He owns a forge in the village of Fornham some four miles or so hence on the Alton road, and I have heard that he makes chain and works his people hard.'

'Your name is?' Arthur's brows lifted.

'Florrie Stewart, sir. I came here when I was close to starving years ago and, though I am a skilled seamstress, I have feared to leave this place though some of the things that go on here make me sick to my stomach.' She clutched at his arm. 'Will you see if Bella is all right, sir? I fear she is too delicate for the work she has been set to.'

'And you care for her?'

'Yes, sir. I helped care for Bella since she was a baby.'

'Rest easy, Mistress Stewart. I shall make it my business to see if the girl is safe. I am staying at the Three Pheasants Inn, which is some nine miles east of here, Mistress Stewart. I might help you to find a good position.'

'Lady Rowntree likes my work. If she would take me into her household I would gladly go, but I was once falsely accused of theft and lost my position. Lady Rowntree knows the employer who dismissed me and I do not think she would have me in her house if she knew.'

'Then I will help you,' Arthur said and smiled. 'You may trust me. You are not the first to have lost your position because of a lie. Leave this place and come to me at the inn before the end of the week if you will.'

'Thank you, sir – but if you could help Bella? She is not strong enough to work in that awful chain-making place, and her mother was a lady.'

'You knew the girl's mother?'

'Briefly, when she stayed here a short time. She told us her name was Marie but I think it may have been a name she chose for herself. Marie died in the fields one bitter night after leaving Bella on the church steps. She was beautiful and gentle, a sweet girl, and we cared for her babe as best we could despite the mistress's spite when it was brought here by the vicar.'

'Yes, I'm sure you did,' Arthur said. 'I intend to speak with Lady Rowntree concerning this place. It may be that things will change here, but I cannot guarantee it.'

Florrie curtsied and thanked him and Arthur left. He knew that, even as he went out to his carriage, Mistress Brent would be complaining to her husband. If he was a man at all he would come after Arthur and try to force an apology from him. Otherwise, the guilty couple would flee. It all depended on whether they believed Arthur's story. If they called his bluff he might not be able to prove anything, but if they ran . . . A smile touched his lips. Florrie had told him what little she knew, but others would tell more if they thought it safe.

In the meantime, Arthur would visit the chain works and hear what this Karl Breck had to say. If he was willing to sell the child Bella to him, he would buy her and take her back to London – and if not? Mentally, Arthur shrugged. He could not rescue every child forced to do unsuitable work, but he would not stand by and see cruelty.

Bella emptied the clothes from the copper where they had been boiled and then left to cool. She put them through the big mangle with its wooden rollers and turned the metal handle. It was almost too hard for her to turn full circle and she was panting by the time she had finished. Now she had to rinse them all in clean water in the zinc bath and then put them through the mangle again. She had filled the bath with cold water and dumped the load of sheets and pillow covers in it, sighing as she stirred with a big wooden stick.

'Bella! Bella, come and help me!' The scream came from the kitchen and Bella rushed in to discover her mistress bent almost double and writhing with pain. She saw that there was a puddle on the tiled floor and where Annie had pulled up her skirts she could see red stains on the cream flannel petticoats.

'My baby!' Annie gasped and clutched at her stomach again. 'It's coming early. Oh, I knew it would happen after what he did last night . . .' Tears rolled down her cheeks and she clutched at Bella's arm. 'He won't leave me alone. He won't see I need rest!' She gave a sob of utter despair.

'Let me help you to bed,' Bella said. 'The beds are newly made and the old sheets are soaking.'

'I need the midwife,' Annie moaned. 'Help me upstairs, Bella – and then run to Fornham for the midwife.'

Bella nodded, looking at her with big, scared eyes. She had not been frightened of the mistress at the workhouse even though she was beaten regularly, but the thought of Annie giving birth terrified her.

Annie leaned on Bella heavily as she helped her upstairs. Once in the bedroom, Bella was kept busy covering the clean sheets with old towels and a torn sheet, but by the time it was done, Annie was panting and grimacing like an animal, her teeth bared as she tried to control her pain.

'Go now and get the midwife,' she gasped.

Bella hesitated for a moment. She'd seen women give birth at the workhouse and she sensed that the babe was coming soon, but Annie gestured angrily at her to go and so she ran. She rushed down the stairs and across the fields at the back of the house towards the village, running as swiftly as her legs would take her. Annie was in terrible pain and Bella was afraid she might die alone with no one to help her.

She ran and ran as fast as she could, her chest heaving as she gasped for breath. It seemed a lot further than it had the day her master brought her to his house and gave her to the mistress. She was gasping and there was pain in her chest by the time she reached the village of Fornham, which was just one street and a huddle of houses to either side, two shops and a larger house that belong to the doctor. She'd run so fast that she was out of breath and it was a few moments before she was able to tell the first person she saw what was needed. The woman looked at her down her long nose when she heard who her employer was.

'Jenny Midwife lives in that cottage at the end of the street,' she said coldly. 'But you'll not find her there – she's at Mr Tucker's farm. His wife is having her baby and she's gone there to nurse her.'

Bella felt the panic rise. 'If no one comes to Annie's aid she will die – please, ma'am, will you come?'

'Me? Come to that house?' The woman's eyebrows arched in horror. 'No, indeed I shall not – fetch Annie's husband to her or someone else.'

Bella looked at her in disgust and ran off. She met three women coming from the village shop but they all shook their heads when she begged them to come to Annie. In despair, Bella ran to the workshop and called for her master. When he came out to her, he looked furious, as if she had committed a sin by asking for him.

'The midwife is away and no one will come,' Bella said. 'Annie is bad and I fear she may die!'

'Get back there and see to her,' Karl said and cuffed her ear. 'You're not a babe. You should've stayed with her and 'elped her.'

Bella knew that any excuse would fall on deaf ears. He went back into the cavernous interior of the dark workshop and Bella began to run back to the cottage. She was terrified of what she would find because she knew that without the midwife it would all fall on her shoulders. She had seen babes born but she did not know what to do for the mother and she feared that Annie might not survive. The babe was coming early and that meant something was wrong. Without proper help, there was little hope for either Annie or her child.

'Where is the midwife?' Annie gasped as Bella returned to the bedroom. 'Is she coming?'

'She was at a farm,' Bella said. 'I know not where – and no one else would come.' She moved closer to the bed. 'I will help you, mistress. I have water on the range. I will fetch it.'

Annie gave a little scream and half rose from the

61

bed. 'No, don't leave me. I can't be alone – it hurts so much. Neither of the others was like this!'

She screamed again loudly and clutched at Bella's arm. 'It is tearing me apart!'

Bella bent over her, stroking the damp hair from her forehead. 'What can I do to help you, mistress?'

'Nothing, I need the midwife,' Annie moaned and screamed again.

Neither of them heard the knock at the door or the voice that called out, nor did they hear the footsteps on the stairs as Annie screamed and screamed. She was panting wildly, her eyes fearful as the pain ripped at her.

'Where is the midwife?' a man's voice asked suddenly and Bella whirled to see a man in clothes that fitted him like a second skin. She had never seen one in her life but she thought he must be a gentleman.

'She is away helping a farmer's wife and no one else would come,' Bella said, a sob in her voice. 'I think Annie will die.'

'We cannot have that,' the man said and smiled at her. 'Are you Bella?'

'Yes, sir.'

'Then take care of your mistress while I fetch the doctor. I shall be as quick as I can . . .'

Bella wanted to beg him to stay but he was out of the door and mounting his horse. She watched Annie writhing in pain, terrified that the gentleman would not return in time and her mistress would die. Going nervously towards the bed, she stroked Annie's sweat-stained brow.

'The gentleman has gone for the doctor, Mistress. He won't be long . . . he promised he would be back soon.'

Annie stared at her wildly, her body tossing as she arched with pain. Unable to do more than comfort her with words, Bella stayed by her side, reassuring her as best she could, until after what seemed ages, she heard the sound of voices downstairs and then the gentleman brought the doctor into the room.

'Fetch up the boiling water, girl,' the doctor said, 'and then you can help me. Now I shall examine you, young lady and we shall see if this child is willing to be born . . .' he said, bending over Annie.

Annie looked at him with frightened eyes as he felt her stomach and then nodded. But for all his brusqueness the doctor's touch was gentle and reassuring. She was panting again. He told her to count and to breathe steadily, and then he reached towards her dilated opening. 'I will try to be gentle . . .'

For answer, Annie screamed as the doctor turned the child. He was working for some moments and she screamed several times, tossing her head wildly in her agony.

'I am so sorry but . . . ah yes, now baby is facing the right way. I think we shall do much better now, Annie . . .'

Annie screamed and began to writhe and push as she felt movement inside her. Her child was suddenly in a hurry to be born; pain caught her, making her pant and push, and then the child's head emerged and with a whoosh and a rush of blood and slime, the large body of a male child came slithering into the world. The doctor tied the birth cord securely and then cut it with the silver penknife he'd earlier taken from his pocket. He picked up the babe and showed him to his mother and then gave him to Bella. After washing his hands and pocketing his knife, he looked at Bella, motioning for her to change the water in the bowl.

'Wash him, child, and then give him to his mother. In a moment you can do what is necessary to make her comfortable but just now she needs to rest and enjoy the babe.'

'Yes, sir,' Bella jumped to obey. She was stunned by what she had seen and watched as the doctor cleared away all the bloody towels and wiped some of the worst from the mother before covering her. She poured fresh warm water into the empty bowl and gently cleansed the babe of mucus and blood, wrapped him in a large clean white towel and took him to his mother. Annie lay still, just looking up at the doctor, clearly shocked and exhausted by the birth. Then, as he was about to turn away, she caught his arm.

'Thank you, sir. My husband will pay you.'

'Mr Stoneham has already paid me; had it not been for him I confess I should have been loath to set foot in this house again.'

Annie looked away in shame, for she knew her

husband's reputation. 'See the doctor out, Bella – and ask the gentleman to step up here please. I wish to thank him.'

Bella did as she was told. In the kitchen the stranger asked the doctor if all was well and they spoke together in hushed voices for a moment. After the doctor had left, the gentleman turned to Bella.

'Is your mistress comfortable? Has she all she needs?'

'She asked that you would step up to her room so that she might thank you, sir.'

'Very well . . .' He followed her back to the room above, where Annie was looking down at the child that had caused her so much agony.

'I am glad to see you safely through your ordeal, ma'am.'

'Thanks to you, sir,' Annie said looking up at him in wonder. 'It was good of you to fetch the doctor for I know well he did not wish to come. May I know your name, sir?'

He smiled at her as she kissed her child and nursed it to her breast. 'I am Arthur Stoneham and I came here to see how Bella was faring . . .' He glanced at the girl. 'Does your master treat you well, child?'

'He gave me to Annie – and I like helping her. It's better than the workhouse,' Bella said truthfully.

Arthur nodded, watching the mother and child for a few moments as they settled and got to know one another, the child snuffling as it latched on to its mother and nuzzled her, seeking warmth and the sustenance instinct told it was to be found here.

'Leave them together for a while and follow me downstairs, child. I would speak with you, Bella – and you should make a cup of something hot for your mistress.'

Annie was looking at her son with tears on her cheeks. She had suffered but now she had the son that Karl had longed for. 'Thank you, Mr Stoneham – I believe you saved both me and my baby for if you had not fetched the doctor we might both have died.'

'I did what I was able, ma'am,' Arthur said.

Bella followed Arthur downstairs. When they reached the kitchen she filled the kettle once more. The gentleman was looking about him.

'Where do you sleep, Bella?'

'In the attic, sir. It is warm and I have a bed.'

'And are you fed adequately?'

'Annie makes the best pies and cakes I've ever tasted, sir.'

'Then you are content to stay here?'

Bella hesitated. She did not dislike the work she did and her mistress was kind enough despite the occasional sharpness of her tongue and a small slap if she was tired and angry.

'It's all right, sir.' Bella did not know what else to say. 'It's better than the workhouse. I hated it there and the food is much better here.'

Mr Stoneham hesitated, and then he nodded. 'Very well, I shall not try to buy your bond if you are content here. Now, please tell me what you know of the babe that was sold at the workhouse.'

'I saw the babe born, sir – and they thought the woman they called Jane would die, but the babe was healthy and then Jane recovered and asked about her child. They told her she was dead, but I'd seen the mistress take her away and the child was crying loudly. Later, I saw the mistress give the babe to someone in a carriage but I saw not who it was.'

'And you were certain it was Jane's babe she gave?'

'Yes, sir. I know it was Jane's child for there were no others in the house that night nor for some weeks after.'

'Good – then I may ask you to sign your name to a paper for me another day. Will you do that?'

'Yes, sir – though I can write no more than my name.'

'That will be fine, Bella.' He put his hand in his pocket and brought out a florin. 'This is for you – I would give you more but you might be accused of stealing it.'

'I've never had a coin before but I've seen one of these – Florrie had one from the lady she works for and she bought some plums for us all and shared them.'

Arthur nodded. 'Is there anything more you can tell me, child?'

'I'm not sure, sir.' Bella looked puzzled. 'Well, there was the boy that disappeared . . .'

Arthur's brow furrowed. 'A boy disappeared?'

'Yes, sir – a few months back, in the autumn last year. He tried to run away and the master caught him and brought him back. He said he would be whipped and told us it was a warning to us all, but we never saw him again.'

'What was the boy's name?'

'It was a bit like yours, sir – Arthur Meaks. But he was not meek, sir. He was always in trouble and being punished, and then he was gone.'

'Did no one tell you where he'd gone?'

'The mistress said he'd been sent to work for a master but I do not know where, for I never saw him again after the master dragged him away – and when I asked Florrie, she was upset and said it was best not to speak of it.'

'Thank you,' Arthur said. 'You have helped me, Bella – and if ever you need my help, you may send word to me here.'

He handed her a small white card with some letters printed on it. The writing meant nothing to Bella but she tucked it inside her bodice with her precious florin. Other people knew how to read and something told her that one day she might want to contact this man again.

'Thank you, sir.' She hesitated but then did not ask for help, because where could she go if he took her away from here? Bella did not want to return to the workhouse and there was nowhere else for her to go. Here her master generally ignored her and Annie was sometimes kind; she thought there might be far worse places than the one she already had and so she held her thoughts inside.

'Goodbye, Bella,' Mr Stoneham said. 'I will come

to see you another day and if there is something you wish to tell me you may do so then.'

Bella watched as he left the kitchen and then set about gathering another kettle and some clean linen. Annie would want to wash and she would need a cup of tea.

CHAPTER 5

'He will expose us and then what shall we do?'
Mistress Brent cried and glared at her husband. 'We
shall be cast into prison and it is all your fault for
selling those babies!'

'You have been quick to take your share of the
money,' her husband grunted. He raised a knotted
fist to her, clenching it in her face. 'Stop your
complaining, woman. This man can know nothing,
for who would tell him? Only a child who is probably half dead by now. The new parents will not
speak for they are equally guilty in this – and this
business with that interfering fool will all go away.'

'But what if they come here and search?' she said
and whimpered as he struck the side of her head.
Her eyes were large and accusing as she looked at
him. 'I have sold children but you have done much
worse and I will not hang for you.'

'Be quiet, you fool!' He rounded on her and struck
her several times about the face and head, making
her shriek and cower in fear. 'Whatever I have done,

you played your part and do not forget it. If they hang me you will hang too – for I'll make certain you're implicated in it all.'

Mistress Brent stared after him with resentful eyes as he left the room. When they'd first come here she'd thought it would be a good life, but he'd made it all go bad. She hated him and yet she feared to leave him. Walter was a violent man and he would never let her go because what she knew could hang him. She went to the little washstand in the corner of her room and bathed her face in cold water. There would be a bruise, which she would struggle to cover with powder and rouge.

She was frightened of the man who had come to investigate them, but even more terrified of her husband. If he thought she had betrayed him, he would not hesitate to kill her as he had those others . . . It crossed her mind that she might throw herself on Mr Stoneham's mercy, confess her part and tell all in return for indemnity, but she could not bring herself to do it. Even if she was not imprisoned, she would never again find herself in a position of trust and plenty. She would be poor and homeless and the thought of ending her days in a workhouse like this terrified her.

No, she must remain silent as Walter bid her. Perhaps this Mr Stoneham would become bored and return to wherever he had come from . . .

Toby Rattan was waiting for Arthur when he returned to the inn later that day. Arthur greeted

72

his closest friend warmly and shook his hand. The younger son of a lord, Toby had helped him with his charitable work many times and he had a feeling he was going to need his assistance before he was finished here.

'It was good of you to come straight down, Toby.'

'I came as soon as I got your note.' Toby arched his brows wickedly. 'How is it that you manage to get into a scrape whenever I am not with you?'

'It must be fate,' Arthur said, and laughed. 'Would you believe it – I come fresh from having overseen a child delivered to the local chain-maker's wife.'

'Good grief!' Toby looked thunderstruck. 'You never cease to amaze me. Now tell me what is behind all this and what you were doing in that poor woman's bedchamber in the first place.'

'I went in search of a workhouse child I'd been told had been sold to the chain-maker.'

'Ah, I might have known it would have something to do with a workhouse!' Toby nodded in perfect understanding. 'Pray tell me more. It was damned boring in London without you so I may as well give you a hand. What is going on down here?'

'You stupid little wretch!' Mistress Brent struck the child in a fury, sending her sprawling to the floor. She stood over the trembling girl and glared at her. 'Get up and stop looking at me as if I were a two-headed monster. If you do not obey the rules, you will be punished.'

Florrie watched as Sophie scrambled to her feet and stood trembling before the mistress, expecting another blow and all because she had dared to ask for a second piece of bread at breakfast.

'Get out of my sight or I will thrash you!' Mistress Brent said, and the small child ran down the corridor and out of sight.

Florrie hesitated and then stepped forward. 'That was not necessary, mistress. The child was given only a scrap of bread for her breakfast and she was hungry.'

'She is a greedy glutton – and you had best mind your tongue, Florrie, or I may rescind your privileges.'

'You do not own me,' Florrie said and raised her eyes to meet those of her furious mistress. She was not sure where the courage to defy Norma Brent had come from, but she was no longer afraid of her. 'I could find work elsewhere, as you well know. I stayed here because it suited me – but you sent Bella away and now you mistreat Sophie. You should be more careful, Mistress Brent. Inquiries are being made concerning you and the master – and some of us know things that you would not wish spoken of!'

'How dare you threaten me!' Mistress Brent raised her hand as if to strike Florrie, her eyes glittering with fury. 'You would find it hard to live outside these walls, Florrie – and if you wish to leave you owe money for your keep.'

Florrie refused to back down and continued to

face her. There had been a time when she feared the mistress, the more so because she had not thought she could manage to live outside these walls, but since Bella had been sent away, Florrie had begun to realise how much she hated her life here and these people who ruled the inmates with harsh cruelty. Of course there were rules; there had to be, for the workhouse was there to ease the plight of the destitute – but when run by corrupt and greedy masters like the Brents it became a place of suffering and sometimes worse.

'I have earned my keep – as any magistrate would testify.'

Mistress Brent lowered her gaze before the accusation in Florrie's. 'You will be a fool if you leave here,' she said at last. 'I'll give you six months before you return here or to another such institution.'

Florrie did not answer her. Much depended on whether or not Lady Rowntree would give her a position in her household. Mr Stoneham had promised to see what he could do to help her – but how much reliance could she place on a man she did not know? If she left here without a position secured she would have nothing to live on until she could find work. She'd been given a few small gifts of money by Lady Rowntree when she was particularly pleased with her work, but the money she earned was taken by Mistress Brent to pay her keep. Like the other inmates Florrie was entitled to a few pennies each week for her work, but she knew that she earned many guineas for the mistress of the workhouse by her exquisite needlework. Surely she could earn enough to keep herself? But she would need help to set up her own little establishment, unless Lady Rowntree would take her on, so it would take courage to actually leave here.

Florrie was thoughtful after her encounter with Mistress Brent. She had threatened her with exposure and it was not only the beatings she inflicted on children and vulnerable old people who had nowhere else to go that she could speak of – there was the mystery of the missing boy. Except that it was not a mystery to Florrie. She knew exactly what had happened to young Arthur Meaks and where he was – and she thought that if Mr Stoneham kept his word to her, she would tell him what she knew. Florrie had hoped he would return, though she knew where to go to find him; it was just whether or not she had the courage to leave the security of these walls that had been her home for so long.

The young woman paused as she entered the inn's private parlour. Toby stood and inclined his head. Although not as tall as Arthur Stoneham, he was lean and strong-looking, his hair light, his eyes hazel green and his complexion clear. His smile was meant to put her at her ease.

'I believe you are Mr Stoneham's friend, sir?' she said.

'Toby Rattan,' he said. 'Arthur told me that your name is Meg?'

'I do not truly know it is, sir – but the name seemed to mean something to me and I do not wish to be called by the name they gave me.'

Something in her eyes touched Toby's heart. He was filled with a sudden fierce anger against the people who had hurt her, both those at the workhouse and the others who had brought her down. He was also aware of a desire to protect her. In that moment Toby knew that he would stay here and help Arthur sort out the nest of vipers at the workhouse, but also that he would help discover who had taken Meg's child – and when he did, he would bring it back to her.

'Meg is a pretty name and it suits you,' Toby said. 'Arthur is a good man – and between us we shall leave no stone unturned in seeking the child you bore.'

'He saved my life and you are kind,' Meg said and blushed because the way he smiled at her made her feel safe and warm. 'I was lucky that Mr Stoneham found me.'

'He has asked me to help him. We shall not allow this injustice to go unanswered, Meg. Believe me, if your babe lives then we shall find her.'

Meg nodded and gave him her hand. 'I thank you, Mr Rattan, and I pray that God will help you in your search.'

Toby kissed her hand gently.

'I am honoured to serve you,' he said. 'Arthur has gone to meet someone but he will be back shortly. I give you my word, both Arthur and I will make certain that in future you are protected and cared for.'

Her shy smile made Toby smile in response. She was lovely and, he believed, innocent of all guile. Her story must be a tragic one and he was determined to discover it.

'It was very good of you to see me,' Arthur said when he was shown into Lady Rowntree's elegant parlour. Its shades of green, rose and cream had a faded, restful aura and suited the beautiful woman in her later years. 'Forgive me for intruding this way but it is important.'

Lady Rowntree smiled. In her day she had been a great beauty, the toast of London drawing rooms, and she still retained the elegance of manner and English-rose complexion that had once had the men vying for her hand. 'Mr Stoneham, we have met on various occasions and I know you to be a man of humanitarian principles which accord with those of my family.'

'I thank you – that is high praise,' Arthur said and went forward to bow over her hand. 'I know it was your family that endowed the Sculfield workhouse.'

Lady Rowntree frowned. 'Have you come to ask for someone to be admitted?'

'No, Lady Rowntree, I come to tell you of injustice – and I believe ill-management on the part of the mistress and master there.'

Lady Rowntree sighed and nodded, showing no

sign of outrage or surprise at the accusation. 'Then I shall hear you, for I have sensed that things were not right for some time past. When I visit, the children are always well-dressed and all say they are fed and happy, but last time I saw fear in some of their eyes and it made me unsure but my husband is unwell, and I fear he may not recover, and I was afraid to stir up something I suspected might be deeply unpleasant.'

'Then I may speak frankly?'

'Of course. Please, do sit down – may I ring for refreshments?'

'I thank you, no. I have breakfasted not long since.' Arthur sat down on one of the beautiful mahogany sabre-leg chairs so that he was on her level and she did not need to look up at him. 'I am sorry that your husband is unwell, ma'am. It is not the time to be worrying you – but it has come to my attention that Mistress Brent is unfit to be a warden of the workhouse. I have not as yet met her husband but she is a liar and a bully. I have been told that she steals the children of unfortunate women driven to have their babies within her walls. I cannot say that she is paid, for I have no proof but I suspect it.'

'Why else would she do it?' Lady Rowntree looked sad. 'When she and her husband were employed, we made it clear that we wished the house to be run on compassionate lines. Naturally, there must be rules, but no woman should be forced to give up her babe without her consent – and I personally instructed that there should only be a physical beating if it was necessary in extreme cases of violence.'

Arthur nodded, because it was what he would have expected of a philanthropic woman. 'Then you would not agree with vulnerable girls being beaten for no reason – and given to masters who may work them to death?'

'Certainly not!' She looked shocked. 'Violent men must sometimes be restrained for they would take advantage and cause trouble for others – but I do not see why a child should ever be beaten. There are other ways to discipline them, if need be.'

He smiled, reassured. 'Then we are in accord, my lady. I know a girl of eleven was recently sent to the local chain-maker's establishment, perhaps in the hope that she might be worked until she was exhausted, for many such children have died in such places. As it happens, in this case the man gave her to his wife who was then expecting and has recently had a child – but it makes me wonder what has happened to other children. I should like your permission to inspect the house and grounds – and examine the records.'

Lady Rowntree hesitated momentarily, and then inclined her head. 'Yes, I believe that must be the way to proceed. My husband and I are the chief guardians but others have made donations and must be told of any wrongdoing – and an investigation will provide the truth. I would not cast Master and Mistress Brent off without proof.'

'You are fair, ma'am, and I cannot disagree with you, though I sense that we shall uncover far more evil than we can yet imagine.'

A little shiver ran through her. 'Yes, I fear you may . . .' She hesitated uncertainly and then lifted her head in resolution. 'Look for proof of what happened to a boy named Arthur Meaks. My husband had thought of taking him for a stable boy but the child disappeared last autumn. I was told that he had been sent to a master in Yarmouth because he had professed an interest in the sea – and when I asked for more details I was promised Master Brent would send them to me. However, he has not done so and may believe my personal troubles have made me forget.' She sighed. 'Had my husband not been so ill I should have pressed them more but I could not summon the will to do it.'

'The name of Arthur Meaks has been mentioned to me previously,' Arthur said. 'Someone told me the master intended to punish him for trying to run away and no one has seen him since, which seems suspicious.'

Lady Rowntree shivered. 'You suspect foul play, do you not?'

'Yes, my lady. I make no accusations yet, but I fear it may be the case. Others of like mind and I are trying to make these institutions more accountable than in the past for we know that many bad things have happened.'

'We appointed the master and mistress with the best intentions,' Lady Rowntree said and her hands

81

trembled, the valuable diamonds sparkling on her fingers. 'I believe they think themselves safe, because my husband is no longer the strong man he once was . . .' She took a deep breath, then, 'May I ask you to discover the truth and do whatever is necessary, Mr Stoneham? I will sign any power of attorney you need in relation to the governance of the workhouse, giving you complete authority.'

'Thank you,' Arthur said. 'I will have something drawn up and call on you again. I think you are very wise.' He rose to leave. 'I wish your husband a speedy recovery.'

'I fear my husband will not see another year out,' she said sadly, 'but I have great hopes for my daughter who is to be married soon.'

Arthur inclined his head and turned to leave, then remembered. 'I believe you think well of the seamstress Florrie's work?'

Lady Rowntree looked surprised. 'Yes, she does the most delicate embroidery – why do you ask?'

'She told me that she wishes to leave the workhouse but is nervous of finding enough work to support herself.'

'Tell her she may come to me and live in here. I can always find work for a woman of her talent – and I am sure my friends might like to take advantage of her services sometimes.'

'She was once dismissed on a false tale of theft and fears you might think ill of her.'

Lady Rowntree shook her head. 'I know what happened and do not believe her a thief, for her mistress at that time was a petty, spiteful woman.' She held out her hand. 'I thank you for calling on me, sir – and please tell Florrie to come to me as soon as she wishes.'

Arthur kissed her hand, bowed and left her. He would still have investigated the master and mistress of the workhouse if Lady Rowntree had not been so cooperative, but her consent made his task so much easier. He intended to seize all the records going back to the Brents' arrival years before and to have a team of men he trusted search the house and the grounds.

CHAPTER 6

'Can yer not keep the brat quiet for a while?' Karl glared at his wife as his son screamed yet again. 'Is there to be no peace in my house? Where is the girl I gave yer – does she shirk her work? I'll give her a thrashing; that will teach her to put her back into it.'

'Bella works hard all day,' Annie said and looked at him resentfully. 'I do not know what I should do without her – those nephews of yours are always hungry and always dirty. We are forever washing their clothes and we have your son to care for now.'

'At least you got one thing right,' Karl said and his expression softened as she picked up his son and put him to her breast. The child sucked lustily, his cries silenced for a time. Bella came in from the scullery carrying a basket piled high with shirts, breeches, napkins and towels. She set the basket down and put two flatirons on the range to heat.

'I think little Karl has soiled himself,' Annie said to the girl and held him out to her. 'Take him in the

85

scullery and change him. I have to start on the baking or we'll have no bread for supper – and then I have to make the cream cheese and butter.'

Karl kept two milking cows and four pigs in pens behind the cottage. Besides all the work of the house and feeding three grown men, the two women had to feed the animals, milk the cows twice a day and muck out their pens. Bella did not have the knack of bringing milk from the cows and so Annie continued her work in the dairy, even though she was only four days up from her bed. That left most of the housework, washing and ironing to Bella – and since little Karl was very good with her, she usually changed his cloths and cleaned his bottom. Thus far she had kept it free from rashes, but he was always hungry and his mother's milk hardly seemed enough for him.

'Do you think baby would take a little cow's milk?' Bella asked when the child's father had gone back to work after eating a chunk of bread and cheese with pickles and drinking a mug of fresh-brewed beer. Besides her other work, Annie was expected to make her own beer, for her husband preferred it to that which the local inn sold.

'I don't know,' Annie said and sighed. 'I'm sore where he's sucked me dry. Mayhap my milk is not rich enough for him.'

'The Jersey's milk is rich,' Bella said, for they skimmed the cream from it and made butter. The rest was turned into the soft cheese which Annie's husband loved. 'It might ease his hunger, mistress.'

86

'If I give the best milk to the babe there may not be enough for cheese and butter . . .'

'Yet if the baby is satisfied he will not cry so much,' Bella said. 'I do not know if he would take any except your milk but he was crying when you slept last night and I was tempted to try him with the Jersey's milk.'

'Perhaps the midwife will call soon,' Annie said. 'If she comes, I'll ask her to decide what he should have . . .'

Bella was silenced. In truth, she had never been called to tend a babe before and did not know what would suit it, but it seemed to her that Annie's milk was not rich enough to see her baby through to his next feed.

Thus far, Mr Stoneham had not returned to see Bella. She thought perhaps he had forgotten her and a part of her wished she *had* asked for his help. Her back ached by the time she went to her bed at night and her hands were sore from all the scrubbing, washing and cleaning she was expected to do – and yet she did not dislike her mistress. Bella had decided that Annie's life was worse than hers for her husband was never kind to her – and he was forever touching her intimately, putting his hands on her no matter who was there to see it. Annie's face told Bella that she hated his touch and feared the time when he would come to her bed again.

Why had she married him if she did not care for him? Bella did not dare to ask. Annie was seldom cross with her but she could turn in a minute if she

87

was upset and with the baby crying most of the time, Karl's complaints, and all the work, Annie looked exhausted. She needed to rest more but there was never any time. Bella did not know how her mistress had managed before she came and so she tried not to dwell on another life. She was better off here than in the workhouse and she did not know what it felt like to have a mother's love or a home of her own – Florrie had been kind, sharing any extra food she earned by her sewing, but Bella had no idea where she might go if she asked Mr Stoneham for help, except back to the workhouse.

So she scurried to do her mistress's bidding and thought herself lucky that she was well fed. Neither the master nor his nephews took any notice of her. Bella knew they thought her a skinny little brat for they laughed about her and asked Karl if he could not have found an older girl they could bed. Annie scowled when they made coarse jokes and reminded them that Bella was but a child. However, she was old enough to have vague ideas of their meaning for the other inmates at the workhouse had often spoken of a time when they had lovers or husbands.

Because the men, women and children were separated at night, husbands and wives seldom met in the workhouse, except briefly on a Sunday if they went to church. Some of the girls could read a few words and write, and though Bella longed to be able to do both, she had only been taught to write her name. During the day, the women looked after the younger girls, teaching them to do the work necessary to the running of the workhouse. Scrubbing, cleaning, washing, ironing and needle-work was undertaken by the female inmates; the men had other tasks, like breaking stones, picking oakum and grinding bones for use in fertiliser or repairing the roof.

Bella had never been to the men's wing and she only knew of Arthur Meaks because he had found his way into their part of the grounds so many times. The dining hall was small so at mealtimes the inmates were given their food in two shifts, the men first and then the women and girls. The workhouse had big gardens which were used to grow vegetables as well as to keep chickens. Arthur Meaks had been given work in the vegetable plot but he'd found a way into the small yard where the women and girls hung out the washing.

He'd jumped out at Bella and startled her when she was hanging out washing on a rope line. He'd teased her and made her laugh and she'd liked him.

'You shouldn't be here, Arthur Meaks,' she'd warned him. 'If the mistress catches yer, she'll flay the skin off yer back.'

'I'm not afeared of her,' he'd boasted, 'and nor the master neither. I ain't gonna stay 'ere long. I can get out easy and I'm goin'. You'll see. I shall run away and find work in a stable or perhaps I'll go to sea.'

'I wish I could come with you,' Bella said but he'd shaken his head.

'I couldn't look out fer yer. Yer need to find

someone to give yer work – I think I know who will take me on in his stables but, if he don't, then I'll go to sea.'

Bella had thought he was just dreaming, but Arthur Meaks had run away and been missing for a day before they found him and brought him back. She'd been looking from her window above the front drive and saw him kicking and screaming as he was dragged back into the building. From the open window she heard him yell that he'd get away again – and perhaps he had, because no one had seen him since. Bella shook her head. She didn't really think so. She thought something bad had happened to him and she believed that Florrie knew what, but she would not be drawn on it.

'Get on with that ironing!' Annie's voice cut through Bella's thoughts. 'If them shirts ain't ready there'll be hell to pay.'

Florrie had made up her mind. She was leaving this place and she would take her chance with Lady Rowntree. She'd waited three days to see if Mr Stoneham would return but thus far he had not, and now she'd made up her mind and there was no going back – she had given notice to the mistress and signed the forms of release.

'I'll want seven shillings for your release,' Mistress Brent had told her furiously. 'You're wearing clothes provided by the workhouse and I want something for your board too.'

'I have my own dress to wear when I leave,' Florrie

had replied. 'Lady Rowntree gave it to me some months ago – it had belonged to her personal maid and was no longer wanted. I can give you the seven shillings for my board, but I have worked and you are not entitled to more. Lady Rowntree would testify that I have earned my keep.'

Mistress Brent had turned bright pink with temper. Florrie had seen her hands clutch at her sides and known that she itched to hit her, but she restrained herself and gave her three forms to sign. Florrie read them carefully and struck out where it said she owed money for bed and board. She had worked and the mistress was only entitled to charge for clothes taken away when someone left and food not earned because the inmate had been too sick to work.

'You'll come crawling back,' the mistress hissed at her. 'Mark my words – you will regret this foolish action.'

'My mistake was staying here so long,' Florrie said. 'I can earn my way and, when I have established myself I shall find Bella and offer her a place with me.'

'You will have to pay her master for her,' Mistress Brent snapped. 'She is indentured to the chain-maker and cannot leave him until she has earned her freedom.'

'You had no right to take money for her,' Florrie said, too angry to think what she was saying. 'It was a wicked thing to do – and if she has been harmed I shall go to someone who will see justice for her. You flout the law mistreating her and think

91

yourself safe, mistress – but there are people who will punish you and mayhap I know more than you think!'

Florrie saw the gleam of anger in the mistress's eyes but she said no more, merely indicating with a wave of her hand that Florrie was dismissed. Unable to rest, she visited the various workrooms and said goodbye to the women and girls she had worked with for so many years. Many of them looked at her enviously because she was leaving but none had her talent with the needle and were too afraid to abandon the safety of the workhouse. The life was hard and the master and mistress were unfair, but life outside was just as hard and most of these women were widows with no home and no one to help them. Most had been destitute before they entered and would never leave.

Florrie glanced at the oak longcase clock at the top of the staircase. It was past eleven in the morning and her time to leave was in twenty minutes. She was wearing her only dress and ankle boots and had nothing to take with her, for everything else belonged to the workhouse. By the time she went down to the master's office her release papers would be ready. She paused at the top of the stairs, heard something behind her and half turned as a hand pushed hard in the middle of her back and sent her tumbling down the stairs. Florrie cried out as she hit her head on a wooden post at the bottom and lay still, her eyes closed . . .

From the head of the staircase a woman looked

down and smiled. However, as one of the inmates came rushing into the hall below, the woman turned quickly and hurried away. Marta glanced up and saw her dress as she disappeared round the corner. Looking down at Florrie's pale face, she gave a cry of distress.

'Florrie! Florrie, speak to me!'

Pressing two fingers to her friend's throat, Marta could feel no pulse. Her eyes closed and tears slipped down her cheeks. This was a woman she'd worked closely with and though she would miss her when she left, Marta had wished her well. Letting out a scream to waken the dead, Marta ran towards the hall door just as it opened and three men entered. Behind them were several more, armed with tools of some kind.

'She's dead!' Marta cried, wild with fear. 'She's been killed because she was leavin'.'

'What has happened?' a well-dressed man asked and looked beyond her. Seeing a woman lying on the floor, he crossed the floor in quick strides, knelt down and pressed his fingers to Florrie's wrist and then bent his head to her chest.

'She's unconscious but still alive, though her breathing is shallow,' Arthur said. He looked at Marta. 'You are her friend?'

'Yes, sir. We worked together in the sewing room. She was leaving – signed herself out, she did.'

'Then, once a doctor has been, I shall take her with me – and if you wish I shall have you signed out so that you may care for her.'

'Me – but what shall I do?' Marta looked at him in awe. 'I could not pay the mistress for my freedom.'

'You will not be asked,' Arthur said. 'I am in charge here now and it seems I have come not a moment too soon.'

'I should have acted sooner,' Arthur said to Toby later, when he had arranged for the two women to be taken to the inn and cared for. Marta was to stay with Florrie and tend her after the doctor had visited. 'If that woman dies it will be because I was too cautious.'

'You wanted all the legal niceties in place,' Toby said and frowned. 'You blame yourself too easily, my friend. You cannot know that this Florrie was pushed – or who did it. Marta only caught sight of a dress she knows to belong to Mistress Brent as she walked away. I do not think it would be enough to hang her.'

'I hope to find enough evidence for that here in the house—' He broke off as the door of the room he'd chosen as his office was flung open and a man walked in. Master Brent was of medium height with a florid complexion and stocky build, his hair thinning on top and his nose bulbous with red veins. Arthur thought he looked like a man who enjoyed his wine – perhaps too much.

'What is the meaning of this? Why have I been summoned?' Master Brent blustered. 'I'll have you know I am in charge here.'

'No longer, for I am ordering you to leave immediately.' Arthur was calm, his tone even as he addressed the irate master. He'd sent one of the magistrate's men to ask Brent to attend him here. 'You might be allowed to return if I find that you have executed your duties within the law – but I think we both know that is not likely.'

'How dare you!' Master Brent was outraged, his face an alarming red that showed his choleric temper. 'I was appointed by Lord Rowntree himself – and if that interfering wife of his sent you here she has no authority—'

'I have the authority here,' Arthur said and took a paper from his pocket. 'This has been signed by a magistrate and two lawyers and it gives me all the powers I need to investigate what has been going on here – and I intend to be thorough. At this moment I have five men searching the gardens and the outhouses – and we may search further afield if nothing is found.'

The effect of his words was dramatic. It was as if all the colour had been swept from the master's face leaving him white and shocked before it flooded back again. He was clenching his hands at his sides, his face working as he sought for calmness.

'This is outrageous!' he spluttered. 'It is lies, all lies!'

'Then you have nothing to fear,' Arthur replied, his tone like ice. 'Here is your formal notice, sir, and a restraining order. I should inform you that you have two hours to leave the building. You are requested to stay in the area and visit me when you are in a more amenable frame of mind – then, as I said, should I find all accusations are false, I may reinstate you.'

'This is grossly unfair!' The master flew into a rage and banged his fists on the table. 'I have no idea who sent you here, but this is all nonsense. I am an honest man. You will find no fault with my finances or the way these wretches have been treated. They continually complain about the food and how hard the work is, but they are lazy creatures and need to be kept in order – as you will discover if you mean to run this place.'

'Oh no, I am merely here to investigate,' Arthur said. 'In time a new master and mistress will be appointed, if necessary. For the moment a woman I trust will take over the care of the inmates. I advise you to go to your wife, sir. I may have serious charges against her – and perhaps you when I've completed my work here.'

'I see you have made up your mind about us,' Brent said and glared at him furiously. 'I have influential friends and this does not end here!'

'You are quite right,' Arthur agreed. 'If I discover that half of what I have been told is true, I believe that both you and your wife will find yourself at the end of a noose.'

Brent's mouth worked but no sound left his lips, though they were flecked with white foam. He turned suddenly and left the room and was heard shouting to his wife.

'I think you were well advised to have the local magistrates on board,' Toby observed as they heard the commotion above stairs. 'Without it, I think we might have had to use force to eject Master Brent and his wife.'

'Disappointed?' Arthur asked, amusement in his eyes. 'I doubt if we've heard the last of those two.' Even as he spoke, the door was thrown open and Mistress Brent entered, her face white with rage.

'I'll make you pay,' she threatened. 'You'll never discover what you seek!' She gave a laugh that sent shivers down his spine. 'Search all you like, Mr Stoneham – you will never find the evidence you need for there is none.'

'Then I shall owe you an apology, ma'am,' Arthur said smoothly. 'But I doubt it will be forthcoming.'

He took her to the door and pushed her towards her husband, who was clutching a leather bag that looked as if it might contain money. As he saw Arthur look at it, he tried to thrust it inside his coat.

'Toby – I do not think these people can be allowed to remove anything from the premises,' Arthur said.

'You have no right – that is mine,' Brent protested as Toby snatched the heavy bag from him.

'Gold sovereigns,' Toby said, spilling them on to the table. 'I wonder where the master of a workhouse came by so much wealth.'

Brent scowled, but as he turned and saw two

burly men standing behind him, gave up his protest. 'What about our clothes and personal things?'

'I shall get one of the inmates to pack them and they will be delivered to the back door this afternoon. You may come to collect them if you choose.'

'You will be punished for this!' Mistress Brent shrilled, but her husband took hold of her arm and hustled her away.

Toby looked through the pile of gold coins. 'There is almost five hundred guineas here. Where do you suppose all this came from?'

'Years of abuse,' Arthur said. 'I dare say the fellow has more hidden about the place. We have uncovered a hornets' nest here, my friend. There may be no records to prove it, but that money did not come from one transaction. I think that pair has been taking advantage of the vulnerable for many years and must have gained a fortune. Babies sold to those who are desperate to have a child, children sold to masters who treat them ill and work them hard – and who knows what else we may find.'

The two men had followed the erstwhile master and mistress to the door to make certain they left and then went out to join the men who were already searching the grounds. Only an hour later one of them returned to Arthur's office and the look in his face warned of dire news.

'The men have found something in the garden, sir. Perhaps we should not have let the Brents go . . .'

Arthur was on his feet, his expression dark and alert. 'So soon? Is it the missing boy?' He had not expected results this quickly but it showed that the master of the workhouse had felt himself totally safe from retribution and made little effort to conceal his evil.

'We're not sure, sir. And . . .' The man paused and his expression sent cold shivers down Arthur's spine. 'There are more bones than could belong to one child – but they haven't found a body and the boy you seek would not be a fleshless skeleton as yet so we haven't found him but evidence of earlier crimes perhaps.'

'Oh, my God!' Toby cried looking thunderstruck. 'I doubted you would find more than some fiddling of the books and babies sold or stolen, but this is obscene – evil.'

'Yes,' Arthur said. 'I felt it when I was first told about the boy. Something warned me not to ignore it. And I believe that if there are many bones, then he is not the only one to have been murdered . . .'

CHAPTER 7

'Are you sure you feel able to cope here, Hetty?' Arthur asked after he had shown her round the workhouse the next afternoon. 'When I begged you to come at once, I had no idea that we should find the skeletons of five children in the gardens – and the body of Arthur Meaks.'

Indeed, it had surprised him that the evidence was so swiftly found but suspected that in his arrogance, the master of the workhouse had never expected to be questioned. So secure did he feel, that he had dug only shallow graves and perhaps he was justified in his confidence. Few cared for the disappearance of workhouse children and his excuses that a child had gone off to find work or had been sent to a master, would have been believed by most. Perhaps if he had not been ill, Lord Rowntree might have questioned further, but luck had been with the Brents until Arthur arrived unexpectedly on the scene. He knew that some of the inmates, particularly the children, were frightened and upset, the women in tears and the men looking sick, as if they had suspected something but now felt guilty by association. For why had no one complained long ago?

'They were children and I should not fear them if they were here, so why would I fear them in death?' Hetty said with a sad look. 'You need someone to look after these poor folk, Arthur. They are in a state of shock, the children terrified and weeping and the women wretched; the men feel resentment and anger, and I cannot blame them after what has happened here.'

'It is shocking and terrible,' Arthur agreed. 'It is the reason I asked for you, because of your compassion and patience. The best thing would be to remove everyone immediately but that isn't easy with so many to house. In time I will find a new home for them all but for now I fear we must care for them here.'

Hetty nodded in agreement. 'They need help and understanding after something like this so the house must continue to function and they must all be fed. I think you have much more to do here, Arthur, and I can be of help to you – and to them in this dark hour.'

'I should have arrested that devil when I had the chance,' Arthur said, both angry and rueful. 'Even though I came here prepared for the worst I wondered if Meg had deluded herself. Bella's story of Arthur Meaks' disappearance was what convinced me to act – but I did not expect this. If the Brents go free I shall blame myself.'

'They have fled?'

Arthur nodded. 'They did not come to collect their possessions. Toby took some of their ill-gotten gains from them, but I think she either had more hidden about her or he had some elsewhere, because we have had men searching and they were seen in the village, boarding a coach for London.'

'Then they will try to disappear or flee the country,' Hetty said and smiled in sympathy. 'You did all that anyone could expect of you, Arthur. Until that grave was found I doubt anyone realised the extent of the cruelty that went on here.'

'The magistrate's men told me they thought some of the skeletons might have lain in the ground ten or twelve years or more. We know when Arthur was killed and it is his body that will convict Brent and his wife – because Florrie has testified that she saw them in the garden and he was digging a deep hole and she saw them place what she thought was a child's body in the grave, though she could not be certain. Mistress Brent did her best to kill her, but fortunately Florrie survived and she has sent word that she is willing to testify against them. She is a brave woman and I am glad she is being cared for by Lady Rowntree.'

Hetty nodded. 'She was lucky to escape with her life. Clearly Mistress Brent feared that she knew too much and hoped to get rid of her.'

'We have had a great deal of luck . . .' Arthur sighed. 'However, Mistress Brent was right in one thing: there is nothing to prove that she sold the living babies of the inmates. She kept no record of any children born here – though that in itself is enough to lose her the wardship of this place, for it is the law that she must keep a register.'

'Then you have little chance of finding Meg's baby?'

'There is no record of it here. Mistress Brent was cleverer than her husband. If he had buried his victims elsewhere we might not have found them so easily, though I was prepared to search the surrounding countryside. However, I have hopes that someone will have heard or seen something to help us. At the moment everyone here is frightened, but perhaps you can convince them that they will not bear the blame for any of this and then they will speak of what they have seen or heard.'

'At least you have stopped those monsters,' Hetty said warmly. 'It must have been fate that brought Meg to that dark road when you were travelling it.'

'Yes, for I have helped her to recovery – but failed to give her back her child.' He looked sad and yet angry, as if he had somehow been guilty of carelessness. 'I realise now that I should have had that pair detained and made them talk.'

'Do not give up just yet,' Hetty said. 'It was never likely that Mistress Brent had kept a record of her wicked transactions, but there are women and men who have been here for years and some of them may know something.'

'That is my hope, for without it I do not know where to begin the search.'

'Someone must have seen something that can help us,' Hetty said and smiled confidently. 'You will win in the end, Arthur – I am sure of it.'

'You have faith in me, Hetty,' he said on a rueful sigh. 'I am not sure that I have deserved it.'

Hetty merely smiled again and he left her to get to grips with the task that awaited her. It was certainly a difficult one. The inmates were unsure of what was happening. For years they had been badly treated and even though the old mistress and master had gone, they could not bring themselves to trust. Hetty would need to be patient and gentle with them, particularly some of the elderly women who looked terrified each time Arthur approached. His rough treatment of their previous masters had made them wary of him, but Hetty was gentle and kind and she would win their trust – and in doing so would bring their best hope of discovering what had happened to the children here.

Hetty watched as Arthur walked away. The search of the gardens was now complete and the bones had been taken elsewhere. Those unknown would be buried in the churchyard with prayers to bless them, but Arthur Meaks' grave would be named. There might be some who would wish to mourn him and she intended to ask if any wished to attend the boy's service.

It was a terrible tragedy that Arthur had discovered here, and although it had come about by chance, Hetty had a feeling that it had been meant to happen.

It was only a fleeting thought, but it was fortuitous that he had been travelling the road and discovered Meg's near-frozen form. Another hour and she might already have been dead – and without her testimony those monsters would have been free to carry on their terrible work.

For the moment Arthur seemed to have forgotten the terrible grief of Katharine's untimely death. It truly was not his fault she had died from falling beneath those horses' hooves, and yet he had blamed himself and it was Hetty who had pulled him from his black mood by telling him it was his duty to Katharine to look for her beloved sister Marianne.

If this new horror took his mind from the grief that Katharine's death had caused, Hetty could only be glad that she had set his feet on the path that brought him here. His urgent message asking her to come had been a surprise, for she ran the charitable home that was part of Arthur Stoneham's good works. She had left it in the capable hands of Lily, a young woman who had come to her from the workhouse, begging for work rather than charity. The young woman had proved a worthy helper and would see that everyone was cared for while Hetty held things together here. It was a temporary arrangement for she knew a master and mistress would be appointed in time by the governors – although, considering what had happened here, it might be better if this house was closed. Who would really wish to live here now? She would speak to Arthur when he had more time to consider the situation.

Hetty had not hesitated when Arthur asked her to come, because she would do anything he required of her. He would never know, must never know, that she loved him with all her heart and mind and body, although he knew that she was a good friend. It was Hetty who had helped him once before when he was in despair, and in turn, he had helped her put her old life behind her.

Sighing, Hetty began to search the desk for any clues to what had happened here. It was Mistress Brent's desk and there were many old bills and oddments. No actual record of the inmates who had come here to shelter from the storm of life had been kept, though there was a recent register of those who lived here now. Hetty thought it had been written hastily and within the last few days – as if the mistress had suspected she might be ordered to produce one. Had the records been kept as they ought it would have been easier to discover who had lived here years ago.

As she was closing the drawer, it stuck. Hetty thought something might have caught and she took it right out to look, and there at the back was an envelope that was yellowed with age. She felt a tingle of anticipation as she wriggled it free, opened the creases and read the words written in faded ink.

I cannot thank you enough for the child. My wife did not know of the substitution and it has saved her life and her sanity for had she lost another child she might have lost her wits and her will to live. I wondered if you might be able to tell me a little more of the child's parents. I know you said that the young woman died – but was she of good birth? It does not matter, for we shall teach our daughter to be a lady, but I am curious.

As to the matter of payment: You question that I paid your husband so much, but I assure you that five hundred guineas was a small price for my wife's happiness.

Your servant,
John Carlisle
Fairview Manor

Hetty looked at the letter, which she had no doubt had been written from the heart. Clearly, the writer had reason to thank Mistress Brent for the child but it proved that payment had been made – and a substantial amount. She could not think that every man or woman seeking a child could afford such a sum, but someone had been glad to pay it. Hetty wondered why Mistress Brent had kept the letter. She must have known that it was evidence against her and could lead to her being arrested – yet perhaps this first transaction had been done with better intentions. It might even have been a gift; but if so it had planted the seed which grew into a monstrous greed that would let nothing stand in its way. The mother of this fortunate child might have died, but other children had been taken for profit from mothers that lived.

Hetty could not know what had changed the wardens from people who had been trusted into the monsters they had become. She would give the letter to Arthur, because it was proof that the wardens had given one child away and been paid – though it did not help in the search for Meg's daughter.

Hetty searched all the drawers but found nothing else. Indeed, she would not have found this letter had it not become lodged behind the drawer. She frowned, sure that somewhere there must be more scraps of evidence that would unravel the awful mystery of this place – but perhaps they lay in people's minds rather than the drawers of a desk . . .

Arthur was glad to be away from the workhouse. He'd felt the desperate hopelessness of its inmates and regretted that he must seem as bad as the former master and mistress to them, because he had been forced to use violence to dismiss their former master. He must hope that Hetty could win their confidence and that one of the older ones would remember something.

He had sent messengers back to London to alert the authorities there but had little hope that Brent and his wife would be apprehended. It had been such a mistake to have let them leave. Had they been locked up in a cell he might have forced some details from them, though he believed that they would just have lied and protested their innocence.

He thought it certain that Brent was responsible for the deaths of the children buried in the garden. From the bones found it seemed they were probably all under the age of ten and believed to be boys. Arthur knew now that the former master was a violent man. He had punished the boys for the slightest fault and some of those beatings had clearly led to death. Arthur could not know whether the boys had been sexually assaulted, but thought it likely. Some boys might be too frightened to resist and would suffer whatever was done to them, but others would fight back – as it seemed Arthur Meaks had before he died. His body had been only partly decomposed and the magistrate's men thought he'd been beaten horrendously, some limbs broken, before he died.

Brent must pay for his sins! Arthur frowned as he rode towards the village. It was in his mind to visit the chain-maker's cottage and see how Bella was managing. She'd said she would stay with her mistress but perhaps she did not expect a good home to be waiting for her? Perhaps he had not made his intentions clear? Arthur would choose his words carefully this time, because if she was not happy he could give her a home in London where she would be safe and could learn a trade that suited her.

'Speak to the workhouse girl?' Karl looked at Arthur belligerently. 'Why? She belongs to me. You may have dismissed Mistress Brent – and I daresay she deserved it for she was an evil bitch – but the girl looks after my wife and is fed and well-treated.'

'Bella may have some information I need,' Arthur said. 'May I speak with her for a moment?'

'She is busy tending my wife,' Karl snarled showing his stained teeth. 'If you want to ask the girl questions come back when there is less work to do – my wife is tired and they have got behind with their day.'

'It would take but a few minutes—'

'I told you – come back another day.'

Arthur could see from the set of the man's mouth and his glare that nothing would change him. It was ill luck that had made him choose this time to ask for the girl. He would return another day, for the more he saw of this man the less he liked him and he was concerned for Bella's safety. Her fate had played on his mind, especially since the discovery of that grave in the workhouse garden. Something was nagging at him, an instinct that told him he should protect this girl. Mistress Brent had hoped to be rid of her by sending Bella here, thinking that she would be put to work in the forge, but she'd been lucky; however, he did not think she would live to become a woman in this household once the chain-maker felt she was old enough to learn his trade. Before he left for good he would try once more to get Bella to leave . . .

CHAPTER 8

Annie woke as Bella was tending the baby. His napkin smelled terrible and the motion was thin and yellow; as she cleaned his bottom he wailed in misery.

'What have you done to him?' Annie demanded unfairly. 'What is the matter with Karl's son?' She rose and came anxiously to look at the babe lying on the bed as Bella wrapped the napkin about his tiny body. He looked thin and unhealthy and was not putting on weight as he ought. 'If he dies Karl will kill us both.'

'I do not know what ails him,' Bella said and looked at her in fear. She had seen the gentleman riding away through the upstairs window and wished that she'd been able to speak to him. He had returned as he promised but would not come again and Bella was uneasy. Karl had beaten his wife the previous evening for the first time and she'd been lying in her bed most of the day. She looked ill and tired and the baby was clearly suffering a nasty tummy upset. Bella was being blamed, though

113

she had done everything she was able. 'You need the doctor or the midwife, mistress.'

Annie picked the child up, her nose wrinkling as he soiled his napkin yet again. 'It's your fault for leaving him dirty!' She reached out and slapped Bella's face, bringing tears to her eyes. 'If he dies I shall tell Karl it was your fault.'

'I have just changed him, mistress.' Bella held up the soiled linen. 'I will change him again.'

'You are a lazy slut and I've a good mind to send you back to the workhouse.'

Bella turned away as she fought her tears. Annie was not always this unkind, but she was feeling ill herself and so was taking it out on Bella. Bella nursed the baby, rubbing his back to make him bring up wind, but as he did so his napkin was soiled once more. His poor little tummy was making him feel ill and he wouldn't stop crying.

She removed the napkin, adding it to the growing pile that needed to be boiled and rinsed. Bella tried as best she could to keep the child clean but she was a child herself and knew nothing of caring for babies. She feared what would happen if anything happened to the babe, because Annie was terrified of the brute she had married and to avoid another beating would blame Bella if the child died.

Was it always so in life? Bella had never known kindness in a man, never felt a father's love, and she did not know whether any could be trusted, though Mr Stoneham had been kind the day Annie's baby was born. Perhaps it was different with gentlemen. A sigh left her lips for she would never know . . .

'Are you warm enough?' Toby asked, solicitous for Meg's wellbeing. They had walked in the countryside for some half an hour and she looked pale. 'Do you wish to return to the inn parlour?'

'Not yet,' Meg begged and looked up at him. 'Sally is very kind and she helped save my life, but I feel restless. I cannot stop thinking of my child and what happened to her. Sometimes, I despair of ever finding her.' A single tear trickled down her cheek.

'We are doing all we can,' Toby said. 'I have hired an agent to make inquiries. Somewhere a woman who did not give birth, or who birthed a dead child, has a new babe and someone will notice. A reward for information has been offered.'

Meg's cheeks tinged with pink. 'You are so kind, sir. Would that *he* had been as kind . . .' She stopped walking abruptly and looked stunned. 'I remember something!'

Toby took her hands, holding them gently as he gazed into her face. 'What do you remember, dear lady?'

'When I knew that I carried the child of a man I hated I ran,' Meg said and her hands trembled in his. 'I cannot recall his name but I know he – he forced himself on me. I cannot think . . .' She pulled her hand away and put it to her face, a little sob leaving her. For a moment she was silent, her fingers covering her

115

face, her shoulders heaving, then she dropped her hands and looked at Toby. Holding her left hand out in front of her face, she stared at her third finger in bewilderment. The words came slowly, stumbling from her lips as though she scarce credited them. 'I was married to a man I detested. My stepfather forced me to it!' She gave a cry of grief. 'I did not want to but he beat me and he threatened to kill my little sister if I defied him and in the end I gave in. God forgive me, I was beaten and I let them marry me to that brute!'

'What happened then?'

Meg lowered her head for a moment and when she looked up, her eyes were dark with remembered misery. 'My husband forced himself on me on our wedding night because I was reluctant to be touched. It happened every night for weeks – and then, when I could bear no more, I ran away . . .' Tears trickled down her cheeks as she met his anxious gaze. 'My name is Margaret and I am Lady Sangster, my husband Sir Gerald.' A sob caught on her lips. 'My sister and mother called me Meg – but my stepfather was a brute like Gerald and he called me Margaret when displeased with me.'

'I *knew* you were of gentle birth,' Toby said and reached out to wipe a tear from her cheek. 'You are safe now, Meg, and I vow that I shall protect you always. You will not be forced to return to the monster that used you so ill . . .'

'He is my husband and he will claim me if he discovers me,' Meg said, her eyes dark with fear. She drew a shuddering breath, trembling and clutching at him for support. Toby put a gentle arm about her, comforting her. 'Things are coming back, rushing into my head!' She pressed shaking fingers to her lips and shook her head. 'It is too much . . .'

'Come,' Toby said softly, supporting her as she almost fell. He held her steady and let her weep into his shoulder until the storm of grief subsided and then drew her towards the inn. 'We shall seek the warmth of the fire in the private parlour and you will tell me everything in your own time. You are safe now, truly for I will protect you, my lady. I give you my word – and I will find your baby. I promise I will, however long it takes.'

Meg smiled tremulously. 'But my husband, sir. If he finds me he will force me back . . .'

'He may try,' Toby said and his eyes glinted like new-polished steel. 'It will be the last thing he does!'

A little smile touched her lips. 'I would not have you risk your life for mine, sir.'

'Would you not?' Toby laughed softly and the light of devilment was in his eyes. 'I would count it as naught if it saved you pain – but come now, the law is on your husband's side, it is true but I shall not allow him to harm you. Trust in me, Meg, for I will prevent him from taking you somehow. We shall order some warmed ale and you may tell me your story for I know there is more . . .'

'Meg was treated badly and that's why she ran,' Toby told Arthur. 'She wandered the countryside for some days until she collapsed and some gypsies found her close to death for she had been badly beaten before she fled. They were good to her, gave her clothes and took her with them on their travels. She cannot quite recall what happened next, but she believes she was out walking alone when she was set upon by some vagabonds who knocked her unconscious and took the gold rings from her ears, but she recalls nothing of that time.'

'That is what happened to her wedding ring, I daresay.'

'No – she threw that away. She says she should have sold it but she threw it into a ditch after she ran from her husband because the memory of his brutality made her wish only to be free of it.' Toby's mouth twisted in anger. 'He beat her into submission when she refused him.'

'Sally spoke of marks on her back. Some were old, she said, but there were newer bruises.'

'They must have been done by the vagabonds who beat her so severely that she lost her memory.' Toby frowned. 'There is much she still cannot recall, but at least she now knows who she is and what happened to her.'

'She has suffered too much,' Arthur said gravely. 'I fear that she may never recover completely, Toby . . .'

'I am prepared for that,' his friend said. 'But I have vowed to care for her – and to find her child if it takes a lifetime.'

'She still wishes for the babe, even though it was the child of rape?'

'Yes, she says the babe was not to blame – the gypsy woman who rescued her, Bathsheba, made her see that. Meg says that she told her a story about a young woman very like her who had been raped some years ago. The girl could not bear the thought of the child and begged her to give her a potion to be rid of it, but Bathsheba would not. And then the woman ran away, though Bathsheba claimed not to know why she went.'

'Bathsheba?' Arthur frowned. 'I have heard of a gypsy woman by that name – but it may be commonly used amongst the travelling folk.'

'Perhaps . . .' Toby frowned. 'It made me wonder – might that young woman the gypsy spoke of have been Katharine's lost sister? Bathsheba told Meg that she died after giving birth to a girl child and was Marianne not supposed by some to have been taken by gypsies?'

'Yes.' Arthur frowned. 'What makes you think that the girl who died might be Marianne Ross?'

'Meg could not recall the young woman's name, but she thought Bathsheba might have called her Marie.'

'Close enough for thought,' Arthur agreed as he felt again the tingling at his nape. Something about Bella had nagged at his subconscious – was it possible that she was the child of Katharine's lost sister? 'So if I could find this gypsy woman I might solve one mystery.'

'It might just be a step too far,' Toby admitted. 'Yet does it not seem to you that this might all be

119

fate? Meg would have died had you not chanced to find her – and perhaps it was meant that she should give you the clue to the mystery that haunts you.'

'If life was so neat it would be fortunate indeed,' Arthur said wryly, a smile on his lips, 'but I shall not dismiss the notion, even though it is a stretch. We need to discover Bathsheba and then perhaps she can tell us where the babe was taken after its mother's death.'

'Meg believes it was to the workhouse, where she herself gave birth.'

'Is that more conjecture?'

'No. Bathsheba told Meg that she had intended to fetch the child out of the workhouse one day, but her brother had been against it and Meg thinks it was because Bathsheba told her she'd taken that unfortunate child there that she tried to reach it herself.'

'And now regrets it.' Arthur nodded. 'If that is true then the Fates are truly at work here, Toby. In any other workhouse the records would tell us the names of the children left with them and their mothers – Mistress Brent has much to answer for if she is ever found.'

'We can only hope that the law is vigilant,' Toby said. 'It is a pity you let them slip through your fingers, Arthur.'

Arthur frowned. 'It was because I believed that we would find wrongdoing – but most certainly not the wickedness that was discovered.'

'Meg told me that Bathsheba and her brother visit the horse fairs and some of the special markets to buy and sell. It might be your best hope of finding the truth – and yet it may turn out to be a wild goose chase.'

'So far I have had no luck whatsoever, but now there may just be a chink of light,' Arthur said. 'Marianne was lost after walking home through the woods – and there was some tale of gypsies having camped there. Some folk thought they had kidnapped her – but supposing the reality was that they found her lying unconscious after a brutal attack?'

'You mean they took her and cared for her, as they did for Meg?' Toby nodded. 'Yes, that makes sense, for Meg told me that Bathsheba is renowned as a healer – and whoever the girl was, whose baby she told Meg is in the workhouse at Sculfield, it has a similar ring to Meg's story.'

'I think I must look for this Bathsheba, Toby.'

'And you may safely leave Meg to me,' Toby said. 'I have already set a search in motion for her babe. I shall protect her and stay here until she is ready to let me provide for her – and Hetty is more than capable of looking after the Sculfield workhouse. You know that Lady Rowntree is consulting with her fellow guardians and a new master and mistress will be appointed soon – so if you have other concerns there is nothing to hold you back.'

'There is a horse fair at Newmarket next month,' Arthur said. 'It is the first of the year and I may find

Bathsheba and her clan there – and if not I may gain some idea of where she may be camped.'

'Mmm. The travelling folk are secretive people,' Toby said. 'It is likely that they will not wish to be found.'

'Well, I shall try – and if I have no luck I will set agents to searching for them,' Arthur said. 'I was delaying my search for Katharine's sister for Meg's sake – but if you are willing to stay and care for her . . . ?'

'For as long as it takes,' Toby said and Arthur nodded, a slight smile on his lips.

'If that is the way of it, I shall wish you good fortune, my friend. I fear that Meg has suffered greatly and the path to happiness will not be easy for either of you.'

'It may never happen,' Toby said soberly, 'but I shall count it a privilege to serve her, Arthur – even if she can never be as other young women are, can never be mine.'

'Then I leave her in good hands,' Arthur said. 'I must speak with Hetty. If she has news of Meg's child she must come to you, Toby, and not wait for my return. Also, may I tell her you will go to her aid if need be?'

'Of course,' Toby said and nodded. 'I pray that I have not set you on a wild goose chase.'

'It will not be the first time,' Arthur said wryly. 'I knew when I set out that I had little chance of finding Marianne unless Fate smiled on me – and perhaps She has . . .'

'How long will you be gone?' Hetty asked when Arthur visited her at the workhouse later that same day.

'Perhaps two or three weeks,' he said. 'It depends on what I find – whether the gypsies are at the horse fair or if I can get word of them.'

She nodded and smiled. 'Then I shall expect you when I see you.'

'Have I asked too much of you?' Arthur said, sensing hesitation in her manner. 'Toby is here if you need help – and Lady Rowntree will appoint a new master and mistress shortly or the house will close and new homes will be found for everyone – and my Cousin Matthew will keep his eyes on the refuge in London. He has proved invaluable and I believe I shall grow fond of him and his family.'

'I hope an alteration is not made here too soon. I am making friends here and I think there is a woman who knows more than she will say.'

'Do you speak of Florrie?'

'No – she visited to speak to those she knew here and I questioned her, but though she knew of Arthur Meaks' fate she knows little more than we have already discovered. Lady Rowntree has taken her on now that she has recovered from her fall, but Marta has returned to us for she has no other home. It was she who told me that Aggie, our oldest inmate, might know something. She has been here almost from the start and Marta told me that she hints at knowing things but her mind wanders and so conversation is difficult.'

'Then you must be patient. She may indeed know something valuable but then again, it may be naught.'

'Yes, I know. Marta has been helping me quite a bit. She is in charge of the sewing department now that Florrie is no longer here and she would tell me everything if she knew it. She says that if Aggie is allowed to sit with her she may start rambling and then perhaps she will say something that may help.'

'I had hoped Florrie might know more.'

'Marta says that Florrie told her she thought the master had killed Arthur Meaks and she believed he was buried in the garden but she knows nothing of the others – or what happened to Meg's baby, other than she was taken by someone in a carriage.'

'Bella told me that – but there was no crest to give us clues.' Arthur frowned. 'I am sorry to take you from London, Hetty – and I hope you will forgive me for asking so much of you.'

'I would do anything you ask,' Hetty said and looked up at him with such sweetness that it took his breath. For a moment his look was sombre and then he smiled, moved towards her and kissed her brow.

'My best of friends,' he murmured. 'I do not deserve you.'

Arthur was frowning as he walked away. For the first time he was aware that Hetty's feelings for him were more than those of a friend. She was a beautiful woman, though no longer young – but then, neither was he. Sensual and warm, she would one day marry, and she deserved that – but Arthur's heart had been bruised and battered. He did not know whether he could ever again feel more than affection for any woman – and he would not offer a woman like Hetty less than a whole heart and mind. Yet he had begun to see that she might be his own path to happiness.

CHAPTER 9

Bella changed the babe's napkin. It was hardly stained, though she knew from the acrid smell that something had passed through the tiny body. She thought that there was nothing left inside the poor little mite to pass, but he cried constantly, as if in pain.

'Hush then, little one,' Bella said, rubbing his back to try and ease him. 'I know you are not well, but the mistress does not care and your father is too busy to notice . . .'

Annie had not risen from her bed yet, though it was well past her usual time. Bella knew that the master had warmed some ale for himself and eaten a hunk of bread and cheese, leaving the remains scattered on the table. She cleared it up and washed his pots, then rinsed the napkins through and put them outside to dry, because there was a watery sun. The baby was quiet for once, so she scrubbed the floor and put a load of shirts into the tub to soak – and still her mistress had not risen.

Anxiously, Bella went up to Annie's bedroom and

knocked. No answer came so she went inside and discovered that her mistress was still asleep – at least it looked as if she slept. She approached the bed cautiously and saw that Annie was soaked in sweat and there were dark bruises all over her arms and her neck. Bella placed a tentative hand on her arm, giving her a gentle shake.

'Mistress, it is late. I've done my chores. What do you want me to do next?'

Annie made no answer and Bella felt the knot of worry twist inside her. The bread was not made and would not be ready when the men came home, and the cows were becoming restless and needed to be milked. Annie always did the cooking and Bella did not know where to start. She gave her mistress a shake, trying to wake her. Annie moaned but her eyes did not open.

She was really ill! Bella hesitated. She knew that her mistress needed a doctor, but should she take it on herself to fetch him? She would be beaten for incurring an unnecessary cost, but surely it must be necessary when the mistress was so ill?

Giving her mistress one more doubtful look, Bella left her. She picked up her shawl and wrapped it around her shoulders, because it was cold out. Before she left, she glanced into the cot. The babe appeared to be resting at last and it would make him cry if she picked him up and ran with him.

'I'm sorry, little one,' she said softly. 'I must fetch the doctor for your mother – and perhaps he will look at you, too.'

128

Once out of the cottage, Bella ran as fast as she could. She saw the plaque on the doctor's wall with his sign and knocked hard, bringing his housekeeper to answer it.

'Please, ma'am, my mistress is sick and needs a doctor – and so does the baby . . .'

'Who are you?'

'I am Bella – and I belong to the chain-maker's wife . . .'

The woman pulled a face of disgust. 'Doctor is busy. I will tell him when he is free.'

'I am afeared my mistress may die!'

'Go back to her then and I'll ask the doctor to call when he has time . . .'

Bella saw the stubborn set to her face and turned away. She was about to leave the village when she thought of the midwife. Perhaps she would come if she was at home. Turning her steps towards the midwife's home, she knocked frantically and this time she was in luck.

'What is it, child?'

'Annie is ill and the baby's been bad more than a week.'

Midwife Janes shook her head. 'Very well, I'll come – this is what happens when you rely on a doctor and not a midwife like me.'

'But you were not here when the child came,' Bella said, waiting as the woman went to fetch her bag and cloak. 'The doctor seemed to know what he did . . .'

'Then why are they both ill?' Midwife Janes asked

crossly. 'I am not responsible if harm was done when the child was dragged out of her – but I will see what I can do.'

She walked swiftly and Bella had to run to keep up with her. She was out of breath when they reached the cottage and the midwife sniffed as she looked about her.

'That smell is not good. Have you kept things clean, girl?'

'Yes, ma'am, I do, and I boil the milk before I give it to the babe . . .'

'You give cow's milk to the child?'

'Annie's milk is not enough to satisfy him and I feed the babe with a rag soaked in the Jersey cow's milk but he still cries all the time.' A thin wail was heard and the midwife scowled at Bella, going over to the cot to pick him up. She wrinkled her nose at the smell.

'This child has a tummy upset. You must give him nothing but sugar in water for a day to get the poison out of his system. Boil the water, let it cool and mix in the sugar and then let him have it in this bottle . . .' She held up a baby's feeding bottle she'd brought with her. 'Tell your mistress I'll want two shillings for it – and remember, no more cow's milk unless the mother's milk has dried up . . .'

Bella nodded, feeling nervous. It was her fault. She had given the master's son cow's milk without being told to and if it had harmed him she would be blamed.

'I'd better look at his mother while you change him again.'

Bella took the babe from his cot, laid him on a big towel on the table, and then wiped and cleaned him, putting on a fresh napkin before soothing him. He quietened at her voice and seemed to fall asleep again. She put him down gently as the midwife came back to the kitchen.

'Your mistress is very ill. Unless the doctor can save her, I think she will die. She has had a fever and it may be that the babe has taken it from her – I shall run back to the village and ask him to call.' She frowned. 'Annie has been sick and she has soiled the sheets. Can you cleanse her and change them by yourself?'

'I will try, ma'am.'

Bella trembled as the midwife left in a hurry. If Annie died she would be blamed – and if the babe died too, Bella would be put to work in her master's chain works. The thought terrified her and she hurried upstairs to do what she could to cleanse her mistress. Annie's eyelids fluttered but she did not open them, though she groaned as Bella rolled her to pull out the soiled sheets and tuck clean ones under her.

Once she had settled her mistress, she opened the window to let in fresh air and bundled the sheets up to take down to the scullery. There she rinsed the things she'd washed earlier and put the soiled sheets into soak. She had just finished putting the shirts through the mangle when the doctor and midwife returned. They did not speak to her but went straight upstairs. Bella took the sheets from the copper and put them in the sink to soak in cold water; she was wiping her red hands when the midwife came back to the kitchen.

'Your mistress is very ill,' she said. 'She has a terrible sickness and Doctor Mason fears she will not last the night. He has asked me to stay here and nurse her – can you find me food and make a cup of tea?'

'Yes, I can find cheese and yesterday's bread,' Bella said. 'I know where the mistress keeps the key to her tea caddy but I am not allowed to use it.'

'Show me,' the midwife instructed. 'I shall take the responsibility – and I shall want more than a bit of cheese. What is in the larder?'

'Ham, cheese, some cold pork – and pickles,' Bella told her. 'The mistress had made a pie for the master's supper but it will need to be reheated today.'

'Does she often reheat food cooked a day earlier?'

Bella nodded and the midwife frowned. 'Do not give me any of that for my supper. I will have ham if it is fresh – or some eggs scrambled on toast if the ham is on the turn.'

'The ham is good,' Bella assured her, 'but I must ask the master . . .'

'Leave Master Breck to me,' Midwife Janes said and set her chin. 'His wife is like to die unless I care for her – and I will not do it unless I am fed properly.'

Bella fetched the key to the tea caddy and then

the ham, which had been sliced only a few times and was still almost new. She watched as the midwife cut herself generous slices and ate them with the cheese and pickles; she also ate the last of the bread and Bella watched in dismay. She would have to try to make fresh, though she knew it was likely to turn out lumpen and misshapen, but at least it would be bread of some kind and her master would be so angry if there was no food for his meal when he came home.

Karl was in a furious mood by the time he arrived. The number-one furnace had cracked, which meant that it would have to be left to cool and then the builders would have to replace or repair it and that meant lost work as well as expense.

He looked for signs of his wife's cooking when he walked in and saw the midwife sitting at his table eating ham and bread with pickles.

'What are you doing here?' he asked rudely.

She gave him stare for stare. 'Nursing your sick wife! You'll be lucky if you have one by this time tomorrow – and if Annie dies, the babe will too.'

'What's wrong with her?' He glared at her and then at Bella. 'Where is my supper?'

'It's in the oven. I will fetch it,' Bella said and brought the pie to the table. She had boiled potatoes to go with it, and root vegetables, also greens, because his nephews would be in shortly and they would demand food too.

'Where is the pudding and gravy?' Karl demanded,

because Annie made a crisp savoury pudding in the oven to accompany every meal.

'I did not know how to make it,' Bella said and shivered as he glared at her. 'I cooked more vegetables.'

'I want pudding soaked in gravy – Yorkshire Pudding they call it. Do you know nothing, girl?'

'I've seen Annie cook it but I did not get time to try . . .' Bella gave a little cry as he cuffed her ear. 'I have been looking after the mistress and the babe – as well as all the work, sir.'

'The girl has done all she can,' Midwife Janes said and glared at him. 'You should have had the doctor to Annie and the babe before this – you are like to lose them both now.'

'She was always a mewling creature,' Karl muttered. 'Weak and forever complaining. I should never have wed her but her father begged me to take her.'

'She has had a hard life,' the midwife said, impervious to his angry looks. 'I think you have ill-treated Annie, Master Brent, and if she dies it will be your fault and so I shall tell any who ask.'

'Damn you, woman! Get out of my house! I'll not listen to your lies another moment.' He jumped to his feet and raised his fist to her.

The midwife hesitated and then nodded. 'On your head be it – if Annie dies it is your blame not mine.' She turned and looked at Bella. 'Look after her as much you are able, but I doubt she will live the night, even if I stay – and I'll not remain here to be shouted at.'

She picked up her things and walked out just as Karl's nephews entered the kitchen and started calling for their dinner. Bella scuttled away to fetch what was left of the pie and vegetables. As Karl had, they asked for the pudding and gravy and scowled at her as she told them there was none.

Karl had seen the loaf of bread on the dresser. 'We'll eat that,' he said and grabbed it, looking at its odd shape. 'I suppose you made this, girl?'

'Yes, sir, I did,' Bella whispered. 'I tried . . .'

'You'll learn to do better or I'll flay the skin from your back,' he said. 'Go up and see to your mistress. See if she has woken yet – and if she has, tell her I want her up and down here doing her job!'

Bella escaped and ran upstairs to her mistress. Annie was lying very still and pale, her arms flung out; there was a trace of vomit on her mouth and Bella wiped it away. She tried to talk to her, but Annie did not answer. She still lived but Bella was afraid that she really would not last the night. Hearing a cry from the next room, she knew that the baby had woken and she rushed through to him. He seemed very hot as she picked him up and she wished the midwife was still here.

Bella had no idea what to do, but decided she would bathe his tiny body and see if it would ease him; if that did not help she thought that he might die almost as soon as his mother.

CHAPTER 10

'It was a pity about the babe,' Aggie said as she sat in her chair by the fire and nursed the cup of hot milk sweetened with honey. She sighed with content for she could not remember when she had last been given so much kindness and attention. ''Tis many years since I tasted milk and honey – my mother was alive then and I a child at her skirts.'

'The babe?' Hetty asked gently, for the old lady tended to ramble and would soon lose her thread if not reminded. 'Do you speak of your mother's babe?'

Aggie savoured a mouthful of the sweet milk and then shook her head. 'No, the young lady I helped to birth her child not much more than a month since. She was a healthy mite and beautiful . . .' Sadness came into her face. 'The mistress said she died but she had strong lungs and I swear I heard her cry that night.'

'The babe lived,' Hetty said. 'Your mistress sold her.'

'Aye, she does that.' Aggie finished her milk but cradled the cup in her hands. Her head nodded wisely, as if remembering. 'So many little ones taken from their mothers and given to others . . . I mind them all . . . She sells the pretty ones to ladies of fortune and the others to any who will pay for them. Sometimes she waits until they are older – as she did with Bella. I liked Bella; she was kind to me and picked me fruit in the garden – mistress would've punished us both if she'd known . . .' A gleam of mischief showed in her eyes but soon faded to tears. She sniffed and wiped her nose with a rag.

'Do you remember where the babies were sent to, Aggie?' Hetty prompted.

'Nay, for there were too many over the years.' Aggie's weak eyes were red and bleary. 'You are kind, mistress, I would help you if I could. I am sorry . . .'

'It is no matter,' Hetty said. 'You must not worry yourself. The new master and mistress will be kinder and you may end your days here in safety.'

'I have seen so many things!' Aggie cackled with sudden laughter. 'The funniest sight I ever did see was Mistress Brent's face when the gypsy laid a curse upon her.'

'The gypsy?'

'Aye,' Aggie smiled toothlessly. 'The colour went from mistress's cheeks when the gypsy woman told her she was cursed unless she looked after Bella. She said she would return one day and if Bella was not hale then she – the mistress – would die in

138

agony!' Aggie's smile vanished. 'I hope the curse comes true, for that witch sent my Bella to die at that terrible place . . .'

'Why do you say that?' Hetty looked at her curiously.

'I worked as a chain-maker until I fell ill and then I was cast off. 'Tis a terrible life for a woman, mistress.'

'Bella is working as a servant to the chain-maker's wife,' Hetty told her. 'She has not been put to the forge.'

'God be praised,' Aggie said. 'It made my heart ache to think of her there, for I know its terrors.'

'You've had a hard life, Aggie.'

'Aye, mistress,' the old woman said and then nodded at something. 'Bella said the carriage had yellow wheels – that's why the witch wanted her dead.'

Hetty stared at her, not quite sure what she'd heard.

'Bella told you the carriage that took the babe away had yellow wheels?' she asked.

'Aye, Mistress Hetty. And I saw it come here a few days earlier – it was a rich man's carriage, for he was dressed fine and carried a cane with a silver head. He spoke with the mistress and I think he gave her money for I heard the clink of coin . . .' Aggie lifted her head, her eyes suddenly bright. 'Did I do right to tell you?'

'Yes, you did. Thank you, Aggie. I am grateful for all you can tell me.'

'I have not told you much, Mistress Hetty, for I know not his name.'

'You have told me more than you know,' Hetty said. She thanked Aggie and told her to join the women in the sewing room, where she could sit and dream by the fire. Aggie was past the age of working, though she could light a candle or carry a drink for others who mended and sewed. Now that Florrie had left there was no one who could do fine embroidery, but the mending and making of clothes for the inmates went on.

Hetty was thoughtful as she wrote down what Aggie had told her. The old woman could not remember things when you asked, but then they came back to her as she rambled and it was likely that she would recall more when she was rested and no longer lived in fear. At least there was a little news for Arthur when he returned, though Hetty did not know when that might be. He had meant to try the horse fair in Newmarket and Hetty wondered if he had found anything of importance, hoped that he would return soon.

The field was thronged with men and horses and the sound of laughter and bartering was loud, a strong smell of horses, stale sweat and beer on the air. A weak sun had filtered through the recent clouds, though it was still bitter cold, but these men were used to hardship and some had their shirt sleeves rolled up to the top of their arms. They wore stained breeches and old leather jerkins and several had black hats, some adorned with brass badges and a feather. The men had little colour about them save for a neckerchief, but the women wore scarlet and yellow and black and looked as fine as birds of paradise, gold hoops in their ears.

While the men bargained over horses and ponies, the women sold all manner of trinkets from the large rush baskets they carried over their arms.

'Buy a sprig of lucky heather,' one of the women accosted Arthur as he watched the vibrant scene. 'Only sixpence a sprig, me lord – and I swear it will bring your luck this day.'

Arthur took a coin from his pocket and spun it into the air. She caught it and grinned as she saw he had given her a shilling. 'I'll take two of your tokens, gypsy – and you could earn a gold coin if you answer me a question truthfully.'

'What would you ask of me, me lord?'

'I seek one of your kind – a woman by the name of Bathsheba . . .'

For a moment the woman stared at him, then she shook her head. She handed him the lucky heather. ''Tis an unusual name for one of us,' she said. 'I know her not . . .'

Arthur watched her as she moved through the field. She did not linger but went to a caravan parked in the far corner and he saw her speak urgently to a man who was standing over his fire and poking it with a long branch. The man looked at Arthur and scowled, then spoke sharply to the woman who walked away, looking annoyed. The gypsy knew that Arthur had watched her approach him and no doubt he'd chastised her for leading him to his caravan. However, Arthur knew better than to follow immediately and when he merely stood and waited, the man came to him. As he drew nearer a feeling of recognition came to Arthur; he had met this man – Jez – once, more than a year ago, and in different circumstances.

The man reached him and their eyes met. The man nodded. 'I remember you. You told my son that he should come with me to Ireland when he wanted to stay in England.'

'Your sister,' Arthur said, 'her name is Bathsheba?'

The gypsy's face was impassive. 'You seek her – why?'

'Some twelve years past, your sister may have inquired after a babe from the mistress of a workhouse . . . the babe of a woman I believe you had previously helped?'

'And what of it? 'Tis not against the law to help a woman in trouble . . .' The man's look was fierce and angry. Arthur understood, for the gypsies were too often blamed for things that were not of their doing.

'No, and Bathsheba is not in trouble. I merely wish to speak with her concerning the child's mother, in the hope that she may tell me if she is a woman I seek. I would reward her with gold for her trouble.'

'Bathsheba is not with us,' Jez said, but Arthur thought he lied. 'I can answer your questions. Many years since, we found a woman lying in a wood by a small village in Hampshire, though I do not recall the name of the place, for we were but passing through. She was beautiful, a lady of quality, and had been abused – and she was unconscious. She would have died had we left her so we took her with us because we could not go to the Gorgio authorities for they would have blamed us for her rape. My sister saved her life.'

Arthur nodded. Everyone believed Katharine's sister had been taken by gypsies or killed by them – but if this story was true they had not harmed her.

'What happened then?' he asked.

'Bathsheba healed the woman's body but she could not heal her mind. At times she was quiet and, though she knew not her name, she thought it might be Marie and we called her thus.' The gypsy frowned, clearly disturbed by the memory. 'At first we spoke of trying to find her home when we went back to Hampshire, next, for she thought her father might be a parson and she believed she had a sister, Kathy, but when Bathsheba told her she was with child, Marie became distraught and refused to talk any more of finding her family, said her memory played tricks on her.'

'Perhaps she was too ashamed to seek out her family,' Arthur suggested.

The gypsy's eyes darkened. 'I cared for her and might have taken her for my favourite woman but she was like a wild fawn, shying at every touch.

As the child grew in her, she became almost deranged . . .' He hesitated and for a moment regret was in the dark eyes. 'I told her I loved her and wanted her to be my woman and it frightened her for she raved at me, accusing me of keeping her prisoner. I believe that all she had suffered had made an illness in her mind and she became more and more confused. When the babe was close to being born she went off and left us without a word and took shelter in the workhouse. And then, later, we learned that she died in the snow soon after the babe was born.'

'Ah, I wondered how she came to be wandering in the cold of winter if you had cared for her, but I see now that she feared you, confusing you perhaps with the brute who abused her. Perhaps she could not have borne anyone to touch her after what she had suffered,' Arthur said but Jez hardly listened, his features twisted with a mixture of anger and pain.

'She ran from me when I told her I would love and care for her.' His eyes were fierce as they met Arthur's. 'Bathsheba would have cared for the babe had Marie stayed with us, for she believed the child would bring us luck and she wanted to take it from the workhouse – but I would not let her and so my sister went to the workhouse and paid the woman to care for the babe. Bathsheba said she would curse her if she sold or harmed the child and I know she hoped to one day reclaim her for her own.' A look of grief came to his face. 'My sister lost her man before they were joined and would take no other, but wanted a child of her own; she has never forgiven me for not letting her keep the babe . . .'

'Can you name the workhouse?'

'It was close by the village of Sculfield but I remember not its name.'

'Then your sister is the one I seek.'

'She can tell you no more than I have.'

'It is small details – a description of the mother's eyes, her hair and her manner, anything a woman might notice. If Bathsheba would trust me, I would reward her.'

The other man inclined his head. 'If Bathsheba thinks she can help you, she will come . . . but I doubt there is more she can tell.'

Arthur nodded. He believed there was more but he would not press the gypsy. Perhaps Bathsheba would give him the answers he still needed, but if not he must be content with what he had.

'I am staying at the Threshed Wheat Inn,' Arthur said. 'I shall be there until the morning – if Bathsheba wishes to speak to me.'

'Very well . . .' He hesitated then: 'Do you not wish to buy a fine horse, Mr Stoneham?' Now Jez had become the true gypsy, a horse dealer, and his eyes gleamed with the light of battle.

'I will look at it and if I like it, we may strike a deal, Jez.'

The gypsy laughed, showing teeth that looked very white against his olive skin. He spat on the palm and held out his right hand. 'Bathsheba will come if she wishes but she is a law unto herself and no man commands her. Now, I will show you a horse that runs like the wind . . .'

Arthur stroked the horse he had bought and smiled. Jez had driven a hard bargain but in the end they had reached an agreement and mutual respect. The horse was broken but still a little frisky and would need a strong hand, but mated with good mares its wild blood would help breed strong foals.

Walking into the inn to order his dinner that evening, Arthur was thoughtful. He now knew that the story of a gypsy cursing Mistress Brent if she ever sold Bella was true and he had been told a story of how the babe came to be given to the workhouse in the first place. It was probably all true in the main, but told him little of the mother's past. He wanted to believe Bella was Marianne's child but knew that he was grasping at straws. Even though the location sounded as if it might be right, and the facts he knew fitted, nothing he'd learned had proved it to him.

Katharine was dead and the ache was still there inside him. If Marianne was also dead then all he could do was to take the child back to London and place her where she would be cared for. It would be an end to his quest, though not an end to his grief.

Arthur ate his meal, exchanged a few pleasantries with the landlord, and then decided to retire. Bathsheba had not come and he was disappointed, but it was late and perhaps she had not returned from her foraging for herbs soon enough to make her journey here before nightfall.

'I trust your meal was satisfactory, sir?' the landlord asked and Arthur smiled.

'Very pleasant. I shall sleep well in your comfortable bed.'

He took the lamp he was offered, its bulbous glass shade casting a yellow glow as he climbed the stairs, feeling unusually weary. With Katharine gone, life stretched endlessly ahead, and though he knew that it was his duty to live and help others, he could find little joy in it for the moment.

Unlatching his bedroom door, Arthur stiffened for he sensed rather than saw the figure by the window and then he smelled the pleasant scent of herbs and instinct told him who his visitor was. 'Bathsheba?' he asked softly. 'Why did you seek me here and not in the parlour?'

A woman moved into the light as he set down his lamp. For a moment he was startled by her beauty and her pride. She looked like an Eastern princess, her face haughty and her nose aquiline, her mouth soft and generous. Her eyes, which held his, were dark and deep like the velvet of night, and then she smiled and he caught his breath as a shaft of desire pierced him suddenly. Her laughter was as clear as a church bell.

'So you are the man Joe my nephew told me of,' she said and her voice was like a caress. 'I came because he liked you – and I am glad I did. I can see that you were in need of me.'

Arthur could not speak as she glided towards him. Her hands touched either side of his face, cupping it as she looked deep into his eyes, and then softly kissed his mouth. He felt naked, as if his soul was bared to her and yet he could not move or speak.

'You carry too much sadness,' she said at last, moving away from him, but her eyes never left his, mesmerising him. 'You think you have lost all, but a greater love awaits you. The woman you mourn would not have loved you the way you should be loved; you are not of common clay and need an equal spirit to match yours – and you would have lived to a time of disappointment.'

Arthur jerked away angrily, breaking the hold of her gaze. He had not asked her to tell his fortune! 'You did not know Katharine,' he said and turned to face her once more.

'No, but I have seen into your heart and you know what I have told you is true, Arthur Stoneham. Grieve for your lost love but know that you will find love again and this one will not disappoint.'

Arthur shook his head. 'What I wish to know is the name of the woman who gave birth to Bella. Do you know aught of her?'

Bathsheba smiled triumphantly. 'You are not ready for the truth, my Joe's friend. Yet it will come and you will not forget me . . .'

Arthur persisted, 'The child's mother – was she Katharine's sister, Marianne?'

'I know only that she was gently born, the daughter of a pastor I believe – and her hair was the colour of moonlight. She spoke of her home near the church, and of a sister she loved, whose name might have been Kathy, but she spoke no other names. Her mind was lost in the terror of the beast's attack and the horror of bearing a child.' She hesitated, then, 'My brother wanted to travel to Ireland and Marie was too ill so we lingered, travelling from place to place, but as the child grew so did her distress.'

'She ran from you – do you know why?'

'Jez wanted her. You know his son, Joe. My brother already had a woman but he wanted Marie and she feared he would keep her his prisoner. My brother is a good man, sir, but he is sometimes harsh in his manner and Marie is not the only one to fear him. I have always stood up to him, but he often intimidates others and she was a gentle soul. I tried to tell her that she was free to go home but she said it would shame those she loved and that in truth she did not know where her home was . . .' A look of sadness came to Bathsheba's face. 'I would have protected her from Jez's lust, but her mind was confused and she ran when my back was turned. Jez searched for her for days but then he grew angry when he discovered she had sought shelter in the workhouse and so we moved on. The weather was bitter and we did not know then that Marie had left the workhouse, had given birth alone and taken her child to the church, hoping the babe would be safe. One of our people had travelled through the village and told me Marie had been found dead, her child taken to the workhouse. I wanted to bring the babe back to us but Jez forbade me and in this even I dared not defy him.'

'Had Marie stayed with you she might have lived,' Arthur said and Bathsheba shook her head.

'I do not think she wished to live. The beast that violated her body destroyed her soul and her mind. Had it not been so she might have been happy as Jez's woman.' She shook her head and her perfume was a heady haze about her that invaded his senses. 'I am sorry, Arthur Stoneham. I know you hoped for more – but I cannot give you the certainty you desire. Yet in your heart, I think you know what you must do to end your torment . . .'

'I feared it would be so,' Arthur sighed. 'Yet I think I have reached the end of my quest, for the child reminds me a little of Marie's sister Katharine.'

'What will you do with the child?' Bathsheba frowned. 'I sense that she is in pain and fear of her life and that is another reason I came.'

'She was well when I saw her. She cared for the wife of the chain-maker near the village of Sculfield. I asked if she needed help but she said no.'

'Yet, she needs it,' Bathsheba said and her hand clasped his arm, sending a shaft of heat through his body. 'Find Bella and care for her as if she were your own and you will receive the gift of peace . . .'

'Yes, I shall,' Arthur said, because he felt it was true. He had come to the end of his quest and in time that would bring peace. 'What do you wish in return, Bathsheba? I promised gold – but what will satisfy you?'

'Not gold,' she said, a twist of contempt on her lips. 'Take the child back with you and see she is safe and I am repaid. I came for her sake, Arthur Stoneham, and because Joe liked you.'

'You do not wish to have her yourself?'

'No, though I would have taken her for my own had my brother not denied me when she was a babe. Her ways are formed now and she could not live my life. She belongs to you, Arthur Stoneham. I give her to you.'

'If you save a life it belongs to you . . .' He saw the answering smile in her eyes and nodded. 'Thank you, Bathsheba. I shall heed your advice.'

'Then I have not wasted my time . . .'

She moved softly towards the door. As she stood with her hand upon the latch, Arthur thought of something. 'The door was locked, I'm sure it was – how did you get in?'

A smile touched her mouth and then she was gone. He stared after her. There was some mystery here, for no one could walk through a locked door . . . could they? She had left in the normal way and yet he had a feeling that she had not been real. Had he conjured her up in his mind? No, the touch of her hands and her kiss had been real and he'd felt her mind probing his. Perhaps he had assumed the door was locked, believed he'd left it so earlier. Unless there was a spare key and Bathsheba had taken it and entered while the inn was busy? Of course that must be it . . . and yet there was still a hint of the power of the woman even after she had gone.

Arthur laughed at his thoughts. He was not such a fool as to believe in such powers, but oddly, his feeling of emptiness and deep loneliness had gone. He felt alive once more and ready to continue with his life – but first he must return to Sculfield and find Bella. Whether she was Marianne's daughter or not, he could not be certain, but he knew that she was a child that needed rescuing and that was more important for the moment . . .

CHAPTER 11

Bella looked fearfully at the woman sprawled across the bed. She'd heard her master raging at his wife, trying in vain to rouse her. Annie looked as though she were a rag doll, limp and lifeless. Approaching timidly, Bella touched her mistress on the arm and discovered that she was stone cold. Was she dead? Her eyes were closed and she might just have been sleeping, but there was no sign of life and she was so cold.

Ought she to cover her mistress and run for the midwife once more? Bella feared that she would not come, for the master had all but thrown her from the house the last time. Perhaps the doctor . . . ? Undecided, she threw a coverlet over Annie's body for modesty's sake and then, as the child whimpered, went into the next room. The babe had still not been named. Annie had called him Karl's son and given him as little attention as possible. His wails had been strong when he was first unwell but they grew weaker all the time.

Bella did not know what to do. She was terrified of approaching her master and the work was piling up in the house. She had washing and cleaning to finish and there was the meal to prepare for that night, but little food in the house. No one had bought anything since Annie fell ill. Bella could boil potatoes and root vegetables but there was no meat to cook, just some cheese and bread she'd baked earlier. Unable to think of anything better, she made a thick vegetable soup with the last remnants of a ham bone to give it flavour. She would serve it with the bread. Bella knew that her master and his nephews would be angry, but she had no money to buy food.

Going back to the child she fed him with a little warmed cow's milk but he brought most of it straight up. Now that the soup was made, she moved it off the hob, wrapped the babe in his blankets and left the house. Perhaps the doctor or the midwife would tell her what to do for the child.

Bella walked as fast as she could to the village. She was lucky and found the doctor at home. His housekeeper took her into the room where he saw patients and he came through to her, still munching some bread.

'What is the trouble now, girl?' he asked impatiently.

'The babe is ill, sir – and I think my mistress is dead. Her eyes are closed as if she sleeps but she is ice-cold to the touch. I tried to feed the little one but he brings the warmed milk straight up again – and his nappies are yellow but hardly filled.'

'Let me look at him. Come, place him on the table.'

Bella did as she was told, looking at the tiny body in pity. He was small and cried so faintly now that she feared he would die – and even if by some miracle he lived, how would he fare with a brute as a father and Annie dead?

'The child is very poorly and like to die without its mother's milk,' the doctor said and frowned. 'If I allow you to take the babe back to that house I condemn it to death. Hmm . . . There is a woman from one of the farms who has milk in her breasts for her own babe died. If she will feed it, the child has a chance.'

'I am not sure my master would let the babe go.'

'I shall send my groom to take the child to the good woman – and I'd best return with you to see whether your mistress is truly dead, girl.'

'Yes, sir.'

Bella waited while the doctor arranged with his housekeeper and groom to take the babe to the farmer's wife who had lost her child. Bella was relieved that the responsibility had been lifted from her but dreaded what Karl would do when he discovered what had happened.

The doctor took his gig after ordering Bella to climb in beside him. She was silent on the return to the cottage, for she did not know what to say. When they reached the cottage she followed the doctor up to Annie's room and watched as he made a brief examination of her mistress. He turned to her, looking grave.

'Her death was imminent but her neck has been snapped by a brutal shaking, possibly after death, perhaps before . . .' He shook his head. 'Who would do such a thing?'

'I think my master tried to wake her.'

'He is a thoughtless brute but I cannot say he caused her death for I think the fever would have taken her.' His eyes narrowed as he studied Bella. 'You did not take it from her even though you nursed her?'

'No, sir. I did what I could to ease her but she was too sick. My master threw the midwife out and I think the birth was too hard for my mistress.'

'Yes, I think that may be the case.' He frowned. 'It is not fitting that you should stay here now, child. You are too young to have all the cares of the house on your shoulders.'

'My master paid for me. He owns me . . .'

'No man owns another – or a woman or child,' the doctor said and looked angry. 'I should return you to the workhouse for there is nowhere else you can go.'

'The mistress there hates me,' Bella said apprehensively. 'She will not want me back.'

'I believe there have been changes at the workhouse, though I do not know exactly how things stand,' he said and ran his fingers through his hair. 'I must inform your master of his wife's death and the situation with his son – but my advice to you is to return to the workhouse. *I* cannot offer you a home but I think you will find they will take you

156

in if you go to the gates . . .' He hesitated as they heard the sound of men's voices. 'Go to your room while I speak to your master, girl – and in the morning, when he goes to work, leave this house.'

Bella saw the door opening and fled through to the scullery. She could hear the doctor's voice and then her master's angry tones. He was shouting at the doctor, threatening him. Bella heard the door slam and knew that the doctor had gone.

She heard the men talking and one of them discovered the soup.

'Is this all there is to eat?' one of Karl's nephews said. 'That lazy slut! She deserves a thrashing. Where are yer, girl – come and get our meal!'

'There is nothing in the pantry,' another voice said. 'Who buys the food here?'

'It was Annie's job!' Karl's furious voice answered the elder nephew. 'We'll manage with the soup and bread tonight. Bella, get out here now or I'll thrash yer until yer bleed!'

Trembling, Bella crept out of the scullery. One of the younger men grabbed her and shook her and then slapped her ear. 'Lazy little slut,' he muttered. 'You're not worth the bread yer eat.'

Bella's stomach rumbled, for she had eaten nothing since a scrap of yesterday's bread at breakfast. 'Where is the meat and pudding?'

'There is no food in the larder,' Bella whispered. 'I have no money to buy food.'

'No, fer yer would steal it!'

'Let her be for now,' Karl commanded. 'Warm

that soup through again, girl, while I cut the bread. I'll order food in the morning – and now that you've nothin' else ter do yer can get this place cleaned up and cook us a decent pie for our supper.'

Bella swallowed hard. She wished that she'd run away while the doctor was still here, because she did not like the way her master's nephews looked at her. She was afraid of what they might do now that she had no mistress to protect her. Annie had kept some sort of decency in the house, but these men looked at her with hard uncaring eyes and she knew they were not above abusing her in any way they thought fit.

While Bella warmed the soup, Karl sliced bread and ate two slices with cheese. His nephews did the same and they broke the rest of the bread into chunks to eat with their soup. No one offered her even a crust and she had begun to feel very hungry.

There was a large pan of soup and she saved a cup for herself and drank it quickly in the scullery while they ate, cowering in there until she heard heavy feet going upstairs.

About to creep back to the warmth of the kitchen, she stopped as Karl's large figure filled the doorway. He stood looking down at her as she waited for the blow she expected.

'Can you cook?' he asked gruffly. 'More than a soup or some bread?'

'My mistress was teaching me but I know very little, master.'

'As I thought . . .' He frowned. 'I should've left yer

at the workhouse and insisted on an older girl or a woman – my wife might have lived then.' For a moment Bella thought she saw regret in his eyes, but then it was gone. 'I've paid fer yer and I'll not get a penny back. Yer will learn ter cook or I'll put yer to the chain-making. Suit yerself, girl. I'll see food is delivered and then it's fer yer to decide – learn fast or yer will discover what work truly is!'

Bella nodded fearfully. She did not doubt he would carry out his threats if she did not please him.

'Get these pots washed and clear up or I'll give yer a thrashin' meself!'

'Yes, sir . . .'

Bella trembled as he left and then she heard him treading heavily up the stairs. She got the pots washed then made a dough and left it to prove overnight, waiting until everything was quiet before running up to her little cubbyhole in the attic. There was no lock on the door but she wedged a chair under the handle just in case one of Karl's nephews decided to visit her in the night. They were brutes and bullies and though they both feared Karl, she did not trust them.

Crawling under her coverlet, Bella shivered in the darkness. She must be up early and give the bread dough its second proving and then bake a loaf for their breakfast, because if there was nothing to eat they would surely beat her.

Hetty stood looking out of the window at the top of the stairs. She thought that she'd seen a movement outside a few moments ago, but since then she had not seen anything more. Was someone lurking out there? Perhaps one of the inmates had gone out into the workhouse gardens? Yet that seemed unlikely for most were elderly or children. Very few of those who lived here now were both healthy and strong. Men forced to enter during the winter months because of near starvation left as soon as there was work in the spring and took their families with them, so only the orphans and the elderly were forced to remain.

She considered going outside to investigate and then decided against it. If someone unpleasant was lurking there she could be attacked. It would be more sensible to walk round the house and make sure all the windows and doors were locked.

After checking all the main doors and the windows downstairs, Hetty walked back to the landing. She thought she'd probably been mistaken and was about to retire when someone approached her.

'It's only me, Mistress Hetty.'

'Is there a problem, Marta? Could you not sleep?'

'I thought I heard something downstairs.'

'I was checking all the doors and windows. It is all safe,' Hetty said and smiled at her.

'I thought . . .' Marta hesitated. 'You will think me a foolish woman, mistress – but I thought I caught sight of the old master through the window earlier this evening.'

'No, I do not think you foolish. I saw a shadow in the garden and that is why I went to investigate downstairs. If you ever see anything like that again, please tell me – though I do not know why he would risk coming back here. He must know that he is wanted for murder as well as other crimes.'

'He is an evil man, mistress. He may have money hidden here somewhere – money that he had no chance to retrieve before your friend Mr Stoneham threw him out.'

'Yes, that is possible,' Hetty said. 'Everywhere is shut up downstairs but you should all make sure that the doors of your bedchambers are well locked for the night.'

'Yes, mistress. I will check the children's dorms are locked and tell the others to be careful.'

Hetty nodded. It was an uncomfortable feeling to know that Master Brent or his equally evil wife might be lurking about, especially as they knew the building so well. Hetty could not help wishing that either Arthur or his friend Toby were sleeping here. Hetty had not thought she needed protection here, but now she wished that Arthur would return sooner than later.

Arthur paid his shot at the Newmarket inn and left. He had done all he'd intended here and though there was no conclusive proof that Bella's mother had been Katharine's sister, he believed that he had likely solved the riddle of Marianne's disappearance and that Bella was the niece of the woman he'd loved and wished to marry. Though Katharine was lost to him and he still grieved for her, the emptiness had begun to lift.

Bathsheba had told him he should take the girl Bella and care for her. Strangely, she was not much younger than Eliza, the girl he believed his own daughter but did not feel he could claim as yet though he longed to. Taking Bella into his home would compensate a little for that, and he was certain that Nana, Katharine's elderly nurse, would welcome the chance to care for a child believed to be Marianne's daughter. And he could hire a governess for Bella, to teach the child her letters. He frowned. If Bella *was* the product of a brutal rape, it would be best kept from her. She need be told only that her mother had died giving birth to her. Still, he wasn't certain that living in a grand London house would be the best thing for Bella . . . He must give this more thought.

Arthur had brought his gig to Newmarket and his groom, Kent, had sat beside him as he drove down, but he'd given the man his new horse to take to his country estate in Sussex and was driving himself back to Sculfield. He was thoughtful as he clicked his long whip. He would be glad when he reached the inn. It was time he fetched Bella from her brutal master in the village of Fornham and he wanted to see how Hetty was faring at the workhouse.

Did he ask too much of her friendship? She had a life in London and friends. At Sculfield there was no one but Toby and he was tied up with helping Meg, for whom he had swiftly developed a fondness.

Arthur frowned as he thought of the young

woman he'd plucked from the jaws of death. He had been able to give her problem little thought thus far. Meg had been badly treated and he was not sure what he could do to help her find her lost babe, but he must try. Surely someone would know something? The agents he'd set to looking must find a clue of sorts . . .

He was suddenly aware that one of his two horses had pulled up sharply and brought the vehicle to a halt. Getting down to investigate, he saw that it had gone lame and would need to be led very slowly to the nearest hostelry. Arthur was both proud and careful of his horses and he would not ruin them by pushing them. He would unharness them both, leave his curricle here by the side of the road and lead them. It was the only way to avoid pain for the horse and perhaps permanent damage.

He looked up at the sky. The hour was wearing on and it would be growing dark by the time he arrived . . .

CHAPTER 12

Three women came to the chain-maker's house to prepare Annie for burial soon after Karl and his nephews had left. Bella had managed to cut herself a slice of bread with some dripping after they'd eaten and she'd drunk a cup of tea. Before he left, her master had told her that the cart would bring provisions for some weeks and she was to see them packed into the pantry.

Bella nodded and agreed that she would. She had still not decided whether or not she was going to risk a return to the workhouse when the women arrived. She took them up to her mistress and they demanded hot water and towels to wash her and clean linen to bind her. Bella heated the water and gave them one of the older sheets. She left them to their work. Now might be a good time to run, but just as she was deciding, the cart came. The delivery man had brought sacks of flour, yeast, vegetables, butter, cooking fat, eggs, milk, cheese, a large bag of raisins and mixed peel, also a whole ham, bacon, chops and stewing meat and various flavourings.

'I've brought what Annie ordered each week but multiplied four times 'cos he said he wanted enough fer the month.'

Bella nodded and showed him where to put the things in the larder, filling the shelves. Besides the food there were three barrels of beer, something Annie had never ordered.

The women came down from laying out Annie while the grocer's man was filling the shelves. They took their leave with a brief nod, not one of them asking Bella if she was all right. Soon after that the delivery man drove away with an empty cart.

Bella hesitated and then started peeling vegetables. She decided to make pies and a big stew of the beef and mutton for it would keep better cooked in the cool pantry, and spent the rest of the day cooking. Karl did not come back for anything midday and when she had the pies cooling she fried all the pork chops. They would serve as cold lunches for the men and the ham and bacon would be saved for later in the month. Karl had purchased too much fresh meat for she knew if she had not cooked it all it would start to go off in a few days.

Once all the fresh meat was dealt with, Bella sat down and ate a piece of bread with a tiny piece of cheese from the new block. It tasted lovely because it was very fresh but by the end of the month it would be getting stale. Karl had thought it simpler to order everything at once – and when he discovered his mistake, Bella hoped to be far away.

She had decided that she would stay until Annie was buried, because it wouldn't be right to leave her alone in the house. It could only be a day or two and then she would go. Where she would go was something Bella had not yet fully considered, for she knew no other life except the workhouse and did not wish to return there for Karl would only fetch her back, but the thought of tramping the roads looking for work terrified her. Yet for now she could not worry about the future. She had done her work and was so tired that she went upstairs to lie down for a few minutes . . .

Bella woke to a rough hand shaking her. She was pulled violently from the bed to the floor and lay there quaking as she looked up at Karl. He was furiously angry and as she tried to rise he kicked her in the side and she fell back.

'You wicked, wasteful girl,' he yelled. 'Cooking all the food that was supposed to last us most of the month . . .'

'The fresh meat would not have kept,' Bella said defensively, looking up at him. 'My mistress bought fresh every couple of days so I worked hard to preserve it.'

Karl glared at her, his anger simmering but perhaps seeing some reason in what she said. 'All those chops – why did you cook them?'

'So that you could take them to work with bread and pickles. The cheese and ham will last longer.'

'Stupid girl,' Karl said but his anger was cooling. 'Come and heat the pie through and serve the vegetables!'

Bella scurried to do his bidding. Their plates were piled high with pastry, meat in gravy, potatoes, pudding and some carrots. She'd partially cooked them earlier and they took minutes to finish. Karl's nephews grumbled that the pastry was hard and the potatoes lumpy, but they cleared their plates. The elder one went into the pantry and picked up a cold pork chop, munching it as he returned and looking pleased. Karl scowled at him.

'They are for the rest of the week. Haven't you had enough?'

'I'm hungry,' Basil grumbled. 'There was no afters.'

Karl looked at Bella. Perhaps he saw that she was weary. 'You demand too much. The girl is learning. She has done well enough for a first time managing alone.'

Bella blinked hard. His praise was slight but he had protected her from the other men's spite.

'I will try to make afters tomorrow, sir.'

'A sponge pudding or some stewed apples and custard,' he said. 'There are apples in the loft if you look.'

Bella nodded.

'Wash these dishes and go to bed,' her master bid her. 'Tomorrow you must clean the house for the next day they will take Annie to the church – and her father will come here to see her leave. If you know how to make a cake and some sandwiches do so. I shall bring him back afterwards for beer and food.'

'I will try, master.'

Bella felt as if she were falling asleep on her feet but she managed to keep going until she had washed the pots and pans and the dishes. She tidied the kitchen and left the table set with plates and mugs for the morning. There was bread in the pantry and the cold meat; she would not have to rise so early to bake next day.

When Bella closed and wedged her door shut that night she was so weary she fell into the bed and went straight to sleep. She did not dream but lay like one dead until the crowing of the cock woke her.

Arthur's thoughts would not let him rest. He rose from an uncomfortable bed at the inn, dressed and went down to the parlour. A candle burned and a maid was clearing cinders from the grate. It wanted at least two hours until first light and as the young girl looked at him in fright and then fled with her bucket, he was aware of the hard life so many were forced to live. He had been born to privilege and wealth, but most worked all their lives and died worn out and exhausted, sometimes in a workhouse. Those too proud or independent to enter such a place often died of starvation by the wayside, having lost their homes when they became too old to serve a master. The system of tied cottages worked well for landowners, providing shelter for their workers, but it left the old vulnerable and often homeless. Arthur and others like him were able to help only a few and until there was social reform nothing would change, particularly for the children of the poor who were forced to work when they ought to have been at school or playing. That focused his thoughts once more on the child who had occupied them for most of the night.

Feeling on edge, he left the inn and went outside for a stroll in the cool air. He would look in on his horses to make sure they were well cared for and then ask the landlord for an early breakfast. He had decided he would return to the workhouse and ask Hetty's advice on what she thought right for Bella. Yes, Hetty would give him good advice, she always did. The thought made him feel lighter and he was suddenly impatient to see and speak to her.

He found his horses in the stable and stroked their soft noses, then left to return to the inn with a new purpose in his stride and because he was busy with his own thoughts of the future, he did not hear the footsteps behind him until it was too late. Alerted by a slight noise, he turned sharply but the cosh hit him between the eyes and he was felled with one blow. A shout came from a short distance away, as the shadowy figure bent over his body, searching his greatcoat pockets.

Afterwards, Arthur would learn that it was the

head groom arriving for work at the inn who had saved him from further injury but that would not be for some days. When they carried him into the inn and put him to bed, he was unconscious and the doctor was summoned to a man they feared might not live . . .

Hetty slept fitfully, dreaming of dangerous intruders and dead children buried in unhallowed graves. When she rose to face the day she was tired and a shadow seemed to hang over her.

How long would it be before Arthur returned? She did not object to the work here and felt sympathy for many of the inmates, but she was uneasy. The elderly men and women who resided in the house had been unsettled by the discovery of the murdered children and some of them looked at her with fearful eyes, as if they thought they might be blamed for the tragic happenings here. The children were subdued and even though Hetty spoke kindly to them, they scurried away if they could rather than face her.

'It's not you they fear, mistress,' Marta told her. 'They think the old mistress will return and punish them.'

'Mistress Brent would be arrested if she came here,' Hetty had told her confidently, but she was on edge, restless. She *had* seen something moving in the gardens late the previous evening and she wished that Arthur or Toby were close, because the man who had been master here was an evil and violent rogue and she knew he would not hesitate to attack her if she opposed him.

If both she and Marta had heard something, then it was likely the intruder had been Master Brent and she could only suppose that he was looking for something that had been left behind when Arthur threw him out. He would return, she was sure . . .

'Mistress Hetty!' She turned as Aggie hobbled towards her. 'I've remembered something.'

'Aggie.' Hetty smiled as the elderly woman reached her. 'What can I do for you?'

'I know who took that baby,' Aggie said and her eyes were bright with pleasure because she had remembered something that had eluded her. 'They came here together and mistress showed them round the dorms. Her name was Sarah Fawcett and her husband Harold was a rich merchant – they came from a place just outside Newmarket, a small village I think they said – but I do not recall its name.'

'How do you know it was they who took Meg's child?'

'I heard them say they would pay two hundred pounds for a girl and three for a boy and mistress looked pleased with herself. I saw her counting gold sovereigns one morning after the babe was born – I swear there were two hundred of them on her desk.' Aggie gave a little cackle of delight. 'She was angry with me for entering without knocking and swept the money into a black velvet purse.'

Hetty nodded and thanked her and Aggie walked away, chuckling to herself because she was pleased to have been of help. Her words were not proof of any wrongdoing on the part of the former wardens and would not convict Mistress Brent, but they showed Hetty the probability of truth.

She decided to send word to the inn and ask Toby to call on her at once. She could tell him of her concern that Master Brent had been searching the grounds for something and give him the news concerning Meg's child. If he wished, he could send agents to look for the couple who lived in a village near Newmarket – a rich merchant and his wife by the names of Harold and Sarah Fawcett. It should not be too difficult to discover where they lived and to confront them with the truth.

CHAPTER 13

'Hetty thinks that she may have discovered who bought your child,' Toby said and reached for Meg's hand as she gasped, her face white and strained. He saw the look of eager hope and his heart filled with love for her and the need to give her happiness. 'I have the names of a couple who paid Mistress Brent a visit. It came from an elderly woman with an unreliable memory so you must not set your hopes too high – but I shall drive there at once and discover what I can.'

'Let me come with you, please,' Meg begged him, her eyes large and bright with tears.

'It would be too distressing for you,' Toby said firmly. 'I shall recover the babe if it is your child, Meg dearest. You must trust me – please.'

For a moment rebellion flared in her eyes but then she nodded. 'I do trust you – but bring my babe back to me, I beg you.'

'I promise I shall do all I can,' Toby said. He took her hands, looking into her face. 'I want you to stay with Hetty at the workhouse while I'm away. She needs a little help and company and I am sending my groom Hobbs with you. He will be there to protect you, Meg. Arthur has been too long absent and Hetty is anxious. If I am to investigate these allegations she needs our help.'

Meg hesitated, clearly wanting to argue but instead, she inclined her head. 'I shall do as you ask, because I know that I am lucky to be alive. If it were not for you and Arthur I might be dead – and if I lived it would be without hope.'

'I give you my word I shall do all I may to protect you and to rescue your child,' Toby promised and lifted her hands to kiss them tenderly. 'Hetty is anxious for Arthur and she also fears Master Brent may return to the workhouse and do harm which is why I am sending her Hobbs. I cannot protect you here at the inn and I would feel happier if I knew you were with Hetty.'

'You are so kind to me,' Meg said and smiled sadly.

Toby's heart contracted. He knew that his love for her might never be fully returned, because she had suffered too harshly at the hands of other men. She was willing to trust him and do as he advised and for the moment it was all that he could expect. Toby had never felt this way about a woman before. He felt exulted and vulnerable at the same time, because his love made him fear that he might lose her even though it might not be possible for her to ever love him as he loved her.

Meg had recovered her physical health. She still could not walk long distances or sit up late in the evenings, but she was growing stronger. It was her mental suffering and her low spirits which made her look so sad sometimes. Toby feared that if he could not return her babe to her she might never be truly at peace again.

Meg watched as the young man rode away. Toby Rattan had promised to protect and care for her and she did not know what else she could do but accept his kindness.

'I could never go to my father's home near Winchester,' Meg told Hetty as they sat together after Toby had ridden away. 'My father would send me back to my husband and I hate him. I would rather die than return to his house.'

'Arthur and Mr Rattan are good men,' Hetty said and looked sympathetically at her. 'I know they will help you – and they would never force you to do something you did not wish to do . . .'

'Thank you,' Meg said and smiled. 'Everything is all so vague after I was attacked by vagabonds but I know that I was very unhappy . . .'

If only Toby could find her child and bring her back to her! She hated the man who had sired her babe but she loved and wanted the child. She needed something to love and cling to for she felt lost and alone. Mr Stoneham had saved her life and his friend had shown her more kindness than she'd ever known, but Meg was not sure if she could ever love a man. It was her babe she wanted, a warm armful that she could nurse and tend – and only if she held the child again could she hope to find some kind of happiness. For the moment she must do as Toby had requested and return to the workhouse.

'Please come back soon,' she whispered when his horses carried him out of sight and she could no longer see his curricle. 'Please bring my baby back to me . . .'

Hetty was pleased that Toby had sent his groom with Meg to watch over them. While she had no fear for herself, she knew that any one of the inmates might be at risk, as might Meg if she had stayed at the inn alone. Only Marta and Aggie had spoken out and given her information about what had gone on here, but others might know things – and if Master Brent feared that knowledge they might not be safe.

'Toby says that he will try to discover why Mr Stoneham tarries so long in Newmarket,' Meg said as they drank a pot of tea together later that morning. 'I daresay he has business for he seemed a busy and clever man to me.'

'Yes, he is,' Hetty agreed. 'He keeps his emotions in check but you must not think him cold or unfeeling, Meg. I know he is as concerned for you as the Honourable Toby Rattan but—'

'Toby is the son of a lord?' Meg stared at her.

'The younger son, yes, but he does not regard it. You did not know?'

'No, he said nothing of it.' Meg shook her head but looked thoughtful. 'I thought him just a friend of Mr Stoneham – he seemed to look up to his friend.'

Hetty smiled, a look of love in her eyes as she spoke of the man she had loved for so long. 'Arthur Stoneham is a forceful man, but do not underestimate Toby. He led a campaign to end injustice towards children who were being abused and has been instrumental in provoking much debate in the House of Lords by persuading his father to speak out for the poor. If there are changes in the laws concerning the wellbeing of young children, he will have played his part . . .'

'I see . . .' Meg looked thoughtful but said no more.

'I am glad you have come,' Hetty told her as she showed her the room she was to use. 'This belonged to Mistress Brent but it has been cleaned and aired and all her things have been removed.'

Meg looked about her. The room was plainly furnished like all the others in the workhouse, but it was so much better than sleeping rough as she had often been forced to after her flight from her cruel husband.

'It will do very well, thank you.' She paused, then, 'You return to London when Lady Rowntree has appointed a new mistress and master here?'

'Yes, and shall be glad to do so – though I know

179

all is well cared for in my absence. But London is my home and I came here only to please Arthur.'

'You are fond of him, are you not?' Meg looked at her curiously.

Hetty smiled. 'He is my dearest friend and I should not know what to do if he were lost.'

'You do not suspect foul play?'

'Who knows?' Hetty frowned for he had been many days on the road, longer than she might have expected, and should surely have returned or sent word by now. She worried that some mischief had befallen him and yet knew that he was prepared for he always went armed when he travelled England's lonely roads. 'Arthur does not suffer fools gladly. He might have enemies anywhere.' Hetty hesitated. 'I told Toby that I sensed something, but perhaps it was just foolishness. Arthur is a strong man and alert . . . perhaps I worry for nothing, as Toby told me.'

'I fear I am the same,' Meg said and smiled. 'I am anxious for news of my child – but I should not want Toby harmed because of me.'

'I doubt it will happen,' Hetty said. 'Both of them carry pistols and they are strong men.'

'Toby left his groom here to guard us,' Meg said and again she looked anxious. 'But Mr Stoneham has his groom with him so I am certain no harm could come to him,' she said and sighed.

'I am not sure what other business holds Arthur here, though he spoke of another child he had concerns for.' Hetty frowned and looked thoughtful.

'I think he may have meant Bella,' Meg said with

a frown. 'She was kind to me when I lay grieving, believing my child dead. It was Bella who first told me that the babe lived and I think Mistress Brent sold her to the chain maker because she dared to help me. I have wondered how she is and whether she is well-treated.'

'Arthur would not leave a child to suffer if he knew of it,' Hetty said confidently. 'Bella you said her name was?' Meg nodded. 'Perhaps I should send someone to the village to inquire for her.' Hetty was uncertain what to do for the best. Arthur had clearly been detained and if a child was in danger, she ought to do what she could to help her . . .

Annie had been buried in the churchyard after several villagers had crowded into the church to pray for her soul. Afterwards, some attempted to offer condolences to Karl but he brushed them aside angrily and invited no one to return to his home for food or drink, though Annie's father accompanied him. Neither of them spoke much and the atmosphere was tense, as if each man resented the other. For the first time Bella thought she understood why Annie had married; her father was not a man to accept her refusal and it must have seemed an escape to the poor girl until she discovered that her husband was even more of a bully than her father.

Bella thought Annie's father, Archie Rush, a morose man; he looked at her with sullen eyes, never speaking a word of thanks. She offered him some of the beer Karl had provided, seed cake and fresh-baked rolls filled with cheese and pickles. He took the beer but refused the food, glaring at her.

'Workhouse brat! Karl should flay the skin from your back – neglecting my Annie and the babe. Had you done yer job, I swear Annie would still be alive.'

Bella would have protested her innocence but knew that Annie's father had been drinking before he came to the funeral and would take no notice of her. He punched her arm spitefully more than once as she replenished the men's beer and filled plates. Karl and his sons ate everything she had prepared and looked for more.

'I have another daughter,' Annie's father announced suddenly. 'Peg is not a beauty but she cooks better than this brat – and she has good child-bearing hips.' He looked expectantly at Karl, as if hoping he would ask for the second daughter.

'I shall not take another wife,' Karl muttered and wiped the froth of beer with the back of his hand. 'They die too easily and complain too much. And I have a son.'

'I'll take her!' The elder of his nephews spoke up, his eyes bright with too much strong drink. 'She'll look the same as other women in the dark – and we need someone to look after us properly.' He glared at Bella. 'The workhouse brat is not much good to us. She can scrub and clean but she's no cook.'

Bella turned away resentfully. She had done her

best, but there was so much to do and sometimes the bread burned on the crust or the stew was cooked too fast and the meat was tough.

'You should put her to work in the forge, as was intended,' he muttered looking at his uncle in anger. 'I'll marry Archie's daughter Peg – and she'll cook and clean fer us.'

'Do you not want her to cook fer yer?' Karl asked Annie's father.

'I'm thinking of takin' a wife,' Archie Rush said and looked sly. 'She's a widow with a bit of a nest egg – and she cooks all the food I like. She also has a daughter who cleans and sews and I'll not want Peg about the place once I've got me new wife.'

Bella turned away in disgust. Annie's father had not come here to mourn her but to bargain away his younger daughter. Peg was to be turned out of her home so that he could take a wife – and it mattered not what she felt about the man she would marry. She would be as miserable, as Annie had been. One thing was certain, though; Bella would have to leave. Karl tolerated her but his nephews did not – and she could see by the speculation in her master's eyes that he was considering whether he should take Archie's advice and put her to the chain-making.

She would run away the next day, Bella decided. She had stayed out of respect for Annie, but now that she was buried and prayed for there was no reason for Bella to stay. The younger of Karl's nephews was staring at her and she remembered that he had made strange remarks concerning her when she first came to the house. Now that his brother was to marry would he consider Bella fair prey?

A shiver ran down her spine. The doctor had told her to run after Annie died but Bella feared life on the run nearly as much as she feared her master and his nephews. If she had somewhere to go she would leave tonight – but Mistress Brent would beat her and send her back if she tried to return to the workhouse. She had to find work for herself – but as far away from this place as was possible. More than anything Bella feared a return to the workhouse where she'd been so ill-treated and thought she would rather starve in the fields than be at the mercy of someone like Mistress Brent . . .

Meg joined the other women in the sewing room at the workhouse. There was always mending to do. She would have preferred embroidery, but now that Florrie was living in Lady Rowntree's house, she did not send work here.

'Does anyone know how Bella gets on?' Meg asked the other inmates and they all shook their heads.

'If she was put to the chain-making she won't last long,' Marta said and shook her head. ''Tis a pity. I liked Bella – she was always helpful and kind, even though the mistress was unkind to her.'

'Her mother was a lady,' Aggie said and for a

moment her eyes were clear as she remembered. 'The mistress treated the child ill her whole life . . .' Aggie shook her head. 'She ought by rights to die in agony for what she did to little Bella.'

They all looked at her, because no one else had lived here this long and they were not sure that Aggie truly remembered. Was this true or just a story she had conjured up from her imagination?

'Did Bella's mother not die in the fields?' Marta asked.

'Aye, of the fever after she'd left her babe at the church,' Aggie said. 'She came here when she was near her time and asked to be admitted but mistress would not take her in. I gave her a bit of bread and a cup of milk and she asked me if I'd seen her sister and she begged me to tell Katharine that she was close to her time, but I knew not who Katharine was or where . . .'

'I knew nothing of this tale,' Marta said and frowned. 'Mistress Hetty will wish to know of this.'

Aggie nodded and smiled a secret smile. 'I told her another secret. I know lots of secrets . . .' Her smile faded and the look in her blue eyes became uncertain. 'I cannot always recall them . . .' She let her head drop, her eyes closing, as if the effort to remember had been too much for her.

'You should not worry,' Marta said, but made a mental note to tell Hetty of Bella's mother's dying wish. 'I am more concerned for how Bella fares now. Someone should go to the village and ask for her.'

She thought that she would speak to Hetty as soon as possible and ask her if she would go.

'I will make inquiries,' Hetty promised. 'In the morning I shall walk to the village and inquire for Bella. If she is unhappy I will offer a home here – or with me in London.'

'Thank you,' Marta said gratefully. 'I ought to have spoken sooner – Florrie would have, but she is not here and I was uncertain what to do.'

Hetty smiled at Marta. 'I meant it when I told you to speak your mind to me – and if you fear to stay here, I can offer you a bed at my house in London.'

'You could not take all of us,' Marta said and looked over her shoulder. 'I have friends here – and the poor children. What is going to happen to us? When the new master and mistress come, will they be as fair and kind as you? No one likes being here – 'tis haunted by the spirit of those unhappy children he murdered.'

'I am not in a position to choose the new master and mistress,' Hetty said. 'Lady Rowntree is the patron here. She and her husband chose the last master and mistress. I can only hope that she chooses more wisely this time.'

'It would be better this place should be closed than another such couple come to plague us,' Marta said and then hung her head. 'I am not ungrateful, mistress. I know what you and Mr Stoneham have done here – but I fear for the future.'

'Yes, I understand that, Marta, and I promise that I shall do all I can to influence her ladyship towards a good choice – but I have little say in what happens when I leave.'

'I know . . .' Marta looked tearful. 'I do miss Florrie. She is happy where she is but this will be a lonely place when you and Meg leave, Mistress Hetty. I fear the future.'

Hetty sighed, feeling saddened by the woman's fear and unhappiness. The workhouse was where Marta must end her days unless she accepted Hetty's offer to live with her in Arthur's house in London – but she knew that Marta could not desert all those others, like Aggie who was too old to move.

'You must trust Arthur,' Hetty said. 'I know that he will do everything in his power to make this a safe place for you and the children.'

'Can any of them ever sleep in peace, knowing that some of their friends and predecessors were buried in the garden? It has given those who understand nightmares. I have heard them crying and calling out in their sleep.'

'Yes, I imagine it might give them bad dreams.' Hetty was thoughtful. *She* found it difficult to pass the spot where the bodies had been buried, so how much worse was it for the children? Perhaps Marta was right and this place should be closed and left to rot. There were fifteen children here and five elderly men, also seven women: twenty-seven people who would need a home if this place was closed. It would be a big ask of Arthur to find places for all of them, for she herself could only take two women and one child. Yet if the children were having disturbed dreams, something must be done.

As the day passed without Arthur's return, she began to feel uneasy. Without Arthur she could offer no hope to any of these folk – and those in London would also be at risk. He was needed by so many people and she did not think he truly understood how much difference he made to the lives of others.

'Arthur, where are you?' she asked aloud. 'I need you – we all need you. I pray you will put your grief aside and return to us . . .'

CHAPTER 14

Bella took only a woollen shawl Annie had given her and the dress she had worn when she left the workhouse. She had baked the bread fresh before her master went to work and made a spare loaf for herself. Wrapping that in her shawl with a stone bottle of water, she slipped out of the back door and into the lane, closing the door behind her.

She knew that the loaf and the small piece of cheese she took with her would be called theft and if she was caught she would be punished severely. She thought it might also be a crime to run away from the master who had paid for her, but she dared not stay longer. She had seen the glint in her master's eyes and knew that he would use her ill – either at his workshops or elsewhere. His nephews were cruel and thoughtless, but her master was worse when he was angry. He had killed Annie by his brutality and Bella knew if she stayed he would turn on her. If he did not work her to death making chains, he would beat her – or perhaps worse. Bella had learned more of life since she came to this house for Annie had spoken freely of what she suffered at her husband's hands.

As yet Bella was too young for him to use her as a woman, but when she was older . . . Bella shivered. She'd seen something in his eyes when Annie's father had spoken of his other daughter. Archie was marrying a woman fifteen years younger and Karl would not hesitate to do the same if he chose – though he might simply take the woman he wanted to his bed and not bother to wed her.

Bella left her master's cottage, heading away from the village because if anyone saw her and told Karl, he would follow and drag her back. She had no idea where she was going; she just knew that she had to get far away from this accursed place before Karl realised she'd gone.

She walked for a long time. It was very cold and Bella felt the bitter wind in her face. She clutched her shawl around her and resisted the temptation to stop and eat. Bella had no money other than the florin Mr Stoneham had given her, because there was none in the house that she knew of and even if there had been, she would not have dared to steal it. It was bad enough that she was wearing boots Karl had paid for and had taken one of the fresh loaves. She comforted herself that she had been paid no wages and was entitled to the things she had, but could not truly believe it.

Bella stopped when she heard a church clock strike the hour of three. She was hungry and thirsty and her feet had begun to hurt. Seeing an old barn just ahead, Bella made for it and discovered that it was merely three-sided and bales of hay were stored beneath the shabby roof. But she could make a place to rest in its warmth for a while, and if she just moved a bale a little, it would shelter her from the wind.

She found a place to sit and broke a piece from her bread, eating that and the tiny piece of cheese, drinking a few sips of water. Bella did not know when she would have the chance to get more food. She would ask for work when she came to a town, but a village, she was certain, would be more curious about where she came from, and Karl might put up posters to advertise his loss.

Sighing, Bella curled up into a ball and hugged her knees. It was lonely but Bella was used to feeling alone. She'd never known the warmth of true love, though Florrie and Marta had been kind, and at least when Annie was alive she'd had regular meals and a bed to sleep in. Now she had nothing but what she found for herself. As she snuggled into the hay, her eyelids grew heavy. She was warmer now and her eyes began to close. For several nights she'd hardly slept and now she was so tired that she could not stop herself falling asleep . . .

Bella was woken by a hand shaking her shoulder. She cried out in fright and shrank back when a lantern was held close to her face as someone peered at her from behind the light. She'd been caught! Karl would beat her black and blue. Trembling, she tried to scramble from her perch and run but a strong hand held her.

'No need to fear me, girl,' a rough voice said. 'I'll not harm yer – but yer'll die if we leave yer out all night.' He turned to someone Bella could not see behind him. 'John, fetch the hay to the horses while I take this little lass to Polly.'

Bella found her arm taken in a firm grip. 'Please let me go. I've not stolen anything!'

'Not even the bread you've been eating?'

Bella's cheeks flushed. 'I baked it myself this morning,' she said defensively. 'I took it instead of wages.'

'Did you now?' the man said. 'You'd best come home with me and tell me your story, lass – my Polly will want to know, and I want the truth or I'll put you straight out.'

Bella looked at him. It was difficult to see his face, because it was nearly dark now and she was very cold, her teeth chattering. As they approached the farmhouse, she saw that a lantern hung outside the kitchen door and the windows were bright. Now she could see that her discoverer was a man of middle age with a bushy brown beard and long, untidy hair. His fingernails were dirty and he smelled of animals and dung, but she did not mind that as long as he did not beat her. She could not escape his firm grip and allowed him to push her inside

the kitchen, feeling the warmth of the range immediately.

'Look what I found in the hay barn,' he said to
the plump woman standing by the kitchen range.
'If we hadn't needed fodder for the horses I reckon
she'd have been dead by the mornin'.'

'The poor child,' the woman said. 'She's shakin'
with the cold and her teeth are chatterin'. Bring her
to the fire, Ernie, and I'll give her a drink of hot
milk and honey.'

Bella was pushed towards the range and the front
was opened so that she saw the red coals and felt
its fierce heat. 'Sit down on the stool, lass,' the
woman said. 'I'm Polly – what's yer name and what
are yer doin' out on such a day?'

'I'm called Bella,' she whispered, feeling pain in
her hands and feet as the numbness began to wear
off. 'My mistress died and I was frightened of my
master and his nephews . . .'

'So you ran off with a loaf of bread and the
clothes you stand up in.' The farmer looked at her
and frowned. 'Did your master beat yer, Bella?'

'Sometimes – and he hit his wife after the baby
was born and she was so weak from the birth. One
of the nephews was to take a wife and they spoke
of puttin' me to the chain-making—' Bella stopped,
realising she had said too much for there would not
be many such workshops in the area.

'Was yer master Karl by name and a brute by
nature?' Ernie asked and his frown increased as she
nodded. 'I've heard of him, though he be set some

miles from here. Yer know what yer risk by running from a man like that?'

'I risked more if I stayed!' Bella lifted her head defiantly. 'I would rather die of cold in the night than return to him!'

'Well, you shall not go back there,' Polly said and placed a cup of hot milk in Bella's hands. 'Drink that and it will put some colour into your cheeks, lass.'

'Yes, mistress.'

'My name is Polly Green, and Ernie is Farmer Green – and you need not fear us. We'll not send you back to the brute that killed Annie Rush and his first wife, God rest their souls.'

'I took Annie's babe to the doctor. I feared he would die too – but I know not what will happen to him if my master takes him back now.'

'I doubt he will; he'll leave him to be fostered until he is grown – and then, when he's of some use, he'll claim him,' Farmer Green said and belched.

Bella drank most of the milk straight down. It was food as well as drink and she needed something more than bread inside her. 'You are kind – did you know Annie? I liked being with her better than the workhouse for Mistress Brent did not like me. She was unkind to us all . . .'

'She is no longer mistress of the workhouse at Sculfield so I've heard tell,' Polly told her. 'She has been dismissed and is being hunted as an accessory to the murders her husband committed.'

Bella's eyes opened wide with fright as she looked from one to the other.

'He is accused of murdering several children placed in his care – you are lucky that you escaped him, lass,' said Farmer Green.

Bella nodded. She had not thought of herself as fortunate but perhaps she had been – but she was not sure what would become of her now. 'What would you have of me now, master?'

'We must discuss the problem,' Ernie said and looked at Polly. 'If we put yer to bed in the warm will you give me your word yer will not run off again?'

'If you give me yours that you will not make me return to the chain-maker.'

'The lass has a tongue on her,' Polly said and chuckled, her chins waggling with mirth. 'We'll not do that, lass. I give yer me word.'

Bella thanked her and Polly led the way upstairs to a small room at the end of the corridor. Inside, there was room for a single bed, which was covered with a candlewick counterpane and had black-painted metal rails at each end, and a few hooks for clothes on the wall.

''Tis small,' Polly admitted, 'but it was meant for a child and it will do. In the morning I shall rouse you and we'll decide on your future.' She turned and the light from her oil lamp went with her, leaving Bella to scramble into bed fully dressed.

At first it was pitch-black but gradually a little light penetrated the tiny window, which was high on the wall and had no curtains. Bella could have managed to undress but because she was still cold, she burrowed under the covers and held them tight around her neck. She was nervous and anxious and it was a while until she could rest, but gradually the exhaustion of the past weeks since the birth of Annie's child stole over her and she closed her eyes. By the time Polly came up to look in at her, she was soundly sleeping.

'She is but a child,' Polly said when she joined her husband in the large double bed they shared. 'She is like the daughter I never had . . .' Polly had given her husband one child, their son John, and she loved him dearly, but he was a big lump and the fragile beauty of Bella's features had touched a soft spot in her heart. 'Could we not keep her, Ernie? She would be no trouble to you, I promise.'

He sighed and hunched his shoulders. 'Polly, I would keep her if I could, but the chain-maker would hear and come for her – and he would demand her return or money.'

'We could pay . . .'

'We have little enough to spare,' her husband reminded her. 'The harvest was poor last year and we had to buy fodder for the cows and pigs. If I offer to buy her – illegal though that would be – I'll have nothing left if the harvest is bad next year.'

'We can't let him take her back. I promised her, Ernie, and I won't give her to him!'

'I'll not ask yer to,' her husband grunted. 'I'll take her into Alton and ask the workhouse there to admit her. I know the master and he's a decent man. If I tell him she was ill-treated by the chain-maker he will not let her be taken back – but it is some miles distant and if we do not speak of her Karl Brett will not know. Even if he did, I doubt he would he dare to go there for the master is an honest man, not like those Brents.'

'I still wish I might keep her. She could help me with the work and the baking.'

'The answer is no,' he grunted and rolled over, pulling the bed covers up around his neck. 'Now hush, wife, and let me sleep.'

Polly sighed but she knew her husband to be stubborn. He might have kept the girl and stood up to her master if he'd not been so worried over losing his farm. If he did not earn some money soon they could not pay the landowner and they would be cast out. Ernie needed his sleep and he needed to be free of this extra problem. She closed her eyes, dashing away the single tear that escaped and trickled down her cheeks.

Her husband would not go to market for three days so she would feed Bella well and care for her in the meantime, even though she knew that she had already begun to give her heart to the young girl . . .

Bella was woken by a gentle hand shaking her. She started up in alarm but as Polly smiled her fear fled as she remembered. She sat up and took the cup of milk that was offered her.

197

'Come down as soon as you are ready. I shall give you breakfast and then you can wash in the scullery when the men have gone. This room would not suit you if you were stayin'.'

'You will not send me back to him!' Bella looked at her in alarm but Polly shook her head.

'Nay, lass, fear not. My husband will take you to the town when he goes to market on Saturday. He will present you to the master of the workhouse and tell your story. You will be properly cared for there, Bella.'

'I hoped you might keep me. I would work hard for you . . .' Bella looked at her pleadingly, tears hovering.

'I know you would, child, and I wish that I could give you a home here – but we are not wealthy. We scrape a living on this land, Bella. Last autumn we lost much of our potato crop to blight because the rains came at the wrong time and we could not get on the field to lift them.' Polly looked grave. 'We shall struggle to pay our rent this year, which is why my husband must travel to the market with goods we wish to sell. I have made curtains and a coverlet to match which should bring a good price and he will sell two pigs. I put a few coins by and if need be I will help him pay the landowner's rent – but we have none to spare to pay your master if he comes here demanding your return nor to fight him at law.'

Bella stared at her in silence. She had thought she might be safe here but now she saw she was not.

Polly had given her a bed for the night and seemed genuinely sad to part with her, but her husband was more practical.

'Thank you for the milk and the bed,' Bella said. 'I slept well.'

Polly nodded sorrowfully. 'I would keep yer if I could, child. Should yer master give yer up, I would take you in and you could be as a daughter to me.'

Bella nodded and tried not to weep. She felt that she could have been happy here but Polly's wishes would not count when Ernie could hardly afford to pay his rent.

After Polly left her, Bella made her bed tidy and brushed at her dress. It was creased where she had slept in it, but it mattered not. She was apprehensive of the new workhouse she was to enter but if the master was a fair man it would be better than staying with Karl and his nephews.

The breakfast that awaited her made Bella's mouth water. There was a slice of fat bacon, an egg with a yellow yolk that ran when she stabbed it with her bread, and two mushrooms, also some fried mixed potatoes with cooked greens. The tastes were so delicious that she ate ravenously.

'Do you like my bubble and squeak?' Polly asked as Bella cleared her plate. 'I have more – but no more bacon or egg.'

Bella accepted another portion of the delicious treat and felt so full she thought she might burst. She had never been fed this well, even when Annie was on her feet and cooking big meals for her husband.

'What would you like me to do for you?' Bella asked when she had cleared her plate. 'I can clean, wash clothes and scrub floors.'

'I need to black-lead my range this mornin',' Polly said. 'If you feel up to it you can wash the pots and then clean the scullery for me.'

'Yes, mistress!' Bella jumped up and started to clear the table. She put hot water and soda crystals into the big stone sink in the scullery and washed all the dishes and pots, stacking them on the dresser and in the plate rack above the range.

After she had finished, she poured hot water from the kettle into a pail and mixed in some cold, then she found a bar of yellow household soap, a scrubbing brush and a cloth. She folded a mat and knelt on it and began to scrub the brick floor of the scullery. It was filthy where the men of the house had traipsed in and out and had not been scrubbed in a while. Bella emptied three buckets of dirty water before she was satisfied. By then her hands were red and she wiped them on an old cloth and went into the kitchen to find Polly, who had finished polishing her range until it shone.

'Have you finished?' Polly went to look at the brick floor and nodded. 'You have done well, Bella. Fill the kettle now and we'll make a cup of tea. The men will be in for their docky soon and after that we must prepare the vegetables for dinner.'

Bella did what she was told and watched as Polly

brought some tins from the pantry. She opened them and told Bella to fetch three plates from the dresser. From the tins she took pastries and cakes, setting them on the plates. To Bella it looked a rich feast, for there were pastry rolls filled with savoury sausage meat, apple turnovers with crisp brown sugar on the surface, and a large fruit cake as well as several smaller pies, one of which had pork meat in the middle.

'My husband and son have hearty appetites,' Polly said, smiling as Bella stared. 'We kill our own pigs and use every bit of them – and the apples come from my orchard. I store them, and I bottle plums, apples, gooseberries and raspberries in season as well as makin' jam. We have enough food – but there is little money for paying bills. If we owned our land then we should want for nothing.'

'You are very lucky,' Bella said. 'I have never seen such food.'

'You must eat and enjoy it,' Polly said, 'for you will leave us on Saturday.'

Bella took her at her word, eating one of the pastry rolls and a slice of the delicious seed cake. She sipped the strong tea Polly had poured for her, finding it a little bitter and strange, but it was warm and she knew that the tea was brewed for the men, who liked it that way.

'Ah, here they come now,' Polly said as the scullery door opened and the men tramped in, bringing mud with them. They washed their hands at the sink in the scullery with the yellow soap Bella had used for the floors and then came into the large kitchen.

'That looks good, Polly love,' Ernie said. 'We've been movin' the last of the roots – the mangles fer the cattle. I've got them stored in the small shed by the byre now so it will be easier for feeding.'

John looked at Bella as she moved away from the long pine table, taking her plate and cup into the scullery. 'You need not move for me, lass,' he said and smiled at her. She saw Polly in his smile and gave him a shy look in return, which made him chuckle.

Polly was busy serving her men for a while but then she brought utensils and empty plates to the scullery. 'John likes you,' she said. ''Tis a pity we cannot afford yer price, child.'

Bella nodded but did not answer. She had met with nothing but kindness and honesty here and she wished with all her heart that she could stay here forever. She would work hard to please them but it seemed the farmer's mind was set and she would be taken to a workhouse once more . . .

CHAPTER 15

'I made inquiries at the forge,' Toby's groom told Meg and Hetty as they sat together in the sewing room that afternoon. 'It seems that the girl Bella has run away. She waited until the day after her mistress's funeral and then she bolted while they were all at work. Needless to say, he is furious. He suspected us of harbouring her but I told him my purpose was to inquire after her wellbeing.'

'Where could she have gone?' Meg asked and looked anxious. 'She cannot be more than eleven or twelve at most and it is a harsh world out there. The nights are still cold, though it is the end of March and she could die under a hedge.'

'We must pray that she has found shelter.' Hetty looked at Hobbs. 'Did you inquire in the village?'

'Yes, Mistress Hetty. I asked at the inn and the doctor's and several women in the street – but no one had seen her since the funeral. The general opinion was that Karl might have murdered her.'

'Do you think he looked guilty?'

'No,' Hobbs said and frowned. 'He was too angry and suspected us of having spirited her away. It seems that Mr Stoneham spoke to him of Bella's future and offered to buy her back from him and he thinks she may have gone to him.'

'Would that she had,' Hetty said and she felt a sharp pang of anxiety for there was still no word of Arthur and it was unlike him not to let them know if he had been delayed. 'I have it in mind to send you to look for Mr Stoneham because I am worried that something may have happened to him.'

Hobbs shook his head. 'Forgive me, mistress, but Mr Rattan made it clear that I am to remain here to protect both you and the lady Meg – and he would not forgive me if I went chasing after Mr Stoneham.'

'I daresay you are right,' Hetty agreed reluctantly. 'Yet I fear that something must have happened, for Arthur would have sent word had he intended to stay longer in Newmarket or go elsewhere in his search.'

'I am sure he will return soon,' Meg said. 'And Mr Rattan promised *he* would not be long absent but he wished to speak with Mr Stoneham before he tried to discover where those who took my child lived.'

Hetty turned to her in sympathy. She was worried for Arthur but he was a grown man and it would take a great deal to kill him – but Meg's child was vulnerable and was growing up without her.

'Mr Rattan will find the child, never fear,' she

said. 'Now that he knows where to look he will discover her whereabouts and demand her return.'

'But will they give her up?' Meg looked at her apprehensively. 'I fear they will lie and try to hold on to her.'

'Toby Rattan has influence and important friends,' Hetty soothed and touched her hand. 'Have faith, Meg. You did not give your consent to the adoption and are therefore entitled to take your child back. The fault lies with Mistress Brent.'

'She has much to answer for.' Anger flickered in Meg's eyes.

'Indeed, and her husband is a wicked devil capable of any evil.'

'Speaking of which, I saw something from my window last night,' Meg said and frowned. 'It was the shadow of a man moving toward the back of the house, but although I lay awake listening I heard no sounds of anyone trying to enter the house.'

'You might have seen me as I patrolled the grounds,' Hobbs said. 'I apologise if I frightened you.'

Meg nodded. 'Perhaps it was. I jump at shadows now.'

'You are safer here with us than at the inn alone,' Hetty said. 'I think Mistress Brent and her husband may blame you for their dismissal, Meg. Arthur was the instrument but you were the cause.'

Meg nodded and bit her lip. 'I fear they might seek revenge for all they have lost.'

'They may simply be searching for something

hidden,' Hobbs observed. 'Mr Stoneham did not give them much time and they may have left money and valuable items hidden here.'

'Yes, that is true, but I would they were in prison where they belong,' Hetty said and frowned. 'Had Arthur suspected such dreadful wrongdoing he would never have let them leave.'

Once again, she wished that Arthur would return. Hobbs was doing his best, but she would have felt safer with Arthur there.

Where could he be after all this time? Why had he not written to her? Hetty's anxiety mounted as the days passed and they heard nothing.

Arthur moaned and moved his head as the light fell on his face and someone came near. He put up a hand to shield his eyes from the light and heard a wry laugh.

'He wakes at last. You had the good landlord worried, Arthur, for he was afraid he would not be paid for all he has done – and that includes fetching a doctor to you and more than likely saving your life.'

'What happened?' Arthur moaned and pushed himself up against the pillows. The back of his head was sore and for a moment he felt dizzy. The room seemed to spin and he moaned. He blinked and then focused, seeing his friend's face and knowing him. 'Did he send for you?'

'I came in search of you because Hetty was worried,' Toby said. 'I also have other reasons for seeking you . . . and you led me a merry dance, my friend. Had I not caught sight of a horse I knew in the stables when I stopped here by chance, I should not have found you, for you had simply disappeared.'

'Someone hit me as I turned,' Arthur groaned and put a hand to his head as the room reeled madly and then settled once more.

'You were set upon, beaten and robbed,' Toby said. 'I spoke to a magistrate and it seems you're not the only traveller to have suffered such an assault in recent times. I thought it might be personal at the start but I am assured it happened also at an inn not ten miles from here. Why did you not stay at one of your usual haunts?'

Arthur looked at him sourly and accepted the cup of water offered. 'The reason escapes me for the moment. I had much on my mind . . .'

'Do you think it was the gypsy you sought?'

'No. I bought a horse from him and sent my man back to my estate with it,' Arthur said. 'In hindsight, that was foolish for I must have seemed vulnerable, travelling alone and with gold to spend.'

'A groom from the inn stables came to your aid and the landlord had you carried to your room and sent for the doctor. It was fortunate – had you lain unseen for hours in the bitter cold you might have caught a deathly chill.'

Arthur returned the cup to him. 'My thanks, but I could do with something stronger. Brandy and then breakfast, I think.'

'It is nearer tea time,' Toby said. 'You've lain in

a daze for nearly three days, my friend. Yet I am sure you may have breakfast if you wish it. Our host is anxious to see you well and gone.'

Arthur nodded ruefully. 'I seem to remember swearing at someone who came near me.'

'You were muttering even as you slept,' Toby said and grinned. 'I am glad to see that your head proved harder than the iron they used to lay you low, my friend; though you may have a slight scar where the doctor sewed you up. I came for reasons other than my care for you and I would have your counsel, but we may speak of that later.'

'Is all well at the workhouse? Has there been any trouble?'

'That is yet another concern. I left Hobbs to look after Hetty and Meg, who is with her – Hetty fears that Master Brent may be lingering with intent to harm.'

'Then I must be on my way for I would see this business settled and a new master and mistress appointed there.' Arthur sat up, threw back the covers and put his feet to the floor. For a moment he felt dizzy but gradually his head cleared. 'You can tell me what bothers you while I dress but first send for the landlord and have him prepare some cold meat, bread and pickles. I am starving!'

'I am glad that Meg is recovering,' Arthur said as they sat over a meal provided by the landlord. 'And if you can recover her child from these people, Toby, it will surely aid her. She has suffered too much and it cannot be right that she be robbed of a child she bore in pain and grief.'

'The law is on our side, though I know these people who took the child will claim they have right on their side. Many young women who give birth in the workhouse willingly give up the babe and other mothers die. These people may have been told such a tale.'

'Offer to reimburse what they paid, if you wish,' Arthur said, 'though they knew they broke the laws of God and man when they purchased the girl – and may deserve to be punished for it.'

Toby shook his head. 'I think mayhap they were desperate for a child and are perhaps to be pitied.'

'Then their story is a sad one, but the child *is* rightfully Meg's.'

'According to the testimony of an old woman whose memory comes and goes!' Toby frowned. 'I cannot in truth be 100 per cent certain that these people have Meg's child. How should I approach them, do you think?'

'You must be forceful. Act as though you are certain of your facts and they will give themselves away – but if they are innocents duped by an evil woman, be generous, Toby. They are losers too.'

Toby agreed and they finished the meal the land-lord had prepared. 'Are you well enough to drive back alone?' he asked when Arthur announced his intention of starting out that evening. 'Should you not hire a carriage to take you back and let a groom collect your horses later?'

'I had a blow to the head, not a sword through my back,' Arthur said grimly. 'However, the landlord assures me that one of his grooms is willing to ride with me for payment. With the money you have advanced me from your purse, Toby, I shall avail myself of his services – just in case the robbery was not a random attack.'

'Very wise, Arthur. I would accompany you myself but I promised Meg I would not delay.'

'You must continue with your journey,' Arthur said. 'I shall not be caught unawares like that again, I promise you.'

'Then I shall take a room for the night and continue my journey in the morning.'

'The landlord's groom knows of a decent inn where we may spend the night, so I will wish you good fortune with your quest, Toby. Meg deserves that you succeed.'

'Then God speed you – and I am glad that I was able to be of service.'

'I stand in your debt and shall not forget,' Arthur said and they shook hands.

Toby was offered the room Arthur had been using and Arthur took his leave. His thoughts were mixed as he drove through the gathering dusk, yet he kept an eye on the road and the trees to either side. He had been taken unawares by a rogue once; it would not happen again. The groom beside him had offered to drive but Arthur's horses were fresh and needed their master's hand to keep them in check.

He and the hired groom drove in silence, making

good speed and reaching a busy inn before the hour was late. Arthur took rooms for them both and then went up to his own after asking for brandy and a cold meal to be served in his, leaving the groom to take supper in the parlour. Arthur would keep to himself this time and not risk raising the interest of a rogue.

Only when he was alone and rested did he allow his thoughts the freedom to roam. He'd denied that the gypsy Jez had been involved in his assault but that did not mean one of the others he'd seen at the fair had not followed with the intention of robbing him. Yet, he still sensed that it had been a random assault, that any traveller with gold in his pockets might suffer.

Dismissing the worry that it had something to do with Master Brent as unlikely, for although that villain might crave revenge, he was, by all accounts, haunting the grounds of the workhouse, Arthur hoped that Hobbs would be sufficient protection for Hetty and Meg, but made up his mind to hire more men to act as guards when he arrived. He must make sure of their safety, speak to Lady Rowntree about the new wardens – and then purchase Bella's bond from her master. Karl Brett would demand more than he'd paid, but it would be worth it to see the child safe. If she was Katharine's niece – and his instinct told him that it was so, though there was no certain proof – then she deserved all his concern.

Arthur felt a surging regret that Katharine would

not know that the child had been her sister's and was not there to offer her the love and kindness of an aunt or mother.

Arthur went to sleep with the same thought in his mind: he must rescue the girl from her situation, but felt it unsatisfactory to leave Bella to the ministration of servants. He'd known how that stung when he was young and his mother paid more attention to her lovers than her son. It was mainly for that reason he'd stopped short of telling Eliza that he believed she was his own daughter. Without a wife, what could he offer to either Eliza or Bella that would make them content?

He slept at last, the thought still unresolved. He must speak to Hetty and ask her opinion. He thought that she had the wisest head and kindest heart of any woman he'd ever known and at last the worry left him and he drifted into the first peaceful sleep he'd known since Katharine's death.

Arthur was able to hire four men at the inn he'd been staying at before his journey to Newmarket. They rode with him to the workhouse at Sculfield and he set them immediately to their task of patrolling the grounds, agreeing that they should take it in turns to stand the night watch.

Smiling, Hetty rushed out to him as he entered the hall, throwing out her arms to embrace him.

'Thank goodness! We feared some harm might have come to you, Arthur. You sent no word!'

'I was unconscious for some time and unwell for

a couple of days,' he admitted ruefully. 'It was a footpad, Hetty. My thoughts were too much centred on my problems and I was unaware of him behind me.'

'Are you better now?' She drew back a little, a look of embarrassment in her eyes because, in her relief at seeing him, she had so willingly embraced him. 'It is not like you to be careless, Arthur.'

'No, it was foolish of me – and I ask you to forgive me if you were worried,' he said and tucked his arm through hers. 'You must tell me all that has happened here.'

'First, you must tell me of your quest. Did you find what you sought?'

'Yes, I did,' he said and smiled at her. 'Perhaps more than I expected. I spoke to the gypsy woman Bathsheba. She is impressive, Hetty, and I think you would like her. Although she could not tell me the name of Bella's mother, I believe it likely that she is Marianne Ross' child.'

'Likely but not certain?'

'Certainty is a luxury in such a case, Hetty. Too many years have passed since Katharine's sister went missing. Bathsheba told me that her brother found her lying unconscious after she had been raped and left for dead. Bathsheba brought her back from the brink and nursed her for many weeks – and by then they knew she was carrying a child.'

'So why did Marianne go off alone to have her child?' Hetty was puzzled. 'If they had saved her life why did she run away?'

'Bathsheba did not truly know – except that her brother wanted Marianne to be his woman when she'd recovered from the birth. Perhaps she simply revolted at the thought of any man touching her and became so distressed that she did not know what she did.' Arthur shook his head. 'Whatever, it was a mistake for she might have lived if Bathsheba had cared for her.'

'She might have given birth in safety,' Hetty said and looked sad. 'Instead, she left her child at the church and died in the fields. Aggie told us a part of what happened, though, as you know her mind wanders and we cannot be sure of all she says. But she claimed that Bella's mother, who she knew as Marie, had, after being refused re-admittance to the workhouse, begged Aggie to seek out her sister Katharine for her. But Aggie had no idea where Katharine was or whether Marie was speaking rationally – and it still proves nothing, I'm afraid.'

Arthur shook his head. After so many years he could never know the whole truth but he believed he had solved the mystery of what had happened to her sister that had haunted Katharine.

'Bathsheba wanted to take the babe as her own but her brother refused her. When she discovered that the child had been brought here to the workhouse, she threatened Mistress Brent with a curse if she failed to take care of Bella because she meant to return and take Bella with her one day – but when I asked if she would take her now she said it was too late.'

'I do not think I should trust her or her brother to tell the whole truth,' Hetty said and Arthur nodded.

'When she came to my room and told me her story I thought it true – but who can say whether she twisted the threads to suit herself.'

Arthur recalled the shaft of desire he'd felt and knew that the gypsy woman had cast her net of sensuality to ensnare him. Yet if she'd meant to lie she need not have come to him at the inn at all. She'd told him he would not forget her and he knew that was true. Yet after her visit he had felt a lessening of the grief that had haunted him since Katharine's awful death.

'What will you do now?' Hetty asked.

'I shall buy back Bella's bond and then find her a home. I was going to ask your advice . . .' He looked at Hetty's face. 'What is wrong?'

'Bella ran away after her mistress died and was buried. Her master is furious and suspects you of stealing her.'

'Then I must make sure he understands the truth – and find her. I doubt she could have gone far . . .'

Hetty sighed. 'You never have peace, Arthur.'

'I think I have reached some peace inside myself,' he said and smiled. 'But I blame myself for not seeing to the child sooner so I must find and help her now.'

'I am sure Katharine would be grateful.'

'Yes, perhaps,' he said and frowned, not wanting to speak of Katharine. 'Now, tell me how you are managing? Is there no word from Lady Rowntree about new wardens?'

'None. Her daughter was just wed and I think she had too many concerns of her own.'

'Then I shall call on her after I have spoken to the chain-maker and settled his claim.'

'Will you not rest for a while?'

'I shall dine with you at the inn this evening, Hetty. My carriage will call for you and we shall talk of the future then . . .'

He leaned in and kissed her cheek softly. 'My very best of friends! I would not have you more put upon than necessary. The sooner you can return to London and your own life the better.'

Arthur took his leave. He would take a fresh horse and ride to the village, knowing that he left guards in place to keep Hetty and Meg safe, as well as the inmates. He had much to think about and much to say – and it was time that he began to open his mind and heart to the one person who deserved to know more of them . . .

CHAPTER 16

Bella looked at the man talking to the farmer who had brought her here. He glanced at her once or twice, nodding as if agreeing with Ernie Green. The wind cut through her thin dress and shawl as she waited for her fate to be decided. Would the master of the workhouse take her in or would she be sent back to her brutal master? She shivered, feeling apprehensive as they looked at her again.

At last they came towards her. Ernie smiled at her encouragingly.

'Mr Thomas is willing to take you, Bella. He knows you have been badly treated and he says you will find it better living under his protection.'

Mr Thomas looked at her but did not smile. 'If what Farmer Green tells me is true and you are prepared to be sensible and work when you are told, I am prepared to keep you. We run a tight ship, Bella, and disobedience will not be tolerated – but you will find Mistress Thomas and myself to be fair,

217

providing you behave. I will not tolerate surly girls who cause trouble.'

'Thank you, sir,' Bella said meekly. She was cold and frightened because she could see no softness or kindness in this man, but Polly had told her he was a decent master and so she must accept that and believe it. He could not be worse than Karl and the master and mistress of her former place.

'Very well, girl, there is no need to be frightened if you behave,' Mr Thomas said and took her arm. His grip was firm but not harsh and he did not hurt her. He guided her to a wagon, which was piled with sacks of produce and pushed her up on to the seat beside the driving position, then climbed up beside her. A moment later a youth of perhaps fourteen sprinted up and jumped on to the wagon.

'Beg pardon, sir,' he said. 'Master Baker delayed me and gave me a message for yer.' He glanced at Bella and smirked in a knowing way, inching up to her so that his knee pressed against hers.

'Well, what was it then, Sidney?'

'He said to tell you the flour yer asked for will be in tomorrow and he will deliver it in the afternoon since it was not here for yer today.'

'Good, thank you, Sidney. You have done well and I shall not forget it.' He motioned towards Bella. 'This is a new inmate. Her name is Bella and I have been told she has a neat hand at sewing – but we shall see.'

'Florrie taught me and she did fine needlework,'

Bella said in a whisper. 'And I was learning to cook until my mistress died.'

'Then you have two trades and will be kept busy,' her new master said and nodded. 'If you do well we shall not need to look for a place for you outside the workhouse just yet. Farmer Green was not sure of your age, girl – how many summers have you?'

'I think this comin' summer will be my twelfth,' Bella said uncertainly. 'I do not know for certain for no one ever told me . . .'

'I think you look older than eleven,' Master Thomas said. 'If you do not know when you were born we shall pick a day for you and on that day you will be thirteen.'

'Yes, sir,' Bella said obediently. It did not matter to her for one day was as good as another and if she was twelve or thirteen made no difference to her. 'I only wish to be safe . . .'

Something made her look at Sidney as she spoke and the gleam in his eyes sent a chill down her spine. There was something menacing in his gaze that made her anxious and when she felt him pinch her arm she stifled her cry for if she made a fuss or told the master, she was certain Sidney would punish her.

Her throat was tight and she felt tears burn behind her eyes. Had she escaped the bullies in Karl's house only to become the prey of another? But perhaps she would not often meet Sidney, because the boys were separated from the girls in the workhouse and she need only endure his looks and little nips until they reached their destination.

She saw the large, grim-looking stone building as the wagon began to slow down. It was situated some three miles or so from the town of Alton but not in complete isolation, because there was a farm just down the road and a smattering of cottages. Women stood at their doors gossiping and shaking mats, and when the wagon approached the farm, Sidney jumped down and waved to Mr Thomas before running towards the gate of a field where some sheep grazed.

'Does Sidney not live in the workhouse, sir?' Bella asked, feeling relief as he disappeared from sight.

'He lived with us until he was twelve,' the master said, 'but then he was apprenticed to the farmer. He accompanies me to market sometimes. I take goods in for his master and he helps me load my supplies.'

Bella nodded, feeling better as she realised she might never have to see or speak to the young farm labourer again. However, she was apprehensive as the tall iron gates of the workhouse were opened by an elderly man who touched his forelock to the master when they drove into the grounds.

There was a short drive at the end of which stood the house. Its windows looked grey and dark and there was only one man working in the beds of shrubs to either side. He was wearing the uniform of the workhouse, dark-blue trousers, and a lighter shade of blue for his shirt, and a black jacket with a cap pulled low over his brow. His clothes looked well-worn and his boots had holes in the uppers where his toes poked through.

Mr Thomas ignored him and drove round to the back entrance. Here, several men were working at various jobs and the noise of hammers breaking stone was loud. All the men paused in their work as the master got down and told Bella to jump. He beckoned to two of the men who wore red trustee badges and told them to unload the stores, and then looked at Bella.

'Come in, girl. Your mistress will see to you now; behave for her and you will have no need to see me again until I sign you out, and that will be next summer when we find a good position for you . . .'

Bella was silent because there was nothing she could say. He was her master until he found a position for her and she had little chance of escaping for the walls were high and the gates securely locked and watched.

She followed him into the kitchen where the smell of soup cooking made her aware that it was some hours since she had eaten. She thought of the good food she'd been given in Polly's kitchen and knew that she would get nothing like that here.

'Ah, Mistress Thomas,' the master said, addressing a tall, thin woman. She was dressed all in black with a high frill around her neck. The severity of her clothing did not suit her and she looked pale, almost ill, dark shadows beneath her eyes. 'Here is another inmate for you. Bella sews and she cooks so you may find her more useful than many.'

Pale-grey eyes looked at Bella without interest but she nodded her acceptance. 'You are small but you look strong. We need help in the kitchen for Martha died last week and as yet I have no one to take her place.'

'I have worked in the kitchen and the sewing room. I was learning to cook and I can stitch neatly,' Bella said hopefully, because there were far worse jobs she might be given. 'I will work hard, mistress.'

'Very well, you shall begin here and then we shall see,' Mistress Thomas said. 'Did you manage to buy all you need, husband?'

'All but the flour, which should come tomorrow,' he said.

The pair moved away, leaving Bella to stand looking about her. It was a big kitchen with two black ranges side by side. Pots were bubbling on both and she could smell bread baking in the oven and her mouth watered. Three women were working, preparing vegetables, one of them stirring the large cooking pot over the heat. Bella's stomach rumbled and she wondered how long it would be before she was fed.

'Hungry, girl?' The woman who spoke wore a turban over her greasy hair but it escaped in wisps and clung to her sweating brow. She brushed it away, eyeing Bella with interest. 'Reckon yer can cook, do yer?'

'A little,' Bella said. 'I was learning from my mistress but she became ill after her babe was born – and then she died.'

'Poor woman,' Cook said. 'I'll bet they worked yer half to death.'

'Yes, it was hard,' Bella admitted. 'But while my mistress lived I was safe.'

Cook nodded and pulled a wry face. 'Men! They are mostly all alike and not to be trusted – but the master here is better than most. He only gets his whip out if one of the men or boys defies him. We don't get much decent to eat, mind, but the bread is good, because I make it and the soup has more than bones in it. The men get bread and cheese for their supper but we usually get bread and dripping, soup or stew at midday, and porridge in the mornings.'

Bella nodded. It was as she'd expected and much as she'd been fed for most of her life, but Annie and Polly had both given her a taste of better food and she thought longingly of her breakfasts in the big farm kitchen.

'Work hard while yer wiv me and I'll see yer right,' Cook said and winked. 'There's scraps from the master's table come our way and I don't go short. Do yer share and I'll look after yer.'

'Thank you,' Bella said. Cook was a big woman and she smelled strongly of onions and sweat, but she was not unkind and for the first time Bella began to feel easier. She had escaped from Karl and his brutish nephews and provided they did not find her and demand her back she would be safe – for a while at least.

'What did you do to her to make Bella run away?' Arthur asked when he cornered the chain-maker in

223

his works. It was noisy, dirty and incredibly hot inside the forge, great furnaces belching out heat and smoke as the men women and children toiled, the noise of hammers against metal chain deafening at times, and he felt pity for those who worked there because the work was relentless. Even the men were paid by weight and it took a long time to bend the really thick iron to make strong links. 'You must have done something, for she was content to work for your wife.'

'The brat was sullen and insolent, especially after Annie died. She was almost useless in the kitchen but I did nothing to harm her. She was my property, mine to chastise as I saw fit, though I held my hand.'

'She was not your property!' Arthur said. 'If you have killed her I shall see you behind bars for it.'

'I didn't touch the brat. She ran off the day after Annie was buried and I've no idea where she went. My nephew has taken a wife and she cooks for us now so if I find that little bitch I'll put her to the chains.'

'She will not return to you!'

'Then I'll have compensation for her.'

'You paid ten sovereigns, I believe.' Arthur threw a leather purse on to the desk, which was covered with stained papers, bits of wood, pencils and an inkwell. 'There is fifteen in the purse – take it and be glad I don't have you arrested for potential murder!'

Karl glared at him but picked up the purse and opened it, looking at the gold coins within. 'Take the brat then if yer can find her – only God knows where she went, unless it was back to the workhouse, though they say not.'

'No, she did not go there, and who can blame her after the way she was treated?' Arthur frowned. 'I should have taken her with me the last time I was here – but I shall find her, never fear.'

'Good riddance! She was of little use or value. I should have taken a woman to care for my wife. She might yet have been here . . .'

Arthur gave him a look of disgust and left. He would have to search for Bella and he had no idea where she might have gone. She had no family or friend outside the workhouse, and he knew she had not returned there. He could only pray that she had found shelter and did not lie dead by the side of the road.

Walking away from the chain-maker's works, Arthur shook his head. If he succeeded in finding the child, he must find a home for her. And having reflected long and hard, despite what Bathsheba had said it could not be with him, for although his servants might be kind enough, they would offer her no real love and certainly not that safety of knowing you belonged. Arthur had spent much of his childhood in a house where the upper servants were left to care for him and he would not condemn a child to that well-meaning indifference.

He would need to speak to Hetty about what was best for Bella. She herself had borne a child out of wedlock and had her child brought up by another and then at a school – but Bella could not read, could write only her name. He shook his head.

So many of the children brought up in workhouses had little schooling and therefore small chance of finding respectable work other than hard labour. He had been thinking that his next charitable venture might be to set up a school for young lads who had little hope in life. If they could be taught a skilled trade then they had a chance to make something of their lives. And perhaps something of the sort could be done for girls? That might be the way forward for Bella – it would depend on what he found when he caught up with her.

Why couldn't she have told him the truth when he'd asked if she was being properly treated at the chain-maker's house? If she'd told him she was fearful of her master, he might have seen her to safety without all this chasing about. Yet in truth he ought to have known and found her another place.

In all honesty, Arthur had had enough of searching these past years. Perhaps it would be enough to have his agents look for the girl . . . No, he would speak to Hetty first and hear what she had to say. He must also speak to Lady Rowntree and discover if she had found new wardens for her workhouse.

'I doubt if she can be far away,' Arthur said later that evening as he dined with Hetty at the inn. The landlady had cooked chicken in a rich wine sauce with sautéed potatoes and greens, followed by a

226

trifle that pleased Hetty's sweet tooth and some good cheese and fresh bread. 'I shall make some inquiries, but if she proves elusive then I must set agents to discover what has happened to her, for it is time I was back in London. Cousin Matthew tends to my business as my secretary but I cannot leave it all to him.'

'Yes, of course you must go,' Hetty agreed. 'I know very little of Bella, but Meg says she is a good girl and kind and everyone here liked her. I just want to know that she is safe!'

'Karl swears she ran from him for no good reason and he was so angry I tend to believe him.' Arthur hesitated, then, 'What should I do with the girl when she is found? If she is Marianne's daughter I would not see her condemned to the life in a workhouse.'

'She could come to me in London,' Hetty suggested. 'I believe that Katharine and Marianne's old nurse, Nana, would love her for Marianne's sake. She is happy enough living with me, but to have a child of Marianne's to care for would delight her.'

'You will soon need a bigger house!' Arthur said and frowned. 'What of your own daughter? Do you never wish that she lived with you?'

Hetty smiled and shook her head. 'She is clever and she can sing beautifully as well as embroider and sew. She wishes to be a school teacher when she is old enough – and the headmistress of the boarding school I sent her to has asked if she will stay on as a pupil teacher when she is sixteen. Mrs Sinclair is very fond of Stella and constantly sends me lovely letters extolling her virtues. Stella loves her and where she lives and I am inclined to allow her to remain there if she wishes.'

'If you had a home of your own – away from the refuge – you could bring her up as a young lady and see her marry well.'

'I could not afford for her to enter society,' Hetty said a little wistfully. 'It is a sweet dream but she is better off where she is, I think.'

'You might not be able to afford it but I could, Hetty.'

Hetty stared at him in astonishment but then shook her head. 'You are generous, Arthur, but I could not accept so much from you.'

Arthur moved forward impulsively. Hetty was a good, honest, compassionate woman and he had the greatest respect and affection for her. He spoke without truly thinking what he said.

'You could if we were married.'

Hetty gasped, her face turning pale as she gripped the arms of her chair. 'You jest, my friend! I could never be your wife – I am not worthy.'

'Oh Hetty, what you did in the past you did out of necessity,' Arthur said. 'It does not weigh with me nor ever will. You have always been a good friend to me and I am very fond of you, Hetty . . .'

Hetty was silent, then she smiled, stood, crossed the room and leaned forward to kiss his cheek. 'Do you think that fondness could be enough for me, my dearest of friends? I thank you for the offer, which I know was well meant – but I shall not deprive you of the chance to find true love, Arthur.'

He shook his head. 'I have loved and lost twice,' he said soberly. 'I should like the comfort of a wife to keep me company and offer me affection and love – but I am not sure I could give my heart a third time.' As he spoke, he began to realise that it would be more than just a comfort to him to make her his wife. She was his friend, the woman he relied on – and far more to him than he had realised before this moment.

'I have loved but once,' Hetty said, 'and I will only marry if I find that love returned.'

'Perhaps one day you may change your mind,' Arthur said. 'We might do much together to help others, Hetty. I pray you think about it.'

She smiled but said no more and he turned away. Something in her eyes told him he had hurt her, though he had not meant to; the words had come from somewhere but he had not planned them. Yet now that they were said he realised that her answer had meant more to him than he had realised. However, to pursue it now would only make her uncomfortable and so he changed the subject.

'You will wish to return to London soon, Hetty?'

'I would not leave you in the lurch,' she said but spoke stiffly.

'I shall speak to Lady Rowntree tomorrow and see how the matter of a new mistress fares,' he said. 'You should be released soon and able to go back to London.'

She made no answer and shortly afterwards intimated that she wished to leave. Arthur accompanied her back to the workhouse and left her in her comfortable sitting room before going out to speak to Hobbs in the drive.

'Have you seen anything untoward?'

'No, sir,' the groom replied. 'Mayhap the ladies were simply nervous – it would not surprise me after what was found here.'

'I think everyone is uneasy. I have been wondering if it might be best to find places elsewhere for those that remain.' The idea came to him just at that moment. 'I have nowhere that could hold them all but I could look for a house that might suit . . .' He was about to turn away when Hobbs detained him.

'I know of someone who would gladly take the position of master in any house you endowed, sir.'

Arthur paused and looked at him questioningly. 'Speak then, for I think this place will always haunt those forced to live here – and though I cannot dictate what Lady Rowntree will do, I could offer the inmates a choice, to leave or stay.'

'I think they would all choose to leave, sir,' Hobbs said. 'The thing is, my cousin was the headmaster of a school for boys which was recently closed down because the man who had endowed it lost his money through bad business and gambling. Ted is looking for a new place – and his wife could care for the girls and women for she was once a lady's maid and has some skill in the care of invalids.'

'And you think them good honest folk?'

'None better, sir. It was no fault of Ted's that led to his loss of position, and Jean is a gentle, loving woman and mother to two grown sons.'

Arthur nodded. 'Write and ask him if he will meet me at my home in London – and if I can second your judgment about these people, we will set up a new house for the unfortunate people here.'

'Yes, sir,' Hobbs looked pleased. 'I know you will like Ted – and his wife is a lovely lady. A change of scene and good people to care for them is just what these children need to comfort them through their nightmares.'

Hetty stood looking at the garden long after Arthur had left. Her eyes were wet and she felt tears on her cheeks. She wiped them away and shook her head as she fought the pain. She had never believed that he would ask her to marry him and his words had been like a knife pricking at her heart. He had offered her marriage – but not because he loved her and that was what made the tears fall. She had turned her face from him in the end so that he would not see her distress and he'd spoken of other things without realising that he had her hurt her more than she could bear.

Arthur had thought that to offer comfort and companionship was sufficient, but she loved him more than he could ever know. She had always hoped that one day he might return her love, but now he offered a marriage of convenience and that made her feel sad, because it could never be enough for either of them. Arthur was a passionate man and had too much to offer a woman he loved. If she had accepted he would have come to regret it – and if, later, he'd found himself a mistress? No, she could not live in a marriage without love.

Sighing, Hetty wiped the tears from her eyes. She must be strong and face the thought of a future without love. She turned as the door opened and Marta entered, speaking her name.

'Mistress Hetty,' Marta said. 'Aggie was asking for you. I think she is not well.'

'Then I shall come,' Hetty said and she turned, forcing a smile.

CHAPTER 17

Arthur was seated in Lady Rowntree's parlour, telling her his plans for the inmates of the workhouse.

'To be honest with you, Mr Stoneham, no one wishes to take the post as master of the workhouse. What happened there has blighted it and they say they could not consider living with such a shadow hanging over them,' said Lady Rowntree with a look of sadness. 'I cannot say I blame them, for it is too shocking for words and I am devastated that such terrible things should have happened there.'

He nodded his agreement. 'I have also thought that it is cursed by the memory and no place for anyone to live. As I told you just now, I am considering setting up another home somewhere hereabouts – and transferring all the inmates. I have someone that may suit as master and mistress in mind.'

'I should be truly grateful if you could take the burden from me,' her ladyship said, clearly relieved, 'for my husband is not likely to live the month and needs all my care. I will have that place razed to the ground once all have gone – and sell the land if any want it.' She looked at him wearily. 'I should be happy to contribute to the purchase of a new abode for those unfortunate people, sir – but I can offer nothing more. I trusted Master Brent and he let me down and I do not wish to feel responsible for such a thing again. I fear those poor murdered children will haunt me forever . . .'

'I completely understand, my lady,' Arthur said sympathetically, for she looked tired and distressed. 'If you wish to contribute to the purchase of the new house, the money will be gratefully accepted and that will be the end of your commitment. In future, those in charge will report to me or my agents – and I shall keep a strict rein, believe me.'

'You are young and strong,' she said in a voice that trembled slightly. 'My father was like you, but my husband was never healthy and he became weak of will as he aged. I tried to keep things on an even keel but it seems I was deceived. I am only glad that you discovered what that evil pair were about before yet more lives were lost.'

'I have men looking for them,' Arthur said. 'Unless they have left the country they will be discovered and then they will pay for their wickedness.'

'I pray it will be so,' she said and, rising from her chair, went over to an elegant satinwood desk; there, she took a pad from the top drawer and wrote something with a flourish, bringing it back to Arthur as he stood by his chair. 'I hope this will be of help to you, sir.'

Arthur glanced at the draft for five hundred pounds on a bank in London and thanked her. 'This will help to purchase a decent-sized house that will be of good use to the community – though I think we shall look a little further afield than Sculfield so that the change of scenery helps to clear young minds of dark thoughts.'

'You might be interested in Houghton Hall,' she said looking thoughtful. 'It is twenty miles south of here and General Houghton was once a good friend to my father. He never married and has recently passed away – his nephew and heir, Sir Mark Houghton, will put the house and its small estate on the market soon.'

'I shall make inquiries and when a purchase is made I shall call to tell you.'

'You are very good, sir. I can only thank God that you chose to take an interest in that place . . .' A little shudder went through her. Gently bred as she was, the news of what had happened in the work-house had horrified her.

Arthur took his leave of Lady Rowntree. It was dark as he rode back to the inn, thinking of the events of the last few weeks. It seemed hardly possible that so much had happened. His brow furrowed as he considered what form his new home should take. Most of those he needed to rehouse were either old or children and it was not an ideal mix. What he needed was a thriving community, a place where craftsmen could work under sheltered housing and begin to make a good life for themselves, and the elderly, destitute, crippled and innocent could find refuge.

Arthur laughed out loud because what he was hoping for was Utopia! Stopping suddenly as his mood lightened, he heard a sound to his left and swung his head round just as a dark shadow launched at him from the side of the road. A man swung a long thick staff at him, hoping to knock him from his horse, but, alert now, Arthur grabbed the weapon and pulled while urging his horse to spurt forward. His surprise action dragged the man off balance and for a moment he was dragged in the mud and stones of the road until he let go.

Arthur calmed his horse and dismounted, walking back to where the man lay sprawled, face down. He held the thick staff at the ready and was prepared to strike but, as he approached, the man suddenly got to his feet and ran off towards the trees. From a distance it had not been possible to see his face clearly but as he turned to glance back, Arthur recognised the man as Master Brent. He sent a look of hatred towards Arthur but did not stay to contest the fight. Clearly, he'd hoped to catch his prey unawares but this time Arthur's senses had not let him down.

He watched the shadows for a moment but nothing stirred. Brent had been alone, waiting. He must have known where Arthur would be and hoped to jump out and murder him. Arthur nodded to himself. Of course, Brent must have been hidden in the workhouse grounds and had heard Arthur tell Hobbs of his intention to visit Lady Rowntree. Hetty and the others had not been jumping at shadows; the man had been haunting the place, looking for something – or the chance to wreak his revenge on the inmates. He must know secret places to hide while he waited for his chance to take whatever it was that drew him back.

It was even more imperative now that Arthur find somewhere new to house the workhouse. He would alert the magistrates to the fact that the murderer was still in the area and arrange for posters to be nailed to trees and the doors of inns and churches. A look of determination settled on Arthur's face. Master Brent would become a fugitive and, eventually, he would end where he belonged, at the end of the hangman's noose.

He walked back to his horse, remounted and rode away. His next task now was to look for the girl he believed to be Katharine's niece. He could not allow her to remain lost. She must be found and given a decent home and a place where she could find affection and safety and Hetty would give her both.

He had already employed agents to look for Bella, but he would also make inquiries himself, because he would not forgive himself if she was in trouble . . .

On the morning after her arrival at the workhouse outside Alton, Bella was greeted by a woman with iron-grey hair, drawn back from her face in a knot. She wore a blueish-grey gown with a white collar and a white apron and she was, the girl had been told, called Matron. Her eyes were a similar colour to her dress and they were cool as they looked at Bella.

'So, you ran away from your master because he was cruel to his wife and you feared what he might do to you, girl?'

'Yes, Matron,' Bella said in a voice that was little more than a whisper.

'Do not try running away again,' Matron said in a severe tone. 'The master is good-tempered but he will punish you if you try to escape – and it is a crime to steal the clothes we give you. Do you understand, Bella?'

'Yes, Matron.' Bella refused to hang her head as most of the girls did when addressed by this woman, yet she tried not to meet her gaze, because she had already made up her mind to run away again as soon as the chance presented itself. No one had beaten her, but the rules were very strict and the food badly cooked and meagre. Bella had thought Polly was her friend, but Polly's husband had sent her here so it seemed she could trust no one.

'Good, I am glad you understand me,' Matron said. 'You will join the girls set to scrubbing out the infirmary today.'

'I was told I would be set to the sewing . . .' Bella ventured and was rewarded by a flash of anger from Matron's eyes.

'The master does not run this wing of the work-house,' Matron said. 'You were brought to me to see if you were fit to work and I have decided that you shall join those set to scrubbing my ward.'

Bella looked at her and rebellion flared, but she kept her mouth shut. Although the master and his wife had seemed calm, sensible folk when she first arrived, she quickly learned that the wife did little but hold the keys of the storerooms and it was this woman who was in charge of setting the work for the women and girls.

It was useless to protest. If Bella was considered impertinent she would be punished until she was broken – and Matron looked to be made of steel.

Bella went with the other young girls set to scrub-bing duties. She was given a bucket filled with hot water, a cloth and a scrubbing brush, and then she was shown where to start at one end and told to move forward towards the door.

'Do not walk on wet floors,' an older girl warned, 'or she will make us do it all again.'

Bella nodded and knelt on the cold flagstones. They were hard and she knew her knees would be sore by the time they had finished here, but there were three of them and they worked in a line, moving toward the far end and the door. Beds were crawled under to wash away any dust, because Matron was particular about cleanliness and would inspect all the nooks and crannies.

'I'm Phyllis,' the girl said as she came out from under the first bed. 'I'm fourteen and I long for an outside job. The master promised he would find me a good position as a maid but thus far he has not done so . . .'

'You might be worse off than you are here,' Bella said as she wiped the soapy water from the floor with her cloth. The floor was not truly dirty. 'How often do you clean this floor?'

'Every morning,' Phyllis told her. 'We clean the bedposts first and then wash the floor so you've missed half the work today. You won't get away with that again.'

'The master's wife said I should be put to sewing or helping in the kitchen.'

'They're the good jobs,' Phyllis said and grinned lopsidedly. 'We'd all like them, but they give them to the favourites – the ones that toady to Matron and I won't do that.'

'I think she is hard and unkind,' Bella said. 'It is in her eyes.'

'She's worse than you can ever imagine,' Phyllis said. 'You're too young to understand – but be careful of her if she starts to smile at you.'

Bella nodded. She had no idea what Phyllis meant, but she hadn't liked the predatory way Matron looked at her. She would do her work, keep her mouth shut and hope she wasn't noticed until she could find an opportunity to get away from here.

'There's always someone to watch out for,' Bella said. 'At the place where I lived for years it was both the master and the mistress – they were as evil as each other, and then I was sold to a harsh master, though his wife was all right until she died.'

'I do not like living here,' Phyllis said. 'As soon as the master arranges it, I shall leave and I'll never come back – even if I starve.'

Bella agreed, though she said nothing. So far she had been treated well enough here, given a thin soup and bread for her meals and a uniform to wear. The red badge she had to wear showed that she had run away from a master and was supposed to shame her but she did not care. There were many people of all ages living in the house, men who worked at breaking stones or picking hemp or sewing coarse sacks, women and children who did sewing, cooking, laundry and cleaning, and all were set to some form of work unless too sick.

In the first few hours Bella had thought that it might not be too dreadful here and she'd looked forward to helping those who did the mending and sewing for the inmates. However, it seemed that she had escaped from a cruel master only to end up at the mercy of yet another spiteful woman who enjoyed taunting and punishing her victims.

At last Bella and the others had finished scrubbing the floor. They exited the door and then Phyllis wiped the doorway over again. They took their pails of dirty water to tip into the latrines, which smelled foul and needed clearing. Bella wrinkled her nose but said nothing, because Phyllis and the other girl, who was named Mariah, but never seemed to speak, appeared to take little notice of the stench.

Phyllis noticed though, and laughed. 'You will get used to it, Bella. You were lucky that Matron did not make that your first job. The men are supposed to clear the ditch but often they are kept to moneymaking duties and the women have to clear it – and that means we have to help if we're chosen.'

'Annie had a closet in the yard,' Bella said. 'We put the cinders down and then one of the men cleared it from underneath when the smell was bad.'

'Then you were lucky,' Phyllis said. 'We have to put up with this all the time – and in the height of summer it is awful.' She frowned. 'Matron complains about it and she says that it is the reason several died of cholera last summer.'

The stink had got into Bella's nostrils and she was nearly gagging on it, so was glad to finish emptying the pails and walk away.

'What do we do now?' Bella asked. 'Are we finished for the day?'

Phyllis laughed. 'We're never done here, Bella. The next place we have to scrub is the master's room and then Matron's and then it will be time for our meal. Come, we must get more hot water and soap; mine is almost finished.'

Bella smothered a yawn and followed her new friend. She had not slept much the previous night for she kept wondering if Karl would find her here and reclaim her. She thought longingly of Polly's warm and comfortable home and wished that the kindly couple had been able to keep her. She would have been happy to work with Polly in the house and in the fields with Farmer Green and his son. She had liked the family but they'd sent her here to this awful place and so they had not truly cared what happened to her. Bella's eyes pricked with tears; it seemed that she would never find the warmth and comfort of being loved.

That first day was long and weary. After they had finished scrubbing and the meagre meal was eaten, Bella was sent to help with sorting the linen ready for the laundry. Torn sheets were sent to be mended first so that they did not rip further in the washing tub and some of them smelled of sweat and urine. She piled armfuls of dirty washing into large baskets, which were then carried away to the laundry to be put to soak overnight and boiled the next day. It took two strong women to carry the baskets and they laughed at Bella as she attempted to lift one.

'You'm not strong enough, my girl,' one of them said. 'Leave it to Peg and the others.'

Bella was glad to do so and relieved when she was informed that her work was done for the day, but then she was told to report to the schoolroom. There, the Master's wife was waiting with five other young girls. All dressed in the same light-grey dresses and white aprons and caps, they sat obediently on a wooden bench in front of a long table, on which lay slates and chalk.

'Sit down, girl,' the mistress said not unkindly. 'The law says we must teach you to read and write as well as learn your numbers. What do you know of writing, Bella?'

'I can form my name,' she answered, 'but I know naught else.'

The mistress clicked her tongue. 'It is often so when young ones come to us from another place. But here you will learn to know all the letters, Bella, and to write them in a neat hand. My husband is a good man and conscious of the law. Before you can leave here to take up work again, you must learn the alphabet and how to add up simple amounts. I shall write the letters on the board and you will spend the next half an hour copying them and learning the sound of them.' She paused and pointed to a girl with dark hair. 'Hannah, you will speak each letter as I write it and the rest of you will repeat it three times and then write it down.'

Bella joined in, listening to the sounds of the letters and repeating them three times and then forming them on her slate. They had reached the letter H before the classroom time ran out and they were told to wipe their slates clean and leave in an orderly fashion.

'Your name is easy to write,' Hannah said coming up to Bella as they left the room. 'But you have a lot to learn.'

'Would you teach me?' Bella asked and the girl nodded.

'If I get the chance, yes, I will. I am in the sewing

room, so if Matron sends you there we can work on your letters as we mend.'

Bella smiled and thanked her. It was another reason to hope that she might be sent to the sewing room sooner rather than later. She had enjoyed the class and thirsted for more knowledge. Perhaps it might be better to stay here for longer than she'd planned. She could learn things that would help her make a better life for herself – and if she gave herself time to really think things through, her plans to escape might succeed. She did not want to get caught within hours and be brought back to Matron for punishment.

Also, she reasoned, some of the other girls were friendly here. Matron was strict and Bella had been warned that she could suddenly be spiteful if she chose, but at least she did not hit the girls all the time and so it was a better place than the one Bella had grown up in.

Bella remembered the gentleman, Mr Stoneham, who had promised to return to Annie's and help her if she needed it. She had missed her chance of that, though she did not know what he could have done to help her. He would probably have taken her to another workhouse, where she might be no better off than she was here.

Given the choice, Bella thought she would like to return to Farmer Green's house, but he could not afford to pay her master for her. When she left, she must have a clear idea in her mind where she was going and what she wanted to do. To simply run away with no idea of where to go would end in her being caught again, so next time she would be prepared. In another year or so she would be old enough to find work for herself – and this place was not so very bad as long as she had friends like Phyllis and Hannah.

CHAPTER 18

Houghton Hall was a good, substantial manor house which had been well preserved and modernised. The old moat had been grassed over and was set with daffodils, which looked glorious on this bright spring morning. There were almost thirty rooms of various sizes, which meant accommodation would be cosier than dormitories, with perhaps three or four beds in each room. Arthur considered whether families should be allowed to live together in individual units, but decided, regretfully, that that idea might be a step too far. However, there were several good reception rooms, some of which would be used for dining, the infirmary and necessary offices, but there was a large one that he thought might be called a meeting room. Here, the men, women and children might be able to meet for an hour at the end of the working day and perhaps on Sundays after the church service they could get together for a few hours. It was more than they were given in most workhouses and would be welcomed by the inmates, he was sure.

Such an innovation would be frowned upon by many who planned, opened and ran workhouses, but would surely contribute to a healthy and happy life for the inmates. The workhouse was intended as a place of refuge where those in trouble could come to rest, recover and then work for their board, and though many signed themselves out as soon as they could find work to their liking, many others preferred its safety. It was not easy when times were hard to keep a roof over a family's head and the work was sometimes scarce outside the workhouse – and every bit as demanding as within its walls. Some were able to secure good, skilled work for their inmates, but others did only menial tasks that paid scant wages. Most were supported at great cost by their local communities, who grumbled at the levy demanded for such things.

However, here at Houghton Hall there were many outhouses which could be turned into craft shops. Arthur's vision was of a disciplined, hard-working community who could support themselves after a period of time. Many of the elderly he wanted to bring here were only fit for light duties, but he would choose the others with care and begin what could be a thriving little community, mostly self-sustaining, on this estate. Some of the children and elderly could even help with the animals: chickens for eggs and eating, cows for milking, pigs and ducks – there were already some clustered around a small pond, making a noise.

The picture created made him smile, though he knew that perhaps he expected too much and would never achieve the half of it, but at least he could give those who wished for such a life a chance. He walked the estate with the agent, inspected all the buildings and declared himself satisfied with the price of five thousand pounds, to include all the land as far as the river.

'It is good land, sir,' the agent declared. 'A farmer who knows his business could keep his family in luxury here.'

'There is enough to keep a community of some thirty to forty folk in food,' Arthur said, 'and that is what I require. Food grown by their own hands, fresh and sufficient to see all well-fed – and craft workshops for those with a trade.'

'It sounds rather like the manor system of old,' the land agent remarked thoughtfully. 'It was a good way too for many years.'

'Yes, something like the manorial system of old, but without a knight or a lord to oversee it. Just a master and mistress to keep things peaceful and see that it does not end in chaos is what I hope for,' Arthur said enthusiastically.

The agent nodded and smiled. 'You will forgive me if I say I think you unlikely to succeed in such an aim – but the estate is good and will not let you down if you use it well.'

Arthur agreed and thanked him and they came to an arrangement for its purchase. It was a pleasant estate and once settled by men and women prepared to work should provide a good living for them all.

'I shall prepare the documents,' the agent assured him, 'and you should be able to move your people within a short time.'

Arthur took his leave and decided that he would return to London and search for the right people to run his new venture, which was perhaps the most adventurous he had tried. It was something new, though its origins were in an old feudal system that had flourished in England for centuries and Arthur had a good feeling about the future there.

His remaining problem was the whereabouts of Bella. Her fate bothered him because as yet there was no word concerning her and he needed to find Bella and take her to safety. Reluctantly, having made inquiries locally himself but found nothing, Arthur had decided that it would be best to leave agents he trusted to search for the girl. They would visit workhouses, make inquiries of magistrates, infirmaries and even nunneries, and he could only pray that she lived and that he would be able to make her life a happy one. In the meantime, he must return to London for there were many matters that needed his attention. He had neglected his affairs and it was time he put his life in order.

Hetty had refused his offer of marriage and he was slowly coming to realise that he had hurt her. Arthur frowned as he thought about her reaction to his offer. She had turned from him as if he had insulted her and he'd seen that she was close to tears and wondered what had affected her so.

Could it be that Hetty was in love with him? And if so – what did he feel? Arthur frowned as he collected his things from the inn and sent a messenger to let Hetty know that he would return in about two weeks' time. He was thoughtful, remembering Hetty's arms about him when he had been torn by grief and in the depths of despair. That had been years ago and he had long ceased to think of those times. Hetty had been a whore then but she had left that place of shame and made a new life for herself and Arthur respected her for her strength of will and her compassion for others. Arthur had come to rely on her for so many things without realising it – and until recently he had not truly understood how much her support and friendship had meant to him.

He knew that they had reached a crossroads in their relationship and he needed to think about what that meant – and to understand his heart before he saw her again. For without Hetty there would be a huge gap in his life.

Bella wiped her hands after scrubbing the floor. Phyllis had been sent to the laundry and she and two other girls had been given the task of scrubbing the dormitories.

'Matron wants you,' one of the other inmates told her. 'You're to go to her office now.'

Bella finished wiping her hands. They were red and sore, the skin starting to crack between the fingers, and she had nothing to rub into them to help the pain. She had hoped that she would be given a different job but for the last two weeks she had been put to scrubbing in the mornings, while in the afternoons she helped sort the dirty linen and put it into the copper to boil, ready for the morning. Every day there were more garments and sheets to wash, because there were more than sixty inmates in the workhouse and the laundry was always filled with steam and wet washing.

Walking swiftly to Matron's office, Bella knocked on the door and then entered. The woman was looking at something on her desk, frowning. She looked up, staring at Bella.

'Your name is Bella – and you were indentured to a man name Karl Brett – is that not so?'

Bella trembled as she looked at Matron, her eyes wide with fear. 'You will not send me back? The master said that I could stay here!'

'Someone is looking for you,' Matron said. Her eyes gleamed. 'A reward of ten guineas has been offered for news of your whereabouts . . .'

Bella moved forward, her heart racing. 'Please, please do not tell him where I am,' she said. 'He will beat me and work me to death. Oh, he is a cruel master.'

'Ten guineas is a small fortune,' Matron said, a spiteful gleam in her eyes. 'Why should I not claim the reward?'

Bella stared at her but said nothing. There was something about Matron that made her shiver.

'You have nothing to say?' Bella shook her head. 'Go back to your work, girl. This afternoon you will join the sewing circle – I shall let you know if I have decided to claim the money – and if I do not, you will be grateful to me.'

There was a barely veiled threat in Matron's words that made Bella feel like running away. She curled her nails into the palms of her hands, willing herself not to show that she was frightened.

Bella was trembling as she went to join the other women and girls for the midday meal. It was a soup made of vegetables with chunks of bread and it filled her up, though it was tasteless. She thought with longing of Polly's kitchen with its enticing smells and tasty pies and bacon. Her throat stung with tears as she joined those helping to clear away the dirty dishes.

'Bella,' Phyllis said coming to her as she left the dining hall, 'I wanted to say goodbye to you – I am leaving this afternoon. I am being sent to a new mistress and my job will be in the kitchens.'

'It is what you wanted, isn't it?'

'Yes, I cannot wait to leave this place,' Phyllis said and gave a little shiver. 'I wanted to say goodbye – and to warn you again about Matron. Be careful of her Bella, she is spiteful and gains pleasure from inflicting pain.'

Bella nodded. 'She threatened to return me to my old master. I would rather run away than go back there.'

'I have often thought of running away,' Phyllis said. 'But if you run away and they catch you, they will punish you.'

Bella nodded. 'I've been sent to the sewing room this afternoon.'

'Then be *very* careful,' Phyllis warned. 'If Matron gives you privileges she will expect something in return.'

'What do you mean?' Bella was puzzled. 'What will she want of me?'

'She will make you spy on others – and if you do not, she will beat you and give you all the worst jobs. I dare not tell you all – but she is not what she first seems, Bella, but an unkind and sometimes harsh woman.'

'So *that* is why she threatened me,' Bella said. 'She wants me to be her spy – but I shall not. Even if she puts me to clearing the latrines I will not tell tales.' She put her hand on Phyllis' arm. 'I am glad you have the job you wanted, but I shall miss you.'

'I shall miss you too,' her friend said. 'If you get the chance ask the master if he will find you a place as a maidservant. It will be better than living here.'

Bella nodded and they parted company. Bella was sorry that Phyllis was leaving but she knew her friend was glad. Phyllis was the only one who had truly been her friend and Bella would miss her. She was apprehensive about what Matron would ask of her and though she was glad to join the women in the sewing room, she wished that she could leave this place.

Hannah greeted her with a smile and told her to sit next to her. 'We have a sheet to mend today,' she said. 'Bide by me and we'll do it together – and I'll help you to learn your letters.'

Bella thanked her. Hannah was no longer in the classroom in the evenings. She was fourteen now and she had been put to the sewing room and the laundry. Her hands looked red and sore.

'We need some balm to sooth our hands,' Hannah said. 'It does not matter for these sheets, but if we were given delicate embroidery our rough hands would snag the silk.'

'Florrie used to do delicate embroidery,' Bella said a little wistfully. 'She used a nice cream and gave me a little sometimes.'

'I asked Matron for some cream,' Hannah said, 'but her price was too high.'

'What did she want of you?'

'She asked me to spy on others!' Hannah looked angry. 'I refused and she put me to the laundry and stopped me attending classes. I am no longer allowed to read books.'

'I have never read a book.' Bella looked at her in wonder. 'Are there books you read for pleasure? I've only seen the books we use for learning – and the Bible.'

'The master's wife used to give me a story book sometimes,' Hannah said, looking upset, 'but Matron told her I did not deserve it and I have been denied all privileges.'

'I'm sorry,' Bella said and felt hot anger stir inside

her. 'It isn't right that Matron should have the power to take everything from you.'

'No,' Hannah agreed and there were tears in her eyes. 'The mistress said that I might be sent to work in a school, because I am a good teacher – but now I have been banned from the classes and my hopes are gone. Indeed, Matron says if I leave here I shall go to the nail factory.'

Bella pressed her hand but there was no comfort she could offer, for such a place would be hell for a girl like Hannah. She knew that most of the girls here were unhappy. They were at the mercy of a mean, spiteful woman and she could do what she liked with them, withholding privileges if they displeased her.

Bella had not been beaten since she'd come here, but she was discovering that there were other forms of punishment and she felt sorry for Hannah.

Bella did her share of the mending and repeated the alphabet after her friend. Hannah was a good teacher and it was unfair that she had been robbed of her chance to do a job she would enjoy, something that might have given her a useful and happy life. Bella wished that there was someone she could turn to – someone she could ask for help, for both her and Hannah.

Her thoughts turned to the gentleman who had come to the cottage. If only she had been able to contact him – and then she remembered the card he had given her. It was tucked inside her bodice with the florin she had not spent. She thought that she could copy the address now, but it cost money to send a letter and she needed paper and a pen and ink.

It was impossible. Bella sighed. Even if she could write the letter, she did not know how to send it. Perhaps if she asked the mistress – the master's wife was not unkind. She seemed to take little interest in the inmates apart from the children in her class, but there was a chance that she would take Bella's florin and post a letter for her. First, though, she had to ask for paper and a pen to write it . . . Another sigh escaped her, because it was unlikely that any would come her way but someone else might know how she could get some.

Bella showed the card to Hannah that evening after supper. She told her that she planned to write a letter asking Mr Stoneham to come and take them both away.

'He asked if I needed help but foolishly I said no and I daresay he thinks I am well settled,' she told Hannah. 'But I am sure he would help us both to find a good position if we asked him.'

'He might do so for you but he does not know me . . .' Hannah looked doubtful. 'I could find a sheet of paper and some wax in the schoolroom desk – but how could we post it? We have no money.'

'I have a florin,' Bella said. 'But I have to send the letter to London and I do not know if it is enough.'

'If you only send one small piece of paper I think

two sixpences would be enough,' Hannah said, looking thoughtful. 'I saw the master's wife writing to her friend in London and she had it franked for two sixpences.'

'Where do we do that?' Bella asked and her heart sank as Hannah told her they must go to the Post Office in the town.

'All post goes from there and the master sends someone to take the letters and bring back his post each morning.' She hesitated, then, 'Usually, one of the servants takes them and she cannot read. If we put your letter in the middle of the pile she would not notice it was different.'

'Yes!' Bella looked at her in excitement. 'Could we do that?'

'I do not see why not.' Hannah caught her excitement. 'You can write the letter but let me do the address. I can make it look a bit like the master's hand and then no one will notice.'

Bella giggled, because Hannah was being wicked and it was fun to share an adventure even if nothing happened.

'What are you doing?' Matron's voice intervened. 'Get to your dorms this instant or I shall report you to the master – and you, girl,' she said pointing at Bella, 'report to me in the morning. It's time I found you more work to do.'

Bella and Hannah fled. Neither of them wanted to be in trouble with Matron. Yet the warm glow they felt in sharing a secret did not leave them and they smiled at each other. If Bella's letter reached

Mr Stoneham, he might come and take them both away – out of reach of Matron's spite.

'I think I may have traced the girl,' Arthur's agent told him when he returned to the inn near Sculfield, after two weeks in London. 'I found a farmer and his wife and they told me that they rescued a young girl who had run away and took her to a workhouse just outside Alton.' He paused as Arthur frowned. 'I inquired of the matron there but she said she could not give me details of the inmates without the master's permission and he had gone to market that day.'

'At last,' Arthur said and looked at his agent with appreciation. 'I should like to meet this farmer and speak to him. If we know where Bella is I shall approach the master and make arrangements to take her away – unless she is content to stay there.'

'I did not like the woman who called herself Matron,' his agent said. 'She has mean eyes and I would say she can be spiteful.'

Arthur laughed and then nodded. 'I know what you mean, Bennett. Thank you for all you've done. You will take me to meet this farmer in the morning, please.'

'Of course, sir,' Bennett agreed. 'He seemed a decent sort – told me he would have kept her but he was afraid Karl Brett would demand money from him if he refused to return her. I have made inquiries and Farmer Green and his wife are considered good folk. They rent their land and are not rich – but his wife Polly said that she had wanted to keep Bella. She thought a lot of her, but her husband told her they could not afford to keep the girl.'

'I wonder what Bella wants,' Arthur said thoughtfully. 'I have not decided what is best for her if she is to be happy.'

'In the morning we could go on to the workhouse and ask to see her.'

'Yes, but I would speak to the farmer first,' Arthur said. 'You have done well, Bennett, and I must pay what I owe you.'

'I would see this business finished,' Bennett said and smiled. 'It has been a pleasure working for you, Mr Stoneham. I am always ready to serve you.'

'Thank you.' Arthur nodded. The man had proved useful many times over the past few years. 'I hope to be done with searching once the girl is found, but there may be other work you can do for me. I can always use the services of an honest man.'

Bennett inclined his head and left. Arthur glanced at his gold pocket watch. He wanted to speak to Hetty as soon as possible but the hour was late. He would wait until the next day, because what he had to say to her was important and should not be done hurriedly.

Hetty glanced out of the window. Arthur's letter had said he would be back soon and she longed to see him, even though she told herself her hopes were foolish – and yet . . . He had offered her a marriage of convenience and she had refused him but he'd hinted in his letter that he had something important to say to her.

Did he mean to ask her again? She had regretted her refusal since Arthur's departure for London. To be his wife – to be his lover – was all that she truly desired of life. Would it be more painful to wed him knowing that he did not love her as she loved him – or worse if her refusal drove a wedge between them? If she lost his friendship and his trust it would be a terrible grief to her.

Hetty looked out of the landing window. Something was moving about out there – was it Hobbs or had Arthur returned? She could quite clearly see a man's shadow approaching the front door and she walked down the stairs eagerly, running to the end of the hall just as it opened and a man entered. The lights were low for she had intended to retire and she had locked the door but not bolted it – and whoever had opened the door must have a key. Hetty frowned as she saw the man was shabbily dressed and looked as if he had been living rough for weeks . . . surely it could not be Master Brent? Had he dared to come here, even though he must know that he was being hunted for his crimes? She sensed that it must be he for there was something about him, and the way he moved, confident of his surroundings and yet wary, that sent shivers down her spine.

Halting abruptly, Hetty stared at the intruder. She felt a shiver of apprehension and fear. He had not closed the door and she considered trying to run past him as he moved purposely towards her, but there were others who were more vulnerable here, children and elderly folk who relied on her, and Hetty was no coward. She planted her feet on the ground and looked at him sternly.

'What are you doing here?' she demanded. 'If you are Master Brent how dare you come here after what you did? You are a wicked murderer and you will hang for your crimes!'

'Be quiet woman,' he grunted. 'I'm here to get what belongs to me – and to teach you a lesson.'

Hetty stood unmoving as he approached her and then quickly dodged to one side as he tried to strike her. He made a grab at her arm, but he was slow and she kicked out backwards, hearing him cry out as her heel struck his shin. She tore herself from his grasp and ran for the door, wrenching it open and calling out for Hobbs. Brent came after her and she saw he had a short club, which he swung at her head. She screamed and ran outside as he struck but he was quicker this time and he caught her a glancing blow on the side of the head, which sent her to her knees in a daze. As he was about to strike her again a shout came from beyond her in the darkness and someone came rushing towards her. Hetty was vaguely aware of shouting and a struggle as she fell to the ground and lay there in a daze while the fight continued.

It was some time later that Hetty came to her senses. She was lying on a settee in her parlour and Marta was kneeling beside her, bathing her head with a cloth dipped in cold water. Hetty tried to sit up and felt her head swim with the effort. Giving a moan, she lay back against the cushions.

'What happened?' she asked, putting a hand to her head, which felt sore and ached dreadfully.

'You were attacked,' Marta said. 'It was Master Brent. He hit you, you screamed, and Hobbs and one of the other guards came and Hobbs felled him – and the magistrates' men have been and taken him away in cuffs!' She rushed the words out without pausing for breath and ended on a little sob. 'It's a mercy you're not dead, Mistress Hetty.'

'You say the magistrates' have him locked up?'

'Yes, they came and took him, chained his wrists and his ankles they did.'

'Thank goodness for that,' Hetty said, because it meant that others were safe from his vindictive revenge. Then she felt the pain in the side of her head and moaned slightly as the room shifted and her senses whirled. 'I remember him hitting me – I think he has money hidden in the house and hoped to find it.'

'How did he get in?' Marta asked.

'I think he must have found a key,' Hetty said. 'Perhaps he had been searching for it and found it at last. I do not know – but he must have had the key hidden somewhere in the grounds or outbuildings, I think, and was only now able to recover it for he would surely have used it before if he'd had it earlier. And the bolts were not drawn as they have been each night. I had left them until last in case Mr Stoneham came . . . If the bolt had been in place his key would have been useless and I think he dared not break windows before this for he knew there were men patrolling the grounds.'

Marta shook her head. 'It is a wonder you were not badly hurt, Mistress Hetty.' She was clearly distressed by the thought. 'That wicked, wicked man!'

'I think he would have killed me if Hobbs had not come.'

Marta dabbed at her wet eyes. 'I would not have liked that,' she said. 'No one has ever been as kind to me as you.'

Hetty smiled at her. 'You deserve kindness, Marta.'

'There's many as deserve it and don't get it,' Marta said and crossed her hands over her middle. 'I'll miss you when you go back to London and there's no saying I shan't. Whoever Lady Rowntree sends to take your place, it won't be like havin' you here.'

Hetty nodded and smiled, but her head ached and she said she would like to go upstairs to rest. Marta asked if she would like a cup of hot milk with honey but Hetty declined. She was feeling distinctly unwell and all she wanted was to lie down and sleep.

Hobbs said he would remain in the house that night, though Hetty believed the danger was past. Nothing had been seen of Mistress Brent since she left the workhouse and she hoped that the former mistress had more sense than to return. Marta insisted on accompanying her up to her bedchamber, fussing about her until she saw how pale Hetty was and apologised, at last leaving her to rest alone.

Hetty could not understand her feelings. She must be having an attack of the nerves for she felt like weeping and it was years since she had let down her guard and allowed tears, but now they came and there was no stopping them. She wept into her pillow as if her heart would break.

When at last there were no more tears, Hetty rested on her bed, though she had not undressed and her sleep was light, restless, and broken by troubling dreams. In the morning she had a headache but was determined not to let it show. She dabbed her forehead with lavender water and combed her hair over a dark bruise. She thought that Arthur would call at some time during the day and she did not want him to see how foolish she had been the previous night, though there was no disguising the large bruise spreading over her face.

CHAPTER 19

The note from Hobbs reached Arthur the next morning as he came downstairs to breakfast in the inn parlour. He took it and scanned it swiftly, frowning as he read what had happened to Hetty.

Damn Brent!

'Is something wrong, sir?' his host asked anxiously as Arthur pushed the hot chafing dishes away and jumped to his feet.

'With your breakfast, nothing,' Arthur said. 'Forgive me, I must not tarry. If my agent calls for me tell him that I shall see him tomorrow. Something has come up and I must postpone our engagement.'

'Yes, sir, of course,' the landlord replied, relieved that his food was not at fault.

Arthur picked up his hat, gloves and riding whip and went out to the stables. His horse was saddled and he set out immediately for Sculfield and the workhouse.

Hetty had been hurt! The words had leapt out at him in letters of fire and he was both angry and anxious. Angry that Brent had managed to slip past his guards and get to Hetty, and anxious for her welfare. If anything happened to her . . .

Arthur realised that he would be devastated. He had always accepted that she was there, ready to smile at him when he was low and laugh with him when he was happy. Her advice was always good and her manner warm and inviting. She was not a lady in the way that Katharine had been, delicate and precious – no, she was much more. Hetty was there to support and comfort, to guide him when he needed it and to love him . . . yes, he realised that he had always known she loved him – somewhere deep inside he had known.

It had been a shock to him when he finally understood that what she had always given him was unconditional love. He had never seen the comfort he'd found in her arms when he was young or the advice and warm friendship she'd given him later when she was no longer a whore as love – but now he saw quite clearly that it was: a very special, unselfish kind of love. Not many men found a love as honest and true as Hetty's and so when he'd offered her less than she'd always given him, he had hurt her and she'd turned him down, but now . . .

Arthur could not be sure what this anxiety and fear meant at the moment. All he knew was that he could not bear to lose her. He could think only of Hetty as he rode and the injury to her head. Katharine had died of head injuries – if Hetty died he might not be able to bear it.

His feelings and thoughts were too muddled to make sense. All he knew was that he wanted to find Hetty well and not lying prone in a bed. He could not bear to see her fade day by day and then be snatched from him. Katharine had been taken from him, but he had always thought of her as a delicate flower that must be nurtured and protected. Hetty was . . . Hetty was his strength, his rock, the life force that gave him strength. Hetty was *everything*. He knew that now. How could he have been so blind all these years? Without Hetty he would not have become the man he was today. He could hardly bear his thoughts as he rode swiftly towards the village and then the workhouse.

When he arrived, dismounting hurriedly, Hobbs and the other guards were talking in the driveway. Hobbs broke off and came to greet him and take the reins.

'I thought you would wish us to continue our patrols, sir. Brent is in the magistrates' cell and they sent for you to go and give evidence this afternoon, sir. I daresay it is safe enough here now but . . .'

'You and your men will continue to patrol until we discover what happened to that murderous wife of his,' Arthur said, restraining his impatience. 'Thank you for your letter – how does Hetty today?'

'I have not seen the lady this morning, sir – but I understand she has a headache and a nasty bruise.'

'I shall go in,' Arthur said. 'You will also give evidence this afternoon, Hobbs, but the other men must remain here . . .'

'Yes, sir, as I thought.'

Hobbs went back to the others to give orders and Arthur ran towards the house and into the main hall. He was about to start up the stairs when Hetty came out of her parlour. She stopped, hesitated, and then smiled and held out her hands in greeting.

'Arthur . . . you're back . . .'

'I arrived last night and thought it too late to call – but I wish I had done so, Hetty!' He took her hands in his and stood looking into her face. 'That brute hurt you, my dearest. Should you be downstairs? Ought you not to rest?'

'It is just a bruise, Arthur,' she said and took her hands from his, touching the side of her face hesitantly. 'Does it look very bad?'

'You look as if you have a black eye and more,' he said with a gentle smile. 'I feared much worse – are you sure you're well enough to be up?'

'I do not like lying in bed for no reason,' she said and turned her face from him. 'I shall not die, Arthur. Fortunately, he only hit me once.'

'Once! That is too much for my liking!' Arthur exclaimed. 'The wicked devil! Why could he not fight me if he wished for revenge?'

'You were not here,' Hetty said and smiled. 'Besides, he was looking for something and I was in his way. Please, come in and sit for a moment. I will ask Marta to make us some tea.'

'I would prefer us to be alone,' Arthur said. 'I have something important to say to you – though perhaps you would prefer me to wait. If your head aches terribly . . .'

'It is not so very bad now,' she said, 'though it did earlier. I suppose it will be sore for a time.'

'Yes, I should imagine so,' he agreed. 'You need something cold to press against the bruise, Hetty.'

Hetty turned and led the way into the little parlour she was using. It was plainly set out, the furnishings old and worn, and yet she had brightened it with sprigs of greenery from the garden. He thought that she deserved a room of pale colours and sumptuous fabrics – and doubted she would ever let him give them to her.

'You must speak to the magistrates this afternoon,' she said. 'Will they also need my statement?'

'I will write it out for you and you may sign it,' he said. 'I am sorry I was not here to protect you, Hetty. Please forgive me. I was wrong to leave you exposed to such danger – and I am pleased to tell you that everyone will be leaving here in three days for a new home. You may wish to see your friends to their new abode before you return to London.'

'Is that what you wished to tell me?'

'Part of it,' he agreed. 'I have bought a small manor house and estate, Hetty. I have wardens to oversee it – but there will be places for craftsmen to ply their trade and it will mean a different way of life. Everyone who can will work – in the kitchens or the bakery or the brewery or the grounds or at some craft of their own, though the children will be taught to read and write and, as they grow older,

271

be given a trade. It will be as much like a large family as we can make it – though a few rules must apply for everyone's sake, the main ones being honesty and decency.'

Hetty looked at him and then smiled her approval. 'I think that would be a wonderful idea, Arthur – to take all these children and old people away from this terrible place and give them a new life.'

'It's the way people used to live on manors, Hetty,' he said, 'but there will be no lord and lady, just two wardens to make sure things run smoothly. The residents will work, as we all must, but they will be treated fairly and not as if being poor was a crime.'

She nodded and looked thoughtful. 'I am sure that is what the workhouse was meant to be but somehow it went wrong,' she said and looked at him in a way that made his heart beat faster. 'Only you would think of such a thing, Arthur.'

'I wanted to take the children away from this house of horror,' Arthur said, 'but when I saw what potential the manor has I realised that the way to make a good life for them was to let them learn a trade in healthy, happy surroundings. They will live on a farm but the craftsmen will have their workshops and the children may be apprenticed to them if they wish. When they are old enough, and have a skill, they can leave and start a new life.'

Hetty stood up and moved impulsively towards him, throwing her arms about him in a loving embrace. 'You are such a generous kind man, Arthur!' He did not push her arms away but looked into her eyes. 'Am I, Hetty? I think I hurt you the other day and that was the last thing I meant to do . . .'

'I know it was not intentional,' she said and tried to move away but he held her fast. 'You loved Katharine and before her Sarah . . .'

'Each in different ways,' Arthur agreed, 'and I thought when I learned of Sarah's death I deserved to die – but you brought me through that crisis, Hetty. *You!* I thought that when Katharine was so cruelly murdered I was broken, but you showed me the way forward . . . you, Hetty; it was you that made me go on living.'

'Arthur – Arthur I do not ask for gratitude . . .'

'And I do not offer it,' he said and his eyes bore into hers. 'I will not deny my love for either lady, for it was true enough in its time – but through it all your strength sustained me. You are the wind that keeps me flying, Hetty. You help me reach for what would otherwise be too far away . . . but more than that, you are warm and real and loving. You are the woman I need in my life. When I thought I might lose you I realised that I could not live without my Hetty, my rock – my everything.'

'Arthur . . .' She shook her head, but tears were trickling down her cheeks. 'I am not worthy of you.'

'Hush, my love,' he said and kissed her mouth softly, tenderly and then with growing intensity. 'You are far above me – so far that I would never marry if I could not have you by my side.'

'But Arthur, I shall not be accepted in society—'

'Be damned to society,' he said and held her. 'You are the one I want and no other will do. If you will not be my wife and my friend then I shall have no one.' He spoke with a finality that she could not doubt.

'How could I refuse when I have always loved you?' she said and her voice was little more than a whisper. 'But we must wait for a few months – you must be sure . . .'

'I shall not change,' he vowed, 'but you may have the time you need, my love. I am yours to command.'

'Then sit here and tell me more of this new home you plan,' Hetty said laughing up at him. He thought how beautiful she was and wondered that he had not seen it before. 'I long to see the manor, Arthur, and I know everyone here will be so happy to know they need not continue to live here. The children are terrified of being left here and the elderly folk are unhappy.'

'Lady Rowntree told me that she could no longer be responsible for this place and made a contribution to the purchase price. She says this house will be razed to the ground and the garden left to go wild. No one would wish to live here again after the terrible things that happened here.'

'I know the children fear the garden where the graves were, and the old folk cross themselves whenever they look out of the window. The sooner Marta spreads the word of their new home the better.'

'Yes, I think it will make many of them feel happier,' Arthur said and smiled at her. 'But do not think you can so easily turn me from my purpose. I pray you tell me you will be my wife.'

'If you still wish it by the summer then I shall be happy to say yes,' she said and her cheeks were pink.

'You're blushing,' he teased. 'Have you blushed before, Hetty? I think I have not seen it.'

'You make me blush when you look at me so . . .' she said and then laughed. 'I am no shrinking violet, Arthur. I know when a man wants to lie with me – and I did not say you need wait for that.'

'Did you not, my love?' His hand reached for hers and he toyed with the fingers. 'And yet I shall. You are not a whore, Hetty, you are the woman – the lady – I wish to marry and I shall not use you, though I was once too young and selfish to see you for the woman you are. I may have used you then in my selfish need, but it will not do so again.'

'You never used me, Arthur,' she said softly. 'You gave me pleasure and respect even then. Why do you think I never took anyone after you? I decided that no other man would do and I made my own way, even though it was hard at times.'

'Hetty . . .' He held her close but made no attempt to kiss her or force her surrender. She must come to him because she chose and for no other reason.

'Give me a little time, Arthur. I want us both to be sure so there are no regrets . . .'

'You may have until the summer as you promised.' He kissed the tips of her fingers. 'More, if you need it – but I may grow impatient.'

Hetty laughed and gave him a little push. 'You

have cured my headache. Go now and see to your business, my friend.'

'Tonight we shall dine at the inn. I shall send my carriage for you.'

Hetty smiled but did not deny him and he left her, whistling a little melody as he went outside to collect Hobbs and warn the others to keep a watchful eye. Master Brent had been captured but his wife was still unaccounted for and might be a nuisance if nothing more. Arthur felt a new lightness in his step. If he could not melt Hetty's reserve before the summer was out then he did not deserve her!

Hannah showed Bella the address she had written. It did not look like Hannah's own hand, but a sprawling script that Bella had not seen before. She looked at it doubtfully.

'Do you think anyone will notice?'

'We'll put it in the pile and see,' Hannah said and winked at her. 'It can't do any harm for I believe they'll just take them all to the post—' She broke off as someone came up behind her, starting in fright as a hand clenched on her shoulder. She turned and saw Matron's eyes glaring at her.

'And what are you two up to?' she demanded as Hannah hid the letter in the folds of her skirt. 'Give it to me, girl – whatever it is!' Hannah shook her head and Matron caught her arm, dragging it round forcefully and making her cry out in pain. 'Serves you right – now give it to me!' She snatched the sealed paper from Hannah and noticed the wax seal.

276

'You wicked girl! Stealing paper and sealing wax! Wait until the master hears of this – he will whip you until you are black and blue.'

'It was me,' Bella said as she saw the fear in Hannah's eyes. 'It was my idea. I wanted to write to a friend – someone who will come and take us away from here!'

Matron swung round, glaring at her. Her hand snapped back and slapped Bella across the face three times. Bella gasped and flinched as Matron prepared to hit her again, but just then the master's wife came round the corner of the hall corridor, crying out for Matron to stop.

'What is this?' she demanded. 'Why are you punishing that girl? What has she done wrong?'

'She stole paper and wax – and they were planning to put a letter in your pile so that you paid for it.'

'Give it to me,' the master's wife said and held out her hand. Matron hesitated and then reluctantly gave it to her. 'Thank you. There is no crime here, Matron. I gave Bella permission to write her letter and to use the wax and to place it with the others for posting.'

Bella stared at her but said nothing, for she could not quite believe that the master's wife had stood up for her like that and felt nervous of what was to come next.

Matron glared at her angrily, sure that the mistress was lying, but could say nothing. Instead, she marched off, every part of her bristling with temper. The master's wife watched her go and then looked at Hannah and Bella, then down at the letter again.

'It is a fair copy of my husband's hand,' she said and a gleam of amusement showed in her eyes. 'Who did this – you, Bella – or was it Hannah?'

'I did it, mistress,' Hannah said and hung her head in shame. 'Bella thought her friend might find us work we liked – and Matron had taken my privileges from me . . .' she faltered.

'Why was that?'

'Because I would not do as she bade me . . .' Hannah hesitated, and then blurted out, 'She wanted me to spy on the younger ones and tell her what they do – she likes to torment them.' Bella thought she looked as if she wanted to say more but was afraid to speak and wondered what else Hannah knew.

The master's wife nodded, her smile fading. 'I see – well, run along then both of you. I shall see your letter goes with the morning post. We have many desperate people needing a home and if Bella's friend can find her a better place we shall not stop her leaving.'

Bella looked at her in surprise. She had not expected Mistress Thomas to say anything like that and she spoke without thinking. 'This place would not be so terrible if Matron was not here!' It was the truth, but she had not realised it until she spoke.

'That is not for you to say,' Mistress Thomas said and frowned. 'I have been lenient, but the next time you want to use my husband's property ask me. And behave yourselves, girls.'

'Yes, Mistress Thomas,' they said in unison and ran.

'I did not think she would be so understanding,' Bella said as they reached their dorms. 'I thought she would send us to the master for punishment.'

'The master is not too bad and his wife can be kind,' Hannah confirmed. 'It is Matron who makes life hard for us whenever she can.'

Bella looked at her curiously. 'What didn't you tell the mistress, Hannah? I knew there was more but you did not say . . .'

'I do not know for sure but I suspect . . .' Hannah said and shook her head. 'If I accuse her of a child's death she will swear she is innocent and how can I prove her evil when I do not know? She picks on those too young or frightened to speak, but I've seen bruises and the look in their eyes tells more than they dare . . .'

'She ought to be stopped,' Bella said. 'We should tell the mistress for I think she does not like Matron.'

'Yet she would not believe us without proof. No, we must try to keep out of her way until we can escape from here, Bella – she can make our lives hell if she chooses.'

'I thought her hard but now I see she is wicked. This place is almost as bad as the one I grew up in.'

'It would be all right if it were not for her,' Hannah said fiercely. 'We must always work wherever we go but she makes our lives miserable . . .'

'I don't mind the work,' Bella said. 'I'll work hard wherever I go – but there are better places to live. It was lovely at the farm. I should like to live like that all the time and Polly was so kind to me.'

'You were lucky. Not many people live like that, even for a short time. I remember my parents before we came here and they both died of a fever. They had worked so hard they were exhausted and stood no chance when the cholera took them.'

Bella looked at her with sympathy. 'I'm sorry, Hannah. It must be worse for you having had parents and losing them. I never knew mine . . .'

'I don't know which is worse,' Hannah said. 'We'd better get in bed now because it will soon be lights out – and if Matron catches us she will be sure to whip us next time.'

They said goodnight and sought their beds. Bella's cheek felt sore where she'd been slapped but she'd had worse hurts and she mumbled a prayer to keep both her and Hannah safe before falling asleep because she was tired.

It was dark when Bella was rudely awakened. She felt a hand shaking her shoulder and then she was roughly jerked from her bed to the floor, tumbling on to her knees. Her hands were pulled together and tied, then a gag was placed over her mouth and Matron's voice hissed in her ear.

'Make one sound and I'll make you sorry, slut!

I'm taking you on a little trip and if you dare breathe a word I shall kill you . . .'

Bella was terrified and shaking with cold as Matron prodded her in the back with something hard. She wore only her nightgown as Matron took her along the hall and down the stairs. At the bottom, she was pushed across the hall and outside and then through the courtyard. Her feet hurt because the stones were sharp and she had no shoes. When they reached an old shed, Matron unlocked the door and pushed her inside. She followed her in and lit a candle, holding it in front of Bella's face. The floor was bare earth and the walls were stout wood and hung with cobwebs.

'You will stay here until you are ready to beg my pardon on your knees,' she said. 'You told the master's wife that I mistreated you and Hannah – and I've been warned. Me! My reputation besmirched!' She shook her fist at Bella, her face twisting with spite and anger. 'Now, I'm warning you. Speak of this again and you'll disappear forever next time!'

She went to the door and began to close it. Bella cried out, 'Don't leave me in here alone!'

'It's what you deserve. Next time keep your mouth shut when the master's wife speaks to you.'

'I don't like being in the dark – and it's cold,' Bella protested.

'Then you know what you'll get if you disobey me again.' Matron laughed cruelly, pulled the door closed behind her and locked it.

Bella tugged at it and shouted but it would not budge. She could see nothing at first because there was only one tiny window at the top but after a while she saw that the shed was filled with sacks and garden tools and she looked for something that might help her to get out but when she tugged at the door handle it came off in her hand and she burst into tears. There was no way she could get out without the key so she must stay here until Matron released her.

She sat on a pile of fusty sacks and pulled one over her lap and another round her shoulders, her bound hands clumsy. Her teeth were chattering with the cold and she was frightened but if she screamed no one would hear her this far from the house. Tears trickled down her cheeks as she sat and thought about her life.

Wherever she went all she got from those meant to look after her was harsh words and punishment; she might as well be dead. She felt lonely and unwanted. It might have been better if she had died in the snow with her mother. Even Polly had let her husband give Bella to the master here.

For a moment Bella felt the weight of all the pain and misery that had been heaped on her and wished she might die, for at least then her suffering would be over. She hung her head, almost ready to give in to the despair that overwhelmed her. Then, suddenly, she started to feel angry at Matron's spiteful act and she lifted her head. She'd been told that Matron liked to torment the young ones but now saw for herself that she was wicked. Bella would not just give in to her spite. She would fight and she would live – and one day she'd see that horrible woman punished. If no one stood up to her, Matron would continue to hurt and punish other young girls. Bella wouldn't let her win!

Jumping up she began to walk backwards and forwards as quickly as she could to get warm and, as she paced, she recited the alphabet over and over and over again. She would live through this bitter night. She would get away from this place and she would make a better life somewhere . . .

CHAPTER 20

'You dined with Mr Stoneham last evening,' Meg said when Hetty met her at breakfast. Her look was petulant as if she felt she had been ignored. 'I should have liked to ask him if he had any news of Toby – I mean, Mr Rattan.'

'I did ask but he said he had heard nothing. I would have told you at once if any news had come,' Hetty said apologetically. She knew that Meg was upset because Toby had sent no word and she'd hoped that he would return and bring her child to her. To Meg it must seem that he had been gone ages. 'I am sure he will come as soon as he can, Meg. He is trying to help you.'

'I know.' Meg gave a little sob. 'I should not be sharp with you, dearest Hetty. You have been so kind to me – and Mr Stoneham has done so much for me. I should not have lived if it were not for him, for I would have died of cold the night he found me – but I cannot forget my child.' Tears trickled down her cheeks and she brushed them away.

'It is hard for you, Meg. I do understand,' Hetty sympathised. 'To have your child stolen from you is unfair and painful, but I am sure Toby will bring news as soon as he is able.'

'Yes, I know.' Meg sipped her tea and crumbled a piece of buttered muffin on her plate. 'You look happier today, Hetty – do you have news yourself?'

'Nothing is settled . . .' Hetty's cheeks were warm as Meg looked at her and then she laughed. 'I may as well tell you, for I am not sure I can keep it a secret. Arthur wants me to wed him. I have not given my answer yet but . . .'

'Oh, you will – you must!' Meg said and smiled. 'You are perfect for each other!' She jumped up and came round the breakfast table to embrace Hetty. 'I am so happy for you. Really, I am.'

'Thank you,' Hetty said. 'I daresay I shall give my promise for it seems churlish not to – and yet I still feel that I am not worthy of such a man or the place in society it will give me.'

'If that is all, do not give it a second thought,' Meg said. 'Few in society could equal Arthur Stoneham. There are many men who bear the title of gentleman who do not deserve it, and ladies who have not one half of your wit or intelligence. You will help him with his work and comfort him – that is all any woman may do for such a man.'

'Yes, I suppose you are right.' Hetty was thoughtful.

'Have you heard anything of that child Bella?' Meg asked, and frowned. 'I do not forget her even though I have my own cares. She was good to me when I lay ill after giving birth and I hope that Arthur will help her.'

'I am sure he will if he can,' Hetty said and smiled at her. 'I believe he has discovered where she might be and he is going to see someone this morning – perhaps he will bring her back to us, Meg. She will be surprised at the changes here . . .'

'Oh, sir,' Polly said and curtsied nervously to Arthur when she answered the door of the farm kitchen and he told her he was looking for Bella. Her hands were covered in flour for she was midway through her baking and she invited him in. 'If only I'd known you was looking for her. We daresn't keep her – not from that brute, her master. He would have made us pay him more than we had.'

'Karl Brett is no longer Bella's master,' Arthur said, 'so if you know where she is I shall be most grateful for any news of her whereabouts.'

'I loved her like the daughter I never had,' Polly told him. 'Farmer Green took her to the workhouse just outside Alton, sir. He visited the market there to sell produce and asked if Master Thomas would take her in. He listened to her story and said that he would make sure she came to no harm – but I miss her, sir, and that's the truth.'

'Would you have kept her if you could?'

'Aye, sir. Farmer Green was sorry to see her go for he knew it upset me – but we don't own our land and we couldn't afford her price.'

Arthur nodded. 'We shall see what Bella has to

287

say,' he promised. 'I'll not keep you from your baking, goodwife. I daresay we shall meet again.'

Arthur left the warm kitchen. The wind was bitterly cold as it whipped across the fields and he approached the agent he had left outside with his groom and their horses.

'Towards Alton, sir?'

'Yes. I think my quest may be nearing its end at last. Mistress Green tells me her husband took Bella to the workhouse near there.' Arthur sighed with relief. He hoped to rescue Bella and take her back to Hetty and Meg, ready to move with the rest of her friends to the manor. Bella could be given a choice. She could live with Hetty, become part of the life at the manor – or return to Polly Green and her husband. He believed that Farmer Green's wife would be more than willing to take her back for a gift of money to set them on their feet. By the end of the day Bella's future would be decided and he could turn his thoughts to his own concerns. A smile touched his mouth as he considered the future and the way he intended to woo his love. Now that he had discovered what had been under his nose all these years, he was impatient to show Hetty all the consideration and love that she had given him so unselfishly.

Bella had fallen asleep at the last, worn out by weeping, raging and pacing the cold floor. She was shaking and her toes had gone numb, but there was nothing she could do except wait until she was released. She'd banged at the door for a long time and called out but the shed door was locked tight and would not budge however hard she pushed and banged against it.

Surely Matron would not leave her here much longer? She was cold, tired and hungry and beginning to feel very frightened. If she was left here much longer she might die and there was no way she could escape until the door was unlocked. Surely Matron would not dare leave her here to die? Mistress Thomas already disliked her and was suspicious of her. If Bella died then Matron could be in serious trouble . . .

'I should like to speak with Master Thomas,' Arthur said as he was shown into the workhouse hallway. 'No, I do not have an appointment.'

'Master Thomas and his wife went to market,' the woman who introduced herself as Matron said coldly. 'I am not sure he would see you without an appointment.'

'No? I have been told he is a reasonable man. When I spoke to the magistrate earlier he assured me I should have no trouble in removing Bella from here as long as all the necessary forms were completed.'

'B-Bella?' The woman swallowed hard, glanced at the large round clock on the wall. 'I will inquire if she is here,' she said, and pounced on a young girl wearing a uniform of blue gown, white cap and white apron. 'Hannah, go and fetch Bella.'

The girl stared at her, her face white, and then mumbled something Arthur could not hear.

'Speak up, girl. This person has come to speak with her.'

'She was not in her bed this morning,' Hannah said shooting a scared glance at Arthur. 'And she didn't come down for breakfast . . .'

'She must have run off again,' Matron said harshly. 'It is the second or third time she's tried since she arrived – and she has been treated with the utmost kindness!'

Arthur did not take his eyes from Hannah's face. She knew, as he did, that the woman was lying; he could see it in her eyes.

'Indeed? That is such a pity, especially if she has been shown kindness, for I should have wished to reward those who had treated her well,' Arthur said. 'I shall return later this afternoon to speak with Master Thomas. If Bella is missing, a search must be made for her – and I shall want to get to the bottom of this.' His eyes swept up to meet the older woman's and saw a start of fear. She glanced at the clock again. 'At what hour do you expect your superior to return, ma'am?'

Colour ebbed and flowed in Matron's face. He saw anger and bile and watched her clench her hands but he had dealt with many her equal in spite and would not let her get away with her obvious lies.

'You may of course visit whenever you wish,' Matron blustered and dismissed Hannah with a curt nod. 'About your business, girl! Have you no work?'

Hannah hurried away, her head down but she looked over her shoulder and something in her eyes warned Arthur. 'I shall take my leave, ma'am,' he said, 'but be assured that I shall return, several times if need be – until Bella is found.'

She made no reply but there was fear in her eyes. What had she done that made her look like that?

Arthur went out of the door and stood for a moment wondering what to do next. He was about to turn away when Hannah came rushing from the back of the house.

'Oh sir,' she cried, 'don't go yet! I am feared for Bella. I think she took her in the night and locked her somewhere.'

'You mean Matron?'

'Yes, sir. Are you Mr Stoneham – the gentleman Bella wrote to?'

'I am Mr Stoneham but I have had no letter from Bella.'

'We addressed it to London,' Hannah said. 'Mistress Thomas promised it would be sent – but that was only yesterday.'

'I would not yet have received it, even had I been there,' Arthur said and nodded. 'What did Bella ask?'

'That you might help us both find work. Matron has turned her spite on us both . . .' Hannah gave a little sob. 'She has locked others she stole from their beds in a cold shed and one boy caught a dreadful chill. He died but no one told the master who made him ill – we didn't dare to say anything against Matron, though we suspected what she'd done. She likes to torment the small ones, you see,' Hannah said, 'and I think I know where she put Bella but the door will be locked . . .'

'Show me!' Hannah set off at a run and Arthur followed swiftly. They entered the back yard where several outbuildings were situated and he caught sight of a woman's gown as she went behind a large building.

'We'd best hurry!'

He increased his pace and rounded the edge of the laundry in time to see Matron use a key to unlock the small shed. She went inside and Arthur followed. He motioned to Hannah to stay well back and stood to listen as the malignant voice rose shrilly.

'I hope you are sufficiently punished, Bella? Remember, I could have left you here to starve had I wished. If you dare to speak out against me again I shall—'

'What will you do, ma'am?' Arthur asked going inside. 'Will you leave her long enough to starve or catch pneumonia or will you murder her and then leave her body here?'

'You devil! You tricked me!' Matron cried and moved to strike him with a small heavy leather knob she held in her hand, but he caught her wrist and twisted it so that she cried out in pain and dropped it. She stood looking at him with hatred in her eyes and rubbing her wrist. 'You can prove nothing! Bella locked herself in here whilst hiding to get out of her duties.'

'What should I wish to prove?' Arthur asked.

'When I have spoken to Master Thomas you will no longer be employed here and I shall circulate your name and description so that no other institution will employ you. But it will be up to the magistrate whether or not he wishes to charge you with the offence of bodily harm.'

'I have never killed or hurt anyone,' she said viciously. 'Children should be disciplined and it is lawful to use the rod – I find they learn quicker if they are shut in here in the dark and cold for a night.'

'You think that justice?' Arthur said, untying Bella's hands. 'Go outside, child, and wait with Hannah.' He turned to look at Matron. 'You think it right to lock small children in here? You shall wait here for your employers to release you. I shall take the children away and wait for their return. It is not the same as being shut in overnight, but it may serve to make you think twice in future.'

'You cannot – you dare not!' Matron looked furious but Arthur smiled, thrusting her back as she tried to push past and escape then went out and locked the door behind him. 'Let me out this instant!'

'You will remain there until Master Thomas decides to set you free,' Arthur said. 'We must leave you now, ma'am, for we have an appointment and these young people need something to eat.'

'Mr Stoneham – you came!' Bella said and stared at him in wonder. 'I thought you might have forgotten me.'

'There are several people who would not let me, even had I wanted to,' Arthur said and smiled oddly. He looked at Hannah, dark brows arched. 'I can find you a new life and work – should you wish it?'

'I should like to stay with Bella for a while . . .'

'Do you have anything to bring with you – anything that is yours?' Both girls shook their heads. 'Then we must pay the master for your clothes and find you new ones as soon as Hetty can manage it . . . come with me.' Arthur led the way to where his agent was waiting. 'I must speak with the master here. Watch the horses for we shall be taking the girls with us shortly.'

'The master arrived back just now and asked me my business. I told him you wished to see him, sir.'

'Come inside, girls,' Arthur said, 'and warm yourselves by the fire. As soon as I have concluded business I shall take you to Polly and ask her to feed you while I send for my carriage – and then I can take you back with me.'

'Where do we go, sir?' Bella asked.

'For a short time to what was the workhouse at Sculfield – fear not, Mistress Brent and her husband have gone. I want to talk to you both so that I may understand what is best for you and then I shall do my utmost to see you settled happily for I will not let either of you be returned here or anywhere like it. Will you trust me?'

'Yes, sir,' Hannah said and smiled. 'Just because of what you did to her – Matron.'

Bella nodded her head in agreement. 'She deserved

it, but I always trusted you, sir. I just had nowhere else to go and I was afeared of Mistress Brent.'

'You will have somewhere better now,' he promised. 'Go along to the fire. I shall not be long and then you will eat some of Polly's good food and I shall make arrangements to get you home to Hetty and Meg. Hetty is a friend of mine and she is looking after the folk at the workhouse for me until I can move them to a new home.'

Bella nodded and bobbed a curtsey. 'Thank you, sir. I am grateful to you. May I ask, what happened to Meg's baby? Did you find her?'

'We are still looking,' Arthur said. 'My friend went in search of the babe and he will not give up until he finds her.'

'Then he will find her,' Hannah said and the look she gave Arthur was little short of adoring.

'Well, sir, I am surprised to say the least,' Master Thomas said when Arthur had told him what had transpired. 'I know Matron to be a disciplinarian, but I did not realise that she was torturing the younger ones.'

'I've been told that one boy died of pneumonia after she'd locked him in the shed overnight – but no one guessed that she was to blame.' The master looked shocked at the revelation and Arthur thought it was genuine. 'She cannot be allowed to continue in a position of authority.'

'Certainly not. Where did you say you left her?'

'In the shed she has too often used for her victims.'

Arthur gave him a hard look. 'I can leave the matter in your hands? I do not wish to learn she has been restored to her post in a few weeks' time. I should then have to take it up with the local magistrate.'

'No, of course not – if I had had any idea . . .' He spread his hands. 'I trusted her implicitly . . .'

'I did mention, dearest,' Mistress Thomas said mildly. 'I did not care for her manner towards myself – and I saw her bullying children on more than one occasion. I should be pleased to take her place for any of her duties, Henry.' Her manner was gentle but underneath she seemed a determined little woman and Arthur smiled inwardly.

Her husband seemed as if he would protest but then inclined his head. Arthur thought that perhaps he might have been attracted to Matron and his wife had been aware of it. Master Thomas knew, of course, that one word from Arthur would see him looking for a new post and had decided that total acquiescence was the better part of valour this time.

'Yes, of course, Helen. I shall be happy for you to do so.' He brightened a little. 'It will save the cost of a new matron . . .'

Arthur hid his amusement as he paid a few coins for the clothes the children were wearing and took his leave. Both girls were standing waiting for him, looking expectant.

'Ready? Good.' His eyes lit from within. 'Polly was baking this morning so I am certain she will have a great deal of food for you – and then you shall come and meet Hetty and Meg and we shall all decide what will be the best future for you . . .'

Polly was so excited that she wept for pleasure. She insisted on feeding not only Hannah and Bella but Arthur and his agent too.

'Well, I never,' she repeated over and over. 'I never expected this – not in all my born days. A gentleman sittin' down to eat in my kitchen and two lovely girls with him.' She glanced at Arthur's agent. 'You be welcome too, sir, whoever yer be, but I do like to have my Bella here and this here gentleman what has brought her to us is a proper saint.'

After the meal, the men left the farmhouse together. Arthur spoke at length to Farmer Green, money was given, and they shook hands before Arthur rode off with his agent. Bella and Hannah were left with Polly and cleared the dishes into the hot water in the sink. Polly washed them with a cloth, Hannah wiped the plates and cups and Bella set them out on the big old dresser opposite the fireplace.

'Well, this is lovely,' Polly said fifty times over as she got out her rug-making kit and the two girls helped her pull strands of rag pieces through the coarse sacking that made the base of the peg rug. All the pieces of cloth had been cut to the same size and were placed in different coloured piles, making a bright pattern as Polly deftly threaded them into place. 'What I wouldn't give of a winter's night to have two lovely girls like yerselves wiv me.'

'I shall never forget you, Polly,' Bella said. 'Mr Stoneham says he will help me choose what I want to make of my life – but I like being here with you, Polly.'

'And I'd have yer, my lovely,' Polly said. 'If I could afford it.'

'I should like to work for a lady sewing fine things,' Hannah said, 'but I doubt I'm good enough.'

Bella assured her she was, though in truth she was not as good as Florrie or Phyllis had been. 'I thought you wanted to be a teacher?' she said.

'Yes, but I need more schooling before I could do that,' Hannah said.

'If you tell Mr Stoneham, he will know what to do,' Bella said and Hannah's smile lit up.

'Yes, I think he will,' she agreed.

When the rattle of wheels outside announced Mr Stoneham's arrival later that afternoon, Polly's face fell but she kissed both girls and told them to visit her if they could and they hugged her and thanked her.

'She is lovely, just like a mother,' Hannah said wistfully as they went outside and climbed into the carriage where a lady was waiting for them. She smiled at them and offered them a blanket to place over their legs.

'I'm Hetty,' she said. 'I am going to look after you until we all go to our new home. Mr Stoneham has bought a lovely place for us all and you will travel there with us and live in our community until you decide what you wish to do with your lives.'

'Will you live there too?'

'Not forever,' Hetty said. 'Just until everyone is settled and happy – and you may not either. Arthur – Mr Stoneham – wants everyone to be happy. You will have the chance to think about what you truly wish and then he will help you find the right place.'

'He's wonderful isn't he?' Hannah said, youthful adoration in her face.

'Yes, I have always thought so,' Hetty agreed. 'Now, why don't you both tell me all about yourselves on the journey home . . . ?'

CHAPTER 21

Toby looked hard at the woman but could not doubt that she spoke the truth. His heart sank as he realised that he must return to Meg and tell her that he had failed her. Her child was dead – had died of a fever just two weeks after she was brought to her new home.

'I am sorry to hear that, ma'am,' he said for the woman had tears in her eyes. 'However, I do not know what I am to tell her mother for the child was stolen and this news will break her heart.'

'It fair broke mine, sir, when the poor little mite breathed its last,' she replied. 'I know you must think us evil, but my brother told us he knew of a house that sent unwanted babes to homes with those that would love them – and as he lives not six miles distant, he went to speak with the mistress there. He was told that a young woman would give birth in a few days and did not want her child . . . my husband and I immediately travelled to my brother's home to await the birth and to bring the babe home.

My brother paid her two hundred guineas to keep the babe for us and we paid her another hundred for we were grateful . . .' Her eyes filled with tears. 'I know it was wrong, sir, but I was desperate for a child and had it lived, I would have loved it dearly.' The tears spilled over and down her cheeks.

Toby nodded, believing her story. Her brother might have known the child was stolen but she'd believed the mother had willingly given up the babe, though still known it was wrong. However, there was no point in raging at her for the child was dead and nothing more could be done.

'I shall take my leave,' he said and turned away but she caught his arm and he looked back at her. 'Yes?'

'I could not bear to hold another child yet but . . .' She looked at him fearfully, uncertain whether to speak. 'My husband said that a young girl – not more than fourteen – in the village some five miles from here, has given birth to a girl child. She was raped and intends to give up the babe for her father will not let her keep it. My husband thought I might take her but I could not bear it yet.' Her voice broke and Toby saw then how much she had grieved for the lost child.

He hesitated, then, 'What is the name of this girl?' he asked and she told him that it was one Gillian Goss of Exening.

'I thank you, madam,' Toby said and left her comfortable home, pausing for a moment before entering his carriage. He was torn by doubt, the thought she had put into his mind growing, and yet horrified at the deceit it meant he must practise if he carried out an act of kindness . . .

Meg had helped to prepare a room for the two girls to share and she was hovering at the window waiting for them when she saw Toby Rattan's carriage drive in through the gates. Giving a cry of joy, she ran downstairs and was at the door to meet him. He was carrying a bundle wrapped in a shawl in his arms, and Meg's heart fluttered, hardly daring to believe what she saw. He had found her child! Tears came to her eyes and she could scarce breathe. He lifted his head to look at her and she saw the joy and triumph in his eyes.

'Is this your babe, Meg?' he asked and she felt a strange light-headedness sweep over her and for a moment she could not move or think, because she was so overjoyed. She had doubted that he could achieve what she thought of as impossible.

'Is it really her?' she asked, moving slowly as if in a dream. It felt as if her feet were stuck in some thick syrup and her limbs were leaden. 'Oh, Toby – is it truly my child?'

'Look and tell me, Meg,' he said softly. He held the babe out and she saw the sweetest little face surrounded by a halo of golden hair; the babe had pink cheeks and large blue eyes that looked wonderingly up at her and she felt an immediate pull of love. She had been devoid of hope and now she had her child returned to her. Nothing else mattered.

'Oh, my darling – my sweet baby . . .' Meg whispered and her voice was thick with emotion, her gaze misty and damp. 'You found her . . .' She looked up at him adoringly: her champion, her hero. 'Toby, you found her!'

'Yes,' he said and smiled as he placed the child in her arms and she cradled it to her breast, tears of joy falling as she gazed down at the beautiful child. 'She is yours, Meg, and no one will ever take her from you again. I promise you.'

'My husband . . .' she said fearfully, glancing up at him. 'If he knew he might try . . .'

'He will have searched for you in vain and I dare say now continues on his merry way to hell,' Toby said, wanting to set her mind at rest, though he knew nothing of the man. From what little Meg had told him, it was unlikely her husband moved in his circles for he never visited London, and if she allowed him to take care of her, he would make sure somehow that the man who had so ill-treated her never came near her again. 'Put him from your mind, Meg. You cannot free yourself of him but if you will entrust yourself and your child to me, I shall protect you for as long as we both live.'

'Oh, Toby . . . Mr Rattan,' Meg said and smiled at him through her tears. 'I am grateful and happy that you offer me your protection.'

'I would offer you marriage but it would cost you too much grief to free you from the bonds of marriage to that monster,' Toby said and the look in his eyes spoke of a love and devotion Meg understood but hardly believed. 'I shall ask nothing of you, dearest Meg, but the privilege of caring for you. Yet it may be best if we change your name to mine by deed poll – and then I can adopt the child so that even if someone came looking for her, she would still be ours. To the world you will be Mrs Rattan, though we cannot seal our union in church.'

'You will be my husband in all but name,' Meg told him, for this was the man who had given her back her life. How could she refuse him anything? She would take all that he offered and smile, even if the scars inside still maimed her. 'I do not know how much of myself I can give you – for what he did to me damaged me emotionally, but I shall always love you in my way. You have given me back my child and my life, and I can never thank you enough.'

'Your trust will be enough,' Toby vowed and went to her. He stroked the tears from her cheeks. 'I will make you happy however many years it takes . . .'

Meg looked from him to the babe in her arms. 'You have already done so. I did not believe they would give her up – how did you manage it?'

Toby hesitated, then, 'Money and the law,' he said. 'I both bribed and threatened and the husband saw sense, though his wife wept to lose the babe. I think she has been well cared for, has she not?' It was partially a lie, for he had given the young mother money, though she'd wept and told him her father

305

had threatened to drown the brat for bringing shame on them.

'I thank you for taking her, sir,' she'd said. 'Give her a good life and I shall not regret what I have done, though I have little choice.'

Toby had felt her grief but told himself that in taking the child its grandfather thought shameful, he would be giving it a chance of a good life and Meg happiness.

'You are happy now?' he asked Meg anxiously.

'Yes, oh yes,' Meg said. 'She is so beautiful. Her name is Elizabeth – after my mother.'

'And mine,' he said and smiled. 'She was called by another name but she is too young to mind or remember.'

'She is almost three months,' Meg said and her face glowed with happiness. 'They never let me hold her once. I saw her for an instant through a haze of pain and her hair was just a dark strand but it has grown fair and beautiful, much like my own when I was small.'

'Your hair is beautiful now,' Toby said and looked at her with love. Meg smiled and then Elizabeth cried and a pungent smell told of a napkin that needed to be changed. 'I shall go upstairs and make her comfortable – and put the clothes I've been preparing on her . . .' Her eyes lit up with happiness as she cradled her lost child to her breast.

Toby nodded and watched her go upstairs. For a moment his face clouded. May God forgive him for the lies! Yet the truth would only destroy the woman he loved. Meg was happy now and he intended that she should live her life in peace and ignorance of what could only hurt her.

'Ah, well met!' A voice from behind made him turn and he spun round to find Arthur looking at him quizzically. 'I take it your mission was successful?'

'Yes . . . it was,' Toby said for that was no lie, though the years would bring many deceptions to cover the one he had wrought here. 'Elizabeth is restored to her mother and I shall adopt her.'

'Yet you cannot marry Meg . . .' Arthur posed an unspoken question.

'She will be my wife in all but name. We shall live together and the child will be presumed mine; Meg will change her name to mine and only a few will know she is not my wife.'

'Will your father know the truth?' Arthur frowned.

'I am not his heir,' Toby said. 'If the time comes when Meg is free of her brute of a husband I shall wed her.' He smothered a sigh. 'And, God willing, we may have other children of our own.' Following Arthur into Hetty's sitting room, he said, 'Hetty is not here?'

'She has gone to fetch two young girls – Bella, the girl I believe to be Katharine's sister's child and a friend of hers from the workhouse where they were found. It was a decent enough place in its way, though the master had allowed a spiteful woman too much power. The girls will come with us to the manor and then decide where they wish to live.'

'I thought you might adopt Bella as your own?' Toby arched his brow.

'Had Katharine lived I should have done so if she wished,' Arthur agreed. 'It is certainly an option I intend to offer Bella, but she has a will of her own and I rather think I know which way her mind tends . . .' Toby looked puzzled and Arthur smiled. 'I think she might like to live with a farmer's wife if they could afford to take her.'

'An easy matter to remedy,' Toby said and Arthur nodded his agreement.

'Money is sometimes a blessing, is it not? Used in the right way it can bring good if not happiness.'

'I think it can bring happiness,' Toby said thoughtfully.

'Is that how you got the child back?'

Toby looked at a point beyond Arthur's head. 'Money was certainly a part of it and a great deal of thought.' He did not elaborate, though Arthur waited for a moment or two. Instead, he changed the subject abruptly. 'So is your business here concluded at last?'

'Once we move to the manor,' Arthur said and looked out at the darkening sky. 'I had hoped for some better weather. It is spring and summer cannot be far away, yet it remains bitterly cold. Much of what we transport will be by cart and that can be sheeted over if it rains – but I'd hoped some of the young ones might ride in a hay wagon and think it a treat. Twelve elderly folk and fifteen children are rather a lot to take in carriages and I'm not sure there are enough for hire locally so they can all leave together.'

'The children will not mind a bit of rain,' Toby said and laughed. 'If they have hay and a sheet up against the worst of it they will treat it as an adventure.'

'Yes, I daresay.' Arthur paused as he heard some laughter from upstairs. 'That is a sound I have not heard much of here and I hope it is a sign that they begin to recover.'

Toby looked about him at the small sitting room. 'Hetty has done wonders with this room, but the whole place is dark and depressing. The manor cannot fail to be better than this and spirits must lift as soon as we are under way.'

'We leave the day after tomorrow,' Arthur said. 'Will you stay and help us – or take Meg to London?'

'Do you need my help?' Toby asked. Arthur was his best friend and he would stay if he was truly needed.

'No, I'm sure we can manage,' Arthur said obligingly for he sensed what was on Toby's mind. 'Take Meg away from this place and get her settled in a new home.'

'No, if you don't mind, I'll let her stay with you until I have things ready and come back in a week or so. She will not be comfortable in an hotel and my lodgings are suitable only for a bachelor.' He paused then, 'It is in my mind to make inquiries in Winchester about her husband, discover if I can whether he still searches for Meg.'

'And what will you do if you find him?' Arthur frowned. 'Remember that murder is still a hanging offence, my friend. You may want to thrash the bastard, but it might be best to stay clear of him.'

'I shall not go myself but send an agent I trust – but I would know Meg is safe until I am certain of his whereabouts . . .'

'Meg is welcome to come with us,' Arthur agreed. 'Another female adult can only be of help keeping everyone together.'

'Thank you,' Toby said. 'I shall speak to Meg and leave in the morning.'

'And now, I daresay you could do with a drink,' Arthur suggested. 'I shall wait for Hetty to bring the girls back safely and then I intend to sup at the inn – would you care to join me?'

'I ate earlier. I would spend as much time as I can with Meg.'

'Yes, of course,' Arthur said, giving him a look that seemed to see into his soul. 'You must love her a great deal, my friend, to do what you have done . . .'

Toby nodded but said nothing. He was almost certain that Arthur knew the truth, though he would not speak of it. As he took the glass of brandy offered, Toby studied its rich glow in the candlelight. The lie was cast and it would live like a dark shadow at his shoulder but he would never reveal the truth because he could not bear to break the heart of the woman he loved. She would never know that the child he had bought and placed in her arms was not her own. He had taken a risk but the look in Meg's eyes had been worth every moment of doubt he'd suffered on the return journey and he would do whatever he must to keep her safe . . .

Arthur was thoughtful as he rode back to the inn. Hetty had brought the two young girls safely home and, far from being afraid, they were chattering excitedly about the move to the manor and he had been aware of Hannah's lustrous eyes on him. He sighed. She had imbued him with the virtues of a knight in shining armour – and it was the name. His mother had named him for the fabled king and now Hannah thought him her saviour. A little smile touched Arthur's lips, for he was nothing like the ancient king!

He wondered if he would have done what Toby had done for love. The change in Meg was there for everyone to see and her light came from within, shining out of her. All the pain and grief of her experiences seemed to have vanished and she had been laughing with Hetty and Toby over a glass of sherry before supper. She was bursting with happiness, seeming to have forgotten the pain that went before.

Yet it was an illusion. Toby had lied to give Meg back her life.

Arthur never left anything to chance and he'd sent his agents to discover what had happened to Meg's babe even before Toby set out in the hope of its recovery, though their report had come too late to save his journey. They had reported back to Arthur that the child had died of a fever scarcely two weeks after it was born. The foster mother had been distraught and blamed herself, but her husband said it was just that the child had somehow contracted an illness and died, as young children so frequently did.

Obviously, confronted with the awful truth, Toby had made a huge decision. In his heart, he must have known that if he told Meg the truth it would break her, perhaps even kill her. Instead, he had looked for and found a babe of the right age, perhaps from a workhouse or a mother too sick to raise it or recently dead; that must have been the reason he'd taken so long and sent no word. It was his secret and Arthur would never ask the details, never tell him that he knew the truth, because that could only destroy both Meg and the man who loved her. Yet he did not think he would have made the same choice. Had Meg been the woman he loved, he would have told her as gently as he could and given her time to heal, standing by her but not intruding – but Toby had begun a lie, a lie that must continue for life. It was not an easy way to live and Arthur would not care for it; he did not think he could live with his conscience – and yet perhaps Toby's way was right, was kinder. He thought that it was not for him to judge.

Arthur shook his head. At the moment Meg was content and that was all anyone could ask – but supposing one day she discovered the truth, that Elizabeth was not truly hers? How would she feel then? Would she love Toby for trying to please her or hate him for his lies?

Life was sometimes hard, Arthur reflected. He had never told Eliza that he believed she was his daughter but now he wondered if he had been wrong. Perhaps she would wish to be acknowledged, to live with him? A wistful longing stirred but he shook his head. It was Eliza's feelings that mattered. When the move to the manor was over, he would talk to Eliza and ask her what she felt about her life as an apothecary's apprentice.

As he dismounted and handed his horse's reins to the groom, Arthur looked over his shoulder. No one was waiting in the shadows. Master Brent was in a cell awaiting trial, and, Arthur had been told, after questioning he had refused to reveal where his wife was hiding. It was suspected that the pair might have fallen out and with Brent's violent past her death was a possibility, because her testimony would have hanged him. But the evidence was damning and even without his wife's testimony, he would hang.

Arthur went into the inn. He had taken a light supper with his friends at the workhouse and though the landlord came bustling forward, asked only for some brandy.

'I shall be leaving tomorrow and will settle my account,' he said. 'You will be glad to be rid of me after so long, I daresay.'

'Indeed, no, Mr Stoneham,' the landlord said at once. 'My Sally has become real fond of you and you've been a generous lodger, sir.'

Arthur nodded, thanked him and went up to his room. The next day he would spend at the work-house helping to pack those things they needed to take with them to their new home. Every pair of available hands would be harnessed and Arthur had arranged for Farmer Green and a friend of his to bring wagons over that afternoon to be loaded ready for the move.

If he was not mistaken, there was just a touch of warmth in the air. Perhaps, at last, everything would look brighter and they would be blessed with the first touch of spring.

The first farm wagons, pulled by a team of heavy horses, arrived as the sun came up and there was a holiday atmosphere as the farmer, his son and several other men set to with a will, packing boxes on to the carts, everyone shouting, laughing and quaffing the good beer Arthur had supplied for them to ease the task.

Some beds, crockery, kitchen utensils, bedding, and other bits and pieces were loaded on to two of the wagons. Much of the heavy, older furniture was left in the house because the manor already had adequate furniture in the main rooms. More beds would be needed, because all the bedchambers would hold several of the narrow cots that accommodated children and elderly alike, and for the homes Arthur intended to give to the craftsmen in the cottages dotted about the estate. It was from their industry that the lifeblood of the manor would flow and he hoped the children would find trades they liked and learn from the skilled men who came to live and work with them.

Some large chests were taken to accommodate the linen, and the children's clothes were packed mainly into large wicker washing baskets; tubs, boxes, pans and utensils were tucked into every corner of the carts. Everything would be unloaded and sorted when they got into their new home.

The mood was one of anticipation and the children were laughing, running backwards and forwards with small treasures they had found and wanted to take.

Lady Rowntree wanted nothing from the house at all.

'It is an episode greatly to be regretted,' she'd told Arthur. 'My family is shamed by association with that dreadful pair, Mr Stoneham. I am grateful to you for bringing Master Brent's reign to an end.'

Arthur had assured her yet again that she was not to blame, that she could not have known what was happening – but in truth the guardians had been lax, allowing children to go missing over the years with no questions asked. It was a terrible thing and a stain on the good name of all workhouses that it could have happened. Laws had not been properly applied and must be examined and tightened, and Arthur meant to make it his business to gather good folk with like minds on the subject to discover what reforms might be made to prevent this kind of thing happening, but he suspected where evil men lurked there would always be shadows and murky areas that others feared to probe. All he could do was to protect those that came within his orbit and that he would do.

The wagons were dispatched as soon as they were packed, and some of the elderly were sent ahead by carriage. Hetty and Bella were going with them to see them settled into rooms that had already been prepared and to oversee the unpacking of the wagons.

Marta, Meg and Hannah stayed with him at the workhouse that night, he on a lumpy settee in one of the abandoned rooms and the others in their own beds, which would be taken on the last wagon in the morning. Hobbs had gone with Hetty and Bella, to help with overseeing things at the other end, and Hannah had been eager to do all she could to assist Arthur.

'I'll make sure the children all have hot drinks and settle for the night,' she promised and Arthur smiled, because she was a caring girl and eager to be of use. He thanked her and she ran off to the kitchen.

'I shall see you tomorrow evening, my love,' Arthur told Hetty before she left. 'Hobbs will see you safely there and George and his wife Betty are good people. I knew at once that they would suit my purpose. You will like them . . .'

'How will you manage the rest of the children?' she asked anxiously.

'I think they are all falling asleep on their feet and I can see little to worry about,' he said and kissed her softly on the lips. 'In a few hours you will all be reunited and this upheaval will be a thing of the past. George and Betty will be there to help settle their charges and in a few days you and I may return to London.'

'You will be glad, no doubt?' Hetty's eyes held a spark of amusement.

Arthur laughed. 'It has all taken longer than I expected,' he admitted. 'I little thought when I first came across Meg, almost dead in the snow that night, that I should remain here so long.'

'And you are happy that Bella is Marianne's daughter?' Hetty looked at him intently.

'As convinced as I can be after so many years – but we shall tell her together and allow her to decide what she wishes to do . . .'

'Given her choice I believe she would return to the farm and Polly,' Hetty said, 'but once you tell her that her mother was a gentlewoman . . .'

'It must wait until we have time – and you must go.'

Hetty laughed and took her leave. Arthur felt a pang of loss as he watched her climb into the carriage. His feelings for her had taken him by surprise but now he knew that he could never bear to lose her.

Perhaps it was thoughts of Hetty that kept him

sleepless or mayhap the lumpy sofa, but Arthur was up before first light. He went through to the kitchen and found a jug of cool cider. He was hungry but there was only porridge, which Marta would cook for breakfast, or yesterday's bread. He'd arranged for food to be brought from the village to sustain the children on the journey to their new home but it was too early for that to arrive so he broke a piece of bread and ate it.

Feeling restless, Arthur went to the doorway and looked out. It was going to be a nice day by the look of that sky. There was dew on the grass and a hush in the air, broken only by a bird trilling in the garden. His thoughts turned to Bella.

He had thought the young girl would be happy enough with Polly, who loved her, and he had been willing to pay them to keep her – but would Katharine have been content to see her niece reared as a farmer's child? He doubted it. In London, she could learn to be a young lady. Arthur came to a decision. He would take both her and Hannah into his care. They would go to school for a while and then Hannah could become a teacher as she wished, and Bella would live with Hetty and him and become whatever she wished.

Once the move was finished, Arthur would offer her the alternatives. He thought that perhaps if he took Bella and Hannah into his care, he might also find the right moment to offer the same choice to Eliza – though he knew she was happy as Miss Edith's assistant, learning to be an apothecary and proving her intelligence and the caring nature she had inherited from her mother. Sarah had been a sweet, gentle woman and he owed it to her to make sure that Eliza was safe.

He had waited long enough, Arthur realised, as the children came pouring downstairs, eager to begin the new day, excitement in their faces and raised voices. They went off to break their fast happily and then to help – or hinder – the last of the packing. Watching them, listening to their laughter, he felt a content he had scarcely known for many years.

He had given them this chance of a new life and already the change in the children, who had been pale, subdued and frightened was worth every penny he had spent. Arthur knew that he had chosen the right life for him and this venture would not be the end of his efforts to ease the suffering of men, women and children who, unlike him, had not been born to wealth and comfort.

CHAPTER 22

Arthur rode with the small convoy making its way to the manor. The sun came out from behind a bank of thick cloud and the children sang and played games, eating the good food that had been prepared for them. When the innkeeper's wife Sally had been told what such large quantities of food were needed for, she had outdone herself, making savoury pies and fruit tarts and fresh-baked rolls filled with cheese and her delicious pickles. To the children of Sculfield workhouse, it was the food of the gods, and they truly felt they were in Heaven. It was the best holiday of their young lives and they cared not that their progress was slow, some of them running beside the wagons for a while before climbing up to sprawl in the scented hay. It was an adventure and they wished it might go on forever, their laughter rang out again and again as the carts trundled towards a new life for them all.

At midday, the horses were allowed to rest by a stream and the children played games on the bank, racing up and down in so much excitement that poor Marta was worn out trying to keep them in order. Arthur advised her to relax and eat her own share of the good food and when one of the smaller children fell in the river to the accompaniment of shrill screams and cries, he plunged in and yanked him out by his collar and Marta pounced on the boy, clucking over him like a mother hen.

Arthur contemplated the likely ruin of one of his favourite pairs of riding boots and emptied the water out of them ruefully. Yet watching as everyone settled down to finish the food and clear up before the start of the second half of their journey, he found himself laughing easily, relaxed in their company.

It was like having a huge family, something he had never enjoyed. He wondered how anyone given the privilege of caring for children and elder folk like these could use them harshly and looked inquiringly at one of the older men as he sat beside him on the bank.

'I mind the time when I could've done that, sir,' he said and touched his forelock respectfully. 'Takes me too long to get up once I'm down now to be of much use in an emergency – but I'm a farmer and I hope you'll have a use for me when we get to this here manor, me lord.'

'What is your name, sir?' Arthur asked. 'And I'm not a lord, you know.'

'Tom, sir. I know you be not a lord but what you've done for us – well, 'tis like the knights of old, and the tales my granny told of chivalry and lords . . .'

Arthur smiled in amusement. 'Well, Tom, my name is Arthur – and I'm sure we can find any amount of work for you at the manor, though you are entitled to rest at your time of life. I daresay you worked hard long enough when you were younger.'

'I did, Arthur, until the agues got me and I was no more use to my master so they put me in the workhouse.' Tom's eyes twinkled. 'I knew you was him – Arthur of legend and his knights what went around doin' good works.' He chuckled as Arthur responded with a shout of laughter. 'Good with horses I be – but I can milk a cow or look after pigs and hens. Too old to do much hard labour but I'd rather work outdoors than sew sacks.'

'I'm hoping there will be small tasks for all those who wish it, even those like you, Tom, who cannot be expected to labour in the fields. I shall bring craftsmen to the manor and they will teach the young a trade – but I hope that we shall be self-sufficient in basic foods once we're up and running. We shall keep a few cows, pigs, sheep and hens – you know what I mean, Tom. You've lived on your own produce all your life. We've plenty of land and can employ men to till our fields and do the heavy labour, but I hope our folk will grow the fruit and vegetables in the kitchen gardens.'

'It will be much like it was not so very long ago, before all the mad rush to the towns,' Tom said. 'I mind my great-grandfather spoke of the good old days – and he said it was the golden age, afore all them trains and the mills and factories. Folk worked on the land then or at a trade, but now 'tis all smoke and noise and dirt.'

'Yes, though sometimes crops failed and pestilence destroyed livestock and people alike, and in the cold winters folk starved,' Arthur said. 'I think we may overcome some of that, Tom – but it is an experiment that can only work if everyone wants it to. I hope for a better life for you all. God willing, it will happen.'

'You've made it better already,' Tom told him and nodded at the others. 'I reckon they're gettin' ready to move, Arthur – and I might need a hand up from this 'ere bank!'

Arthur laughed then stood and offered his hand, giving the elderly man a haul to his feet. Tom thanked him, nodded and went off to help load the things they'd used back on to the wagons.

Turning his head, Arthur saw that Hannah was looking at him adoringly again. His prompt plunge into the river to rescue the young lad had been heroic in her eyes and he sighed inwardly. She was a nice little thing and Bella's friend, and he wanted to do the best he could for her, but the sooner she understood that he would be marrying Hetty the better, because at the moment she thought herself falling in love with him.

The new wardens, George and Betty, had spent a few days at the manor preparing things, and although the arrival of some of their inmates and half the goods and chattels had upset the order, Arthur could already see that his instructions had been carried out. The men's and older boys' bedchambers were in one wing and the women and younger children were in another.

However, unlike the workhouses, here there were also communal rooms where the men and women, girls and boys could spend time together after the work of the day was done. At the moment there were no married couples or families residing at the manor – that was something for the future.

Even amongst the old folk, the atmosphere was much lighter now that the people were away from the gloomy old building where so many terrible things had happened. At first it was all noise, mess and bustle as the wagons were unloaded and the farmers stayed to eat and rest their horses before starting their journey home. They had arranged to stay overnight at an inn nearby to break their journey and thanked Arthur for securing rooms and paying the cost of their stay. They had been more than eight hours on the road since leaving Sculfield but everyone had enjoyed themselves, for time meant nothing to country folk when money was to be earned, gold that would stand them in good stead even if the harvest was poor that year.

'It has been a pleasure working for you, sir,' one of them said. 'Anytime you need a man and wagon you ask for Alfie Brown and he's your man.'

They clearly felt it had been a holiday, away from

the back-breaking hard slog of their everyday lives. Arthur gave them some more beer for their journey and they left in high good humour, waving their caps to the children who called out and thanked them.

'You survived in one piece then,' Hetty said teasingly as Arthur went back inside the manor, and found her talking with Bella and Hannah in the hall. Bella took Hannah off to see the room they would be using while they stayed there. 'I am told you saved a child from drowning on the way here.'

Arthur gave a short laugh. 'Hardly that. I only got wet up to my backside and he was only in there seconds before I yanked him out – hardly heroic, Hetty.'

'Hannah found it so!' Her eyes teased him and he shook his head at her, reaching out to pull her close to him. 'I think she likes you, Arthur . . .'

'Jealous?' he asked huskily and kissed her passionately. 'I want only you, my love.'

Hetty moved away from him, her cheeks warm. 'This is a wonderful place, Arthur. You said it was charming and I understood you had big plans – but I never dreamed it would be so beautiful. I went for a walk to the lake this morning . . .'

'Yes, the view from there is lovely,' Arthur agreed, his eyes on her face. She had surprised him, for he thought her most at home in London. 'I have a beautiful country estate, not unlike this but larger . . .' His gaze intensified. 'Do you not prefer the town, Hetty?'

'Me?' She seemed surprised. 'Perhaps sometimes, but . . .' She shook her head. 'I am full of fanciful ideas since I came here, Arthur.' She walked away to the window to look out as George, the warden, entered the room.

'Ah, Mr Stoneham,' he said. 'I wanted to tell you – we have a candidate for our first craftsman. He came to me yesterday and asked if he could have one of the larger barns. He is a cooper and his landlord recently doubled the price of his workshop rent, thereby putting him out of work. When I told him the rent here was based on what he could afford, plus some time given to training youngsters and helping out when it was harvest time, he begged to be our first tenant and I told him to return today and speak with you. He is waiting in the kitchen.'

'Then I shall come at once,' Arthur said and sent Hetty an apologetic smile. 'We shall speak later.' He joined his employee. 'You are at liberty to call me Arthur, George, for I hope we shall be friends and that this is the start of a long and rewarding friendship.' Then, glancing over his shoulder, Arthur saw that there was a wistful expression on Hetty's face as she looked out of the window.

Hetty turned to an empty room. The sun was still shining in at the window but some of the sparkle had gone and she knew that it was Arthur – he brought so much energy and purpose to all he did. He was such a busy, important man and much sought after in London society, though he seldom attended the larger society events, preferring an intimate dinner with close friends. However, he had several influential acquaintances, a great many charitable projects, art galleries he patronised, and a life he enjoyed – and he wanted Hetty to share it.

She loved Arthur and wanted to be his wife more than she could ever say, but could she be the wife he needed? His house was one of the most admired in London's fashionable quarter, rich with silks and gleaming wood and the glitter of precious objects in French cabinets. Hetty enjoyed pretty things but to be mistress of all that . . . ? Her eyes swept the large, comfortable sitting room and the slightly shabby drapes at the windows, the sofas that had worn into shapeless comfort, their faded shades of rose, gold and deep-emerald greens muted into softer hues. Now this was a room she could happily be mistress of . . . She heard laughter and then a group of young children burst into the room carrying something. They stopped as they saw her and looked hesitant, a little uncertain.

'What have you got there?' she asked and a little girl called Millie came forward with a tiny rabbit in her arms.

'We found 'im in the garden, miss.'

'He looks very young to leave his mother,' Hetty said. 'I think he might be lonely, don't you, Millie? Shall we take him back where you found him? There are lots of little animals here for you to see – some you can pet but rabbits don't really like to be in the house.'

She ushered the children from the room and they took her out to where they had found the rabbit at the back of the house. Hetty bade them put it down and it shrank to the ground for a moment in fear and then went loping off.

'Will it find its mother now, miss?' one of the boys asked and Hetty smiled.

'Yes, I should think so, Georgie. I don't suppose any of you have seen animals like that before?' They all shook their heads. 'Well, here you will have hens to feed and ducks – and there will be babies. You children will learn to collect the eggs and that can be fun. Shall we go and see if there are any now?'

Hetty took them off on an egg hunt, explaining that hens often laid their eggs in the strangest places. She told them how she had collected the eggs for her mother when she was a child living in the country and kept them all amused and happy. By the time they went in for supper, they had found three eggs and the children had begun to learn how very different their lives would be here at the manor. They would still have their jobs to do, because the manor must run by everyone's efforts, but they would also have time to run and play outside and become healthy and strong in the fresh air, boys and girls mixing together.

Millie slid her hand shyly into hers. 'Will you stay here with us, Miss Hetty?'

'You have Master George and Mistress Betty now to look after you, and they will be kind,' Hetty told her. 'Perhaps I can visit sometimes, but you will be so busy and happy you won't miss me.'

'Yes we will,' a chorus of voices said and Hetty felt unexpected tears sting her eyes.

She turned to see that Arthur was standing in the doorway watching them. Hetty smiled as she moved towards him, surrounded by a cluster of happy children.

'Enjoying yourselves?' he asked and nodded as they all thanked him.

'We want Miss Hetty to stay with us,' one little boy said. 'She's like my mother used ter be afore she died of the fever.'

'Miss Hetty will visit you sometimes,' Arthur said and frowned. 'Off you go, then. Miss Mary and Marta are waiting to get you your tea. Oh, and children, this is your home now and you will have many privileges you did not have at the old workhouse.'

'Is it still a workhouse, sir?' one of the boys asked.

Arthur was silent for a moment. 'Sort of, Charlie, because we all have to work to make it pay – but we shall call it the manor and I want it to feel like a home where you can learn good things. When you are older you will choose what you wish to do with your life. None of you will be sold to a master. You will all learn a trade and jobs will be found for you when the time comes.'

'Thank you for answering me proper, sir,' the lad said and grinned as he ran off. 'I ain't never 'ad a real 'ome!'

'That was well done, Arthur. The children were not sure what was expected of them now.' Hetty smiled as she followed him through to the parlour where they had spoken earlier. 'Did all go well with your visitor?'

Arthur nodded and looked pleased. 'Very well, I'm glad to say. We have our first craftsman – and a cooper is very traditional. I believe we shall get some more unusual crafts as time passes, and I hope to build some more cottages for married couples who can manage to support themselves if they have a little help. I should like the boys to learn carpentry, boot making and other leather crafts. Pottery is an idea I've had and I'm keen to try it myself, but we should need a kiln for that . . .'

Hetty laughed. 'You surprise me, Arthur. I thought you a man of business affairs.'

'Oh, I enjoy working with my hands at times,' he said. 'If I can start up a pottery here I might try my hand at throwing a pot when I visit.'

'You intend to visit regularly then?'

'We shall want to keep an eye on things,' he said. 'I trust George and his wife – but I do not intend to be a patron in the background only. Complacency leads to carelessness.'

'I should like to visit sometimes,' Hetty said wistfully.

'When we are wed you have only to ask . . .'

'Arthur . . .' Hetty paused as Marta entered the room.

'Oh, Hetty, I wondered if you could come,' she

said. 'The children are quarrelling over who sleeps where and I know you said where they should be and Mary says I'm right but two of the girls have fallen out and . . .'

'Yes, I will come,' Hetty laughed. 'There are bound to be squabbles until they settle down. It is only natural. They've never had so much freedom and personalities are coming to the fore!' Freedom brought a different kind of problem, which was why there still had to be certain rules and regulations.

Arthur sighed as Hetty was taken away to perform yet another task. There were half a dozen jobs he had seen needing a man's attention and he might as well get on with them. Moving so many people into a new home was a huge undertaking and there were bound to be sparks flying until it was all settled again.

It was after they had dined that Arthur finally found time to be alone with Hetty. He went outside to smoke a cigar and stroll on the lawn and she came out to him, a warm shawl about her shoulders because the air had cooled once the sun had gone. It was not yet warm enough to be strolling at night and she shivered in the night air.

'A busy day,' he said and smiled at her. 'Are you tired, my dearest one?'

'Yes, a little – as you must be. I'm sure I saw you chopping logs just before supper.'

'Tom was showing me the correct way to split them,' Arthur said and grinned. 'He is a countryman and we've had some interesting talks.'

'I think you already knew, did you not?' Hetty looked at him in amusement.

'Perhaps, but it does no harm to listen to sage advice,' Arthur said and smiled.

'You're a kind man, Arthur Stoneham.'

'Am I?' he said huskily and moved closer to her, throwing his cigar into the earth. 'Kind enough for you to marry, Hetty?'

'I love you,' she said simply and smiled as he touched her cheek. 'You only had to ask me enough times – though I do not think I shall make a grand society hostess.'

'Nor will you be asked to attend the kind of affairs that would make you unhappy,' he said softly. 'Would you live in the country with me, Hetty, devoting our lives to our family and to those we choose to take in and care for?'

'Here?' she asked but he shook his head.

'George and Betty will take care of our people here and we may visit as often as we like. I meant at my estate in Devon. It is much larger, the house too big for one family, which is why I never bothered with it. With some thought, it could be both our home and another place like this – with children, elderly folk, working families and craftsmen in one wing. We will build cottages there too so that families can stay together. Everyone will work together and we will have a pottery, a carpentry shop making special furniture – and other trades. It will be like the manor here but we shall take it further.'

'Oh, Arthur . . .' Hetty's eyes lit up. Arthur's smile

told her that he thought her lovely and she felt his love as their lips met in a kiss of sweet passion that held them fast until they were trembling with love and desire. 'You have just offered me heaven on earth!'

'I'm going to ask Bella and Hannah to visit with us for their holidays, but they will go to school – and they will become whatever they wish. I think Tom might like to come with us to our home, because we have become friends, but everyone else will stay here. We shall take in those in need locally when we are settled and ready.'

'What of the refuge in London?' Hetty asked, for it had been her task to care for the inmates there.

'It will continue with Ruth and Lil, and my Cousin Matthew will oversee it for me. His daughter, Lucy, has written to tell me of her hopes for the future and I believe she may wish to help others less fortunate. She might help to run the refuge for she could still do her sewing – and teach others if she chose. We shall stay in town from time to time, for I think you would like to visit the theatre and the shops, but I believe I shall sell my father's London house and buy something more suited to my lifestyle. The money can be used for better purposes, helping to support the manor, perhaps, though I hope it will become self-sufficient in time.'

Hetty looked at him. 'You do not have to give up all your pleasures for me, Arthur. What of Toby and your other society friends?'

'Toby will be living with Meg and we might buy

something near them for our visits to town – and my true friends will visit us wherever we are, my darling. I do not intend to give up my campaign to improve the lot of the poor of London, for there is much to do there. What we can achieve, even if we devote our lives and fortune to it, is a mere drop in the ocean. Reform is needed so that children do not go hungry and are not abused, and the elderly must be treated with dignity and understanding. I shall lobby those in power to use their influence towards improving the lot of the destitute.'

'You hope for Utopia,' Hetty said and smiled up into his loving eyes.

'Yes, I strive for it but know I can never achieve it,' Arthur admitted ruefully. 'I will do what is in my power to help all those I can in whatever way I can – and that is all any man can do, my darling.'

'Yes,' she said and kissed him. 'And I love you for trying . . . it is all anyone can ask.'

'I love you, Hetty. Can you forgive me for not knowing it years ago? I have wasted so much time!'

'No, never wasted,' she said. 'We have been friends and we have both learned. Until we came here I did not know what would truly make me happy, Arthur.'

'And now you do?'

'Yes – but there is one more thing we both need before we can be truly content . . .'

He looked into her eyes. 'You mean Eliza, don't you? You think I should tell her about Sarah and why she was left at the workhouse.'

'She has a right to know, Arthur – and unless you tell her, you will never be at peace, my love. Speak to her, if not for your own sake then for mine.'

'How wise you are for one so young and beautiful . . .'

Hetty laughed and shook her head. 'I am not truly young, Arthur, but I do love you and I hope that we may have children of our own – although I know that if we do not we shall have others, all those lost and lonely little ones that we can rescue . . .'

'Your daughter, Hetty, mine, Bella and Hannah . . .' he said softly. 'And so many others . . .'

CHAPTER 23

'I am glad to have caught you,' Toby said as Arthur was about to leave his London house. 'I wanted to tell you my news.'

'From your expression I would judge it to be good news?'

'The best,' Toby said. 'My agent discovered the whereabouts of Meg's husband – and it is a churchyard in Winchester. Meg's father lives there and her husband had an estate close by. Apparently, this past winter, her husband caught a putrid chill and died in his bed.'

Arthur arched his brow. 'Is that the truth or what you will tell Meg?'

Toby frowned. 'I swear it is the truth,' he said. 'I will not lie – had I found he was alive and still looking for her I might have killed him, but it seems the bitter winter did it for me. I consider it justice for all he made her suffer.'

'So now you may make Meg your wife?'

'Yes, if she will have me,' Toby said and then swore. 'God forgive me, I know I should not rejoice in another's death – but I cannot help it. Had that devil lived I know she would always have feared he would come for her.'

'You have my blessing, my friend, and I wish only happiness for the both of you.'

Toby's face lit with a genuine smile. 'I must go and tell Meg my news – but I wanted you to know . . .'

'Go with my good wishes,' Arthur said. 'I have things I must attend to.'

Eliza was busy mixing a remedy for the rheumatics. Miss Edith had shown her that there were different kinds of ailments that people grouped as rheumatics or the agues, and they each required a different herb to be effective. She had carefully measured and chopped and now the herbs were soaking in pale natural vinegar that would draw out all the healing properties.

Miss Edith was sitting in the chair by the fire, dozing. Her chest had been bad this past winter and Eliza worried about her cough. She did not want the woman she loved almost as a mother to die, and sometimes, when Edith was very ill, she feared that the time was creeping closer.

'Eliza, there's a gentleman asked to see you. He said is it all right if he comes through?' Bess, the little serving girl they'd taken on to help in the shop, came through to the kitchen.

Eliza glanced up and saw the man standing just behind Bess. A little jolt of surprise made her cry out as she saw it was Mr Arthur Stoneham.

'Yes, of course, sir,' she said. 'Go back to the shop,

Bess. In half an hour you may go home. Let me know and I will come and lock the door after you.'

'You are very busy, I see,' her visitor said and advanced into the kitchen. He looked a little nervous and Bella wondered at it, because although she had not often seen him these past months he had regularly sent her hampers of lovely things for her to share with her beloved Miss Edith. 'What may I do for you, sir?'

'Have you time to sit and talk with me for a few minutes, Eliza?'

'Yes, of course.' She glanced at Miss Edith but she was fast asleep. 'If we go a little further away we shall not disturb her.' They retreated to the far end of the kitchen and he sat down at the table.

'Is she no better?' he asked and Eliza shook her head sadly. 'If there is anything I can do . . .?'

Eliza shook her head again. 'She is comfortable and I care for her.'

'You love her.'

'Yes, very much. She took me from the workhouse and gave me a home – but more than that, she taught me to read and write, she showed me how to make herbal preparations that ease pain – and she taught me to drink tea!'

Eliza's eyes sparkled with mischief at that last remark and Arthur felt a pang of recognition. She had his sense of humour and that look of mischief in her face was his own. If he had ever been unsure, he knew now that Eliza was his daughter with Sarah, the girl he'd loved as a young and headstrong man.

'I never know why folk like tea,' Arthur said. 'I prefer wine or ale.'

'I prefer a cup of good ale,' Eliza admitted. 'A bad habit I learned in the workhouse, I imagine.'

'Yes . . .' Arthur sobered immediately, his conscience smitten by the memory of what she had endured there. 'You should never have been there. Forgive me for all you suffered, Eliza. I shall never forgive myself but I hope you will at least understand when you know the truth.'

'I fear I do not know of what you speak,' Eliza said puzzled. 'I was abandoned by my mother and left there years before you knew of me.'

'Not by your mother. She died and someone else took you to the workhouse and gave you to that foul woman.'

Eliza stared at him in silence, her eyes widening in disbelief. 'How could you know?' she asked but her voice was no more than a whisper. 'You know of my mother?'

'I knew her, Eliza,' Arthur said, and she saw that he too was much affected. 'When I first discovered you in that place I had no idea whose child you were – nor even that Sarah had had a child. I learned it a few months back, because I made it my business to . . . and it is a strange and involved story. One that leaves me culpable, though I vow I never knew of you until recently.'

Eliza's hands were trembling. She sat down abruptly in a wooden armchair and stared at him, clasping her hands to stop them shaking.

'Sarah died with only strangers to care for her and that is a bitter thorn that pricks me endlessly, for I did love her. But I was a young, heedless creature and cared too much for my own pleasure. Eliza . . . Eliza, I seduced Sarah and then I left her but I swear that I did not know she carried my child.' Arthur paused to let her take it in. She nodded, her face expressionless, and he continued, 'Her brother kept the truth from me for years. I learned of my child only when it was too late – and I did not know that both Sarah and my child had lived until I met you and saw this – and then I searched for the clues that led me to the truth.'

He held out a trinket that sparkled. Eliza took it wonderingly. It was a halfpenny set in gold and ringed with diamonds and had once been his watch fob. 'Ruth, who looked after you, kept this for you when she found it in your shawl when you were brought to the workhouse. She wanted to give it to you when she knew you were safe here, but she dropped it in my presence and I saw it. I knew at once it had been mine, and Ruth guessed what it was from my reaction when I first saw it and she waited to ask me for permission to give it to you. I persuaded her to let me give it to you.'

Eliza was still bewildered, unable to take in more than the knowledge that he had not only known her mother, but was her father, here to declare it to her. The rest concerning the shawl and the trinket hidden in it went over her head for it was too much to absorb and she would need to ask

Ruth for the details when her head was clear. For the moment emotion gripped her, bringing her close to tears and she could hardly believe that she had heard aright.

At last she spoke again, 'Her brother denied you the chance to give Sarah love and make amends. Do you not think that he deserves much of the blame?' Eliza's eyes never left his as she waited for his answer.

'Sarah's brother John was angry, because he felt that she had shamed his name, though I think after her death he may have blamed himself – yet I know that I alone must bear the blame and I know that you must hate me for my spineless desertion of your mother – thereby condemning you to years of hurt and pain.'

Eliza was silent, looking at him thoughtfully as she saw the emotions working in his face and felt his tension. It was true that his careless treatment of a young gentlewoman had caused much distress, but he had suffered for it. She saw the deep sorrow in his eyes and found there was no anger or bitterness in her.

'It hurts me that she died alone and believed herself abandoned,' Eliza said at last. 'Yet I do not think you can blame yourself for her death – had her brother not forced her from her home she might never have taken the fever – and as for the rest, anger and blame will not bring her back from the grave nor will it give me the mother I never knew.' Eliza held the halfpenny, which hung from a clasp, clutching it tightly. She looked at it, thoughtfully. 'It is a gentleman's watch fob, I think.'

'Once mine, thrown away in anger, found and taken up by your mother and concealed in your shawl – and now yours. It was the clue that led me to the truth of Sarah's death and your fate.'

Eliza looked at the trinket in silence, then, 'There was a time when I might have sold it to buy food but now I shall keep it to remind me of my mother . . .' She slipped it into her apron pocket and then gazed calmly at him. 'Do you not think you should tell me all of it?' she asked, and so he did.

Arthur described the complicated story of how she had been given to a childless couple, who longed for a babe of their own, but the husband had died and the woman had decided she could no longer cope with caring for her.

Eliza repeated the tale in wonder. 'I was given to a woman who longed for a child but her husband died of a fever and so she was forced to give me up . . .' She looked at him strangely. 'Without this trinket you would have had no clue, so are you certain that I am your child, sir? Could it not have got into my clothing some other way?'

'Until today, Ruth's testimony was the closest I could come to certainty,' he said, 'but now I know that you are my daughter.' He smiled. 'It is a certain expression in the eyes; a way you have of laughing that reminds me of myself – and also of your grandmother, my mother. You are a little like her in looks, though thankfully not in nature. Forgive me, Eliza.

I should have told you the truth as soon as I discovered your story, but I did not know what to do for the best. I did not want you brought up by servants as I was, unloved, neglected and yet given every material comfort.'

'Is that how you lived as a child?' She looked at him curiously.

'Yes – but I do not say it for sympathy, merely for understanding why I did not tell you as soon as I discovered the truth of your birth and the reason you were given to the workhouse.'

Eliza was silent, gazing at him in wonder and disbelief. Could it really be true? For all her life she had been a nameless brat with no mother or father, and although Ruth had cared for her and Miss Edith loved her, there had been a huge gap in her past that left an empty space inside her.

'I have a father – and a mother who loved me and would have kept me had she not died?' He inclined his head, his eyes filled with tears that spilled over and trickled down his cheeks. Eliza looked at him and realised that she was crying too. 'Thank you – thank you so much for telling me of her!' She smiled through her tears. 'I have known love from Ruth in the workhouse and from Miss Edith – but now I know my mother loved me too.'

'Your mother loves you,' the gypsy woman had told her once and Eliza had begged her to tell her more but she had had nothing to tell. Arthur Stoneham had just told her the true story of her birth and she felt the wonder of it overcoming the stunned disbelief, filling her with a warmth she had never known. She had a mother, and her mother's name was Sarah.

Her father held out his hand towards her, asking for her to take it and forgive him. 'I would like the chance to make it up to you – to show you a father's love if you are prepared to give me a chance.'

'You said that if you took me into your house, I would be brought up by servants, neglected and unloved?' She was puzzled, not understanding what he was offering or asking.

'Things have changed,' Arthur said and gave her the smile that seldom failed to charm. 'I have a loving home to offer now – and I have learned what a family could be. It does not have to be the way mine was, Eliza, and I pray that you might one day be a part of my home and my family.'

'Tell me what has changed,' she asked gently, for she saw something in his eyes that spoke of hope and happiness.

Her father's face softened as he told her of his love for Hetty. He spoke at length of their plans – of the journey to the manor when he'd jumped into the river after a small child and discovered what it felt like to know real happiness, the contentment of family and friends, and Eliza's tears flowed. She understood that he too had known loneliness, not just of the person but of the spirit; he had suffered as much as she because her mother's brother had destroyed the chance for them to be a family when he lied to Arthur and told him Sarah was dead while she yet lived.

'Yes, I do see that things have changed and that there would be a chance for us all to begin again.' Eliza looked at him and there was tenderness and understanding in her eyes.

'You have your mother's capacity for kindness, Eliza. I see it in you – and it humbles me.'

'My poor father,' she said and got up. She put her arms about him and put her face to his chest, holding him. 'I think you were very lonely – more than I ever was in the workhouse.'

Arthur caressed her blonde locks with a father's hand. 'Do you truly forgive me?'

'Yes, I do,' she said and looked up at him. She had admired him for a long time, now she believed that she could love him and be proud that he was her father. Eliza knew that from now on she would be acknowledged as his daughter and loved, as she should always have been. 'I should like to live with you and one day I will ask you to come and fetch me, Father – but not yet.' Her eyes went to Miss Edith who was stirring and she left him and went to the sick woman, kneeling down to smile at her. 'Mr Stoneham came to visit us, Miss Edith – was that not kind of him?'

'Goodness!' Miss Edith said, startled. 'Did you offer him some tea, Eliza? You should have done, my dear.' She looked at Arthur. 'We have tea and cake and you are very welcome to share.'

'You are very kind, dear lady,' Arthur said in a gentle voice, for she was clearly fragile, 'but I shall take no more of Eliza's precious time. I hope to see

346

you better soon, Miss Edith – and if there is anything you need you have only to send word. My own doctor shall call if you wish it.'

Miss Edith smiled and shook her head. 'Eliza knows how to look after me, dear Mr Stoneham. And you have been so very kind to us.'

He went to take her hand, looking down into a face so pale and delicate that he knew she could not live long. His gaze returned to Eliza and the smile he gave her told of love and reassurance.

'Take care of your friend, Eliza, and send for me whenever you need me.'

'I shall, you may be certain.' Eliza's eyes smiled at him. 'If you're sure you will not stop for tea, sir . . . ?'

He saw the hint of wickedness in her eyes and smiled. 'One day you and Miss Edith will have the pleasure of sharing a pot of tea with me – on the day of my wedding to Hetty . . .'

Eliza had a new dress for her father's wedding. Hetty visited her and brought a large box containing the dress, a hat, shoes, silk underwear and stockings and little white lace gloves.

'It is a gift from both of us,' Hetty said. She had also brought a box of almond comfits for Miss Edith that Ruth had baked for her, but the poor lady was ill in bed and unable to eat them.

'She will be sorry to have missed you,' Eliza said. 'I thank you for the new dress and the comfits, Miss Hetty, but I fear I shall not be able to attend the wedding, though I do wish you both much happiness.'

'You do not wish to leave your friend?' Hetty nodded her understanding. 'You would never forgive yourself if she passed while you were gone.'

'Thank you for realising why I cannot come,' Eliza said. 'Ruth offered to sit with her but I will not leave her. I love her for her kindness to me – and I hope my father will not feel that I have slighted him or you.'

'Of course not,' Hetty said and took her hand. Eliza was on the verge of tears and grateful for her warmth. 'Arthur very much wants you to live with us when you are ready – but he knows this shop is to be yours and that you may wish to continue in your work.'

'I shall certainly continue my work,' Eliza said. 'As for the rest – I hardly know. Trade has not been as brisk since Miss Edith no longer runs the shop and I might not be able to carry on. In the eyes of the law I am still a child and Miss Edith's cousin and his mother may try to take the shop from me by any means they can.'

'Eliza, we will stand by you – and if it is your wish to continue . . . ?'

'For the moment I cannot think ahead,' Eliza said sadly. 'My place is here – and I do sincerely wish you both happiness and a good life.'

'I am excited by what lies ahead,' Hetty told her. 'If you asked, Eliza, your father would send you to school – you could learn more of herbs and medicines. And if you wish to continue with your healing when you are older the schooling will only lend credit to your cures.'

For the moment Eliza could not think of her future. She knew that once Miss Edith was dead and buried the legal wrangles with Miss Edith's relations would begin. Even if the will was watertight they would make trouble for her – and already some of her clients questioned whether she was able to make their medicines up properly. It might be better to have that schooling so that she could claim more knowledge than even Miss Edith had – but that really was for the future.

She glanced at the clock on the mantel. 'It is almost time for Miss Edith's medicine,' she said. 'Thank you again for my dress – and I do wish you great happiness.'

Hetty stood up and moved to kiss her cheek. 'I am glad I came to see you. I know Arthur wondered if you could truly forgive him but I see that you have. Take care, dearest Eliza, and remember that we will come to you if you need us. You have only to send us word . . .'

Eliza thanked her and impulsively hugged her. 'I am so glad he has found you,' she said. 'I think he was very lonely and unhappy for a long time – and he is a good man.'

'Arthur does not think of himself in that way,' Hetty said and her love for Eliza's father was in her face. 'He does kind, generous and thoughtful things but always finds himself lacking. I know that I am lucky to have found love and that I shall be happy. I shall pray for Miss Edith and for you.'

Eliza went to the door with her. The shop had been closed for a few days now, because the bell disturbed Miss Edith and she needed peace. Returning to the kitchen, Eliza began to grind the herbs, nettles and berries that would give her friend ease for a few hours, sieving the mixture and adding water. The mixture was strong and too much would give Edith the everlasting sleep that men called death, but Eliza regulated the dose carefully so that her friend felt hardly any pain and yet was able to talk and drink a cup of the tea she so much enjoyed. Eliza hated the thought of losing her, cherishing these last precious days and every moment that they spent together. She wished she could cure her dearest friend, but there was no cure, only the kindness of freedom from pain.

She would think of Hetty and her father the next day as they married and wished them well, but she would not leave Miss Hetty even for an hour. She hoped her father would understand and not think she was angry with him or resentful. Hetty had told her they were having a short honeymoon in France but would be home in a couple of weeks.

'We have too much to do setting up the estate as we wish it to stay away long,' she'd said. 'Once it is up and running it will be a good place to live for as many as we can take in.'

'I like the way you want to live,' Eliza told her. 'Like you, I could never live in my father's London house – but the life you describe sounds as if it could be interesting and fun, as well as serving others.'

'I'm glad you see it as we do – it will benefit us as much as those we give a home,' Hetty said. 'It is a life I can live with Arthur and be truly happy.'

She'd given Eliza Arthur's address in the country. 'Ruth has it too,' she said, 'and you can contact us there – or a letter to his London house will reach him; he intends to sell that great house, though he keeps his refuge for fallen women.' She'd smiled at Eliza. 'Everyone would be happy if you came to live with us – but it is your choice.'

Eliza was not sure what she would do when the time came, because she did not wish to think about it. Miss Edith was her friend and when she was sedated she was still happy to sit and talk and Eliza was content to be with her. There was time enough to think of Eliza's future, though knowing she had a father who cared for her made her feel warm and happy inside.

The wedding ceremony was short and held in a small church that was more than adequate for the few guests invited. A reception at Arthur's house had been arranged for those of his London friends he'd chosen to invite, and a much larger family party would be held when they returned from their visit to France.

Arthur lifted the small veil that covered Hetty's face and kissed her softly. 'You look beautiful, my love,' he said. 'I do not deserve such happiness . . .'

351

'Foolish one,' Hetty returned and touched his cheek with her hand. 'We shall discuss this later, dearest Arthur. For now we must see to our guests . . .'

'I am sorry Miss Edith was too ill to come,' Arthur said and could not keep the disappointment from his voice. 'I had hoped Eliza might.'

'As I told you, she does not want to leave her friend just now,' Hetty said. 'Yet she wished us happy . . . and I am sure she meant it, and I believe she will come to us when the time is right.'

'Yes, I am certain you are right,' Arthur agreed. 'She has her mother's generosity. I do understand that she could not leave Miss Edith.'

He took her hand and led her from the small church to the sound of joyous bells. Ruth showered them with rose petals and Bella and Hannah, dressed in pretty clothes fitted to their new lives, gave Hetty a shiny horseshoe tied up with blue ribbons and lace. Lucy and Kitty, Cousin Matthew's daughters, gave Hetty a beautiful basket, lace-trimmed and filled with scented flowers in blue and pink.

'You look lovely, Miss Hetty,' Bella said and Hetty bent to kiss her cheek. 'I cannot tell you how happy I am to be here today. Until Mr Stoneham found me I had known nothing but abuse and unhappiness – now I have friends and all I could want.'

'He is happy to have found you, and you should hold up your head, Bella. You are the daughter of a gentlewoman brought down through no fault of her own. She saved your life by taking you to the church the night she died in the snow and though her mind was disturbed by what had happened to her, I am certain that she loved you. Her mind was clear enough to place you where you would be found and cared for. She could not have known that you would be cruelly treated by that woman . . .'

Bella's cheeks were wet with tears, but they were happy ones, and she hugged Hetty as she thanked her for her kindness.

'Mr Stoneham looks handsome,' Hannah said to Ruth and sighed. 'He's sending me to school to learn to be a teacher – is that not kind of him?'

'It's Mr Stoneham's way,' Ruth told her and smiled. 'Lovely man, he be! He rescued me and Cook from the workhouse – that's 'er over there talkin' to Mr Rattan and 'is lady. Married, Cook be now, and happy as a lark.'

'Bella told me about her,' Hannah said. 'Mr Rattan looks handsome too in his way – but his lady seems more interested in her baby than him . . .'

Ruth nodded and frowned. 'Aye, well, she lost the babe for a while, didn't she?'

'Yes, so Bella told me. It was wonderful that Mr Rattan got her back for Meg, wasn't it?'

'Yes, wonderful,' Ruth said but her frown didn't lift. 'Though, it was a bit odd . . .' She broke off as the bride and groom were driven off to their reception in a carriage tied with horseshoes and white ribbons. 'We've been invited to the reception. I'm lookin' forward to seein' inside that big 'ouse of his.'

'Yes, we're all going,' Hannah said. 'I bet the food will be lovely. I'm going to eat and eat and eat!'

'Don't make yerself sick,' Ruth warned and went off to join Cook, Meg and Toby, who had married quietly, with their baby as the other carriages drew up to convey the guests to the reception.

The reception was over and their guests had all gone. Hetty was alone in the bedroom they would use for this one night before leaving for the coast and their ship to the South of France. She had just undressed with the help of her new maid, Minnie, and was now sitting in her elegant silk and lace negligee before the dressing table, brushing her hair. She turned to glance at Arthur as he entered the bedchamber and dismissed the girl.

'Thank you, Minnie, I can manage now.'

Arthur came to stand behind her as the maid left. He looked at her in the dressing mirror, taking the ivory-backed brush to stroke it over her hair, which reached below her shoulders, a slight wave in the rich reddish brown where she had taken it down from the coils that had held it in place earlier.

'You should wear your hair down more,' he said and kissed the top of her head. 'You smell of flowers . . .'

'I am not a young girl,' Hetty said and laughed at him in the mirror. 'Besides, I wear it down at night for the only man I wish to admire it . . .' Her eyes lit with mischief and he bent over her to kiss her throat, making her tingle with need. His fingers caressed her neck and the white skin at the nape, lifting her hair to kiss her on her most sensitive spot. She shivered with pleasure as she felt the tip of his tongue licking sensuously at her there.

'You remembered,' she said softly, because it was many years since they had pleasured each other. Hetty had been a whore then and Arthur had been the only man who had ever taken the time to discover what aroused and pleased her instead of simply taking his own pleasure. It was no wonder that she had never allowed another man to touch her after she'd discovered what it was to find true happiness in a man's embrace. He had been the spur she needed to try again – and because he'd shown her kindness and helped her, she had found a new life for herself. And now at last, she knew that the man she'd adored all those years loved her in return.

'Of course,' he said huskily and drew her up into his arms so that she felt the length of his strong body holding her against him and his arms enfolding her in an embrace that told her she was where she belonged. 'I was such a fool not to know what a treasure was mine all these years . . . forgive me for the wasted years, my love.'

Hetty turned to face him, reaching up for his kiss, quivering with the need and desire she had suppressed through so many long years when she had believed she could never have what she longed for – would never hear him say such words. Now at last she had her heart's desire and she wanted him so much that she burned with need and longing to lie with him and feel him possess her once more.

'I love you, Arthur,' she said. 'I want you so much. I did from the first moment I held you and gave you comfort all those years ago. I knew then that you were the only man I had ever loved or would love – and I never expected that one day you would love me but I was prepared to accept friendship as long as you were happy . . .'

'It took me much time and pain to learn,' he said humbly. 'Can you forgive and forget all that went before – and look only to the future and to mutual happiness?'

'Yes,' she said simply and pressed her lips to his, feeling the heat of his desire as he pressed her against him. The time for words was over and now was the time for love, pleasure and a future yet to be explored; a future that would include friends and family and touch the lives of many yet unknown.

They had both travelled a hard road but together life would be sweeter and they could face whatever came. Secure in love, they would devote their lives to saving and caring for those less fortunate – the lost and lonely, the destitute, the sick and the poor – and most of all, the children of the workhouse.